Leaving *Yesterday*

**Center Point
Large Print**

Also by Kathryn Cushman
and available from Center Point Large Print:

Waiting for Daybreak

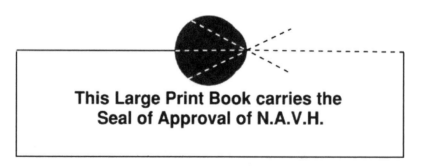

**This Large Print Book carries the
Seal of Approval of N.A.V.H.**

Leaving *Yesterday*

Kathryn Cushman

CENTER POINT PUBLISHING
THORNDIKE, MAINE

This Center Point Large Print edition
is published in the year 2010 by arrangement with
Bethany House Publishers,
a division of Baker Publishing Group.

Copyright © 2009 by Kathryn Cushman.

Scripture quotations are from the HOLY BIBLE,
NEW INTERNATIONAL VERSION.®
Copyright © 1973, 1978, 1984
by International Bible Society.
Used by permission of Zondervan Publishing House.

The text of this Large Print edition is unabridged.
In other aspects, this book may vary
from the original edition.
Printed in the United States of America
on permanent paper.
Set in 16-point Times New Roman type.

ISBN: 978-1-60285-753-7

Library of Congress Cataloging-in-Publication Data

Cushman, Kathryn.
  Leaving yesterday / Kathryn Cushman.
    p. cm.
  ISBN 978-1-60285-753-7 (library binding : alk. paper)
  1. Mothers and sons--Fiction. 2. Large type books. I. Title.
PS3603.U825L43 2010
  813'.6--dc22
2009052567

To Melanie Cushman—

I've watched you smile your way through things
that would bring most people to tears of despair.
Your courage inspires me more than I can say.

One

My son was dead. I knew it the minute I saw the black-and-white car pull to the curb in front of my house.

Clods of potting soil still clinging to my gloves—like the debris of the last few years clung to everything in my life—I turned back to my house, walked up the porch steps, opened the front door, then closed and locked it behind me. Perhaps a reasonable person would understand that the clink of the deadbolt sliding into place did nothing to stop the impending news. Well, show me the mother who thinks with reason when faced with the news that her only remaining son is dead.

I walked into my kitchen and tossed my gloves on the counter, ignoring the splatter of soil they left over what had been spotless granite. I grabbed a cup from the top shelf and shoved it against the slot in the refrigerator door, holding it in place with such force I thought the glass might shatter. Cold water filled it almost to the rim. Just taking a little break from gardening, that's what I was doing. That policeman outside had turned onto the wrong street, that's all. He had probably realized his mistake and was gone by now.

I took a seat at the kitchen table and opened the home improvement catalog that sat atop the mail pile. I thumbed mindlessly through page after page until one particular ad reached out and wrapped its fingers around my throat. The boys in the photo looked nothing like Nicolas or Kurt, other than the fact that my sons had once been boys that size. Still, looking at the picture, I couldn't help but remember them as their eight- and ten-year-old selves. A smiling father held up the latest power drill beside the tree house in progress; his smiling wife stood atop the latest greatest ladder. Even the chocolate Labrador at the bottom of the picture appeared to be smiling at the two boys, who stood beside the pile of lumber. A world so full of promise.

Just like ours had once been.

The chime of the doorbell brought me back to the present. And reality. A reality I didn't want to face, but I had to. Time had just run out.

As I walked toward the front door, it occurred to me that these would be the last steps I would ever take without knowing for certain that Kurt was dead. I needed to hold on to this time for as long as I could, remember each step as something precious. One step. Two. Three . . . At ten, I reached the door.

I took a deep breath and put my hand on the brass handle, still smeared with dirt from my use-less attempt to shut this moment out. In spite of the fact that I didn't want it to, the lock pivoted beneath my fingers. There was no turning back now. I tugged at the front door, surprised by how heavy it felt, and then came face-to-face with my worst nightmare. Only what I saw did not match the image I had expected.

Everything about the officer's appearance surprised me. Missing was the grim undertaker expression on a face sagging with age and sorrow. At the very least, I expected a strong undercurrent of discomfort from the poor unfortunate officer saddled with delivering this kind of news. Instead, his demeanor was pleasant, almost amiable as he looked at me. His reddish hair and youthful freckles reminded me of a grown-up version of Opie from *The Andy Griffith Show*. "Alisa Stewart?"

I held on to the doorknob for support, waiting for the blow to come. "Yes."

"I'm Detective Bruce Thompson from the Santa Barbara Police Department." He didn't say more. I supposed he was giving me a chance to respond with some pleasantry, or to ask about the nature of his visit.

I didn't.

What could I possibly want to say to him? We both knew what was coming. Why would I want to ask the question that would bring on the inevitable? I simply stared at him and waited.

He shifted on his feet and finally looked down at a small pad of paper he carried in his right hand. "You are Kurt Stewart's mother. Is that correct?"

"Yes."

Again, he waited. His military-short haircut stood at attention, as if it, too, anxiously anticipated my response. What was he expecting? I'd answered the question; that was more than enough talk for me.

Finally, he asked, "Do you know where we might find him?"

"What?" The doorframe beside me seemed to waver. I reached my left hand to grab it for support. "You're not here to . . . you're looking for him?"

He looked as confused by my response as I was surprised by his question. "Yes. Is he here?"

I turned to lean my back against the doorframe and slid to the ground.

Detective Thompson knelt beside me. "Are you all right?"

"I'm, I'm fine. It's just that, I thought you were here to tell me that he was . . ." I rested my head on my knees and took deep breaths. Deep, freeing breaths.

My son was still alive.

To Detective Thompson's credit, he waited quietly beside me, giving me a chance to pull myself together without any clumsy attempts to be helpful. Finally, I looked at him and shrugged. "I thought you'd come to tell me that you'd found my son dead." How many years now had I dreaded just such a visit? To an addict's mother, it was woven into the fiber of daily existence as completely as the fragile thread of hope—and often with more clarity.

Detective Thompson rubbed his hand to his forehead. "I am so sorry. If it had occurred to me what you might think, I would have stated up front that everything was okay."

I became aware of a woman walking her golden retriever on the sidewalk across the street, eyes fixed right here on my front porch. It didn't take much of an imagination to know what kind of story this could make around the neighborhood. I stood up and gestured weakly back inside. "Would you like to come in?"

He nodded and followed me in. Whatever his reason for the visit, it didn't matter. My son was alive. "Here, let me get you some water."

A moment later we were seated at my kitchen table, the magazine still opened to the family tree house picture. I touched the face of the smallest boy, suddenly thankful for his presence.

"Back to my earlier question, is Kurt staying here? Do you know where I might find him?"

I shook my head. "I haven't seen him in over a year." I took a sip of my water, feeling the coldness slide down my throat. "We have a young daughter, and my husband believes . . ." I stared out the back window at a group of crows roosting in the giant oak on the other side of our fence. I envied the lack of complication in their existence.

"Well, at some point a parent has to quit enabling bad choices. You know, tough love, all that." I looked into his eyes, wondering what a police officer thought about tough love. Did he see it as the cruel, uncaring act that it often felt like, or did he see it as the necessity that Rick did? As a mother, my head told me one thing, my heart another.

"I understand that." It was stated as a fact, nothing more. Not an agreement or a disagreement, just the truth of his understanding. "So, you have no idea where I might find him?"

"No. The last I heard he was working odd jobs at construction sites around town, but that was a while ago." As the fear of Kurt's death ebbed away, reality set in, and another fear began to grow and take its place. "Why are you looking for him?"

"Just routine questioning." He flipped up a sheet on his pad of paper.

I reached my hand across the table and grabbed his. He looked up, his eyes wide with surprise.

"Detective Thompson, in the last few years I've lived through one son's violent death and the debilitating addiction of another. My husband has recently left home, and I am using the last ounces of strength I possess to make it through each day and be here for my daughter. I cannot afford to be blindsided. I need to know how bad this might be."

He drew his hand away, studying my face as he did so. Surely a detective trained in interrogation could take one look at me and see the depths of desperation, know beyond a doubt that I spoke the truth. After a moment, he shrugged and said, "A drug dealer was killed downtown last weekend. I'm just looking to ask some questions."

"Why would you want to question Kurt?"

Again, he searched my face before deciding to offer a response. "Do you know what a pay-owe sheet is?"

"No."

"It's a record that drug dealers keep of people who owe them money. In that line of work, somebody always owes you money."

"I guess so." I focused on my glass of water. The ice cubes were slowly shrinking and disappearing, just like I was. "Am I to assume that Kurt's name is on the—what did you call it?—pay-owe sheet of this drug dealer?"

"Yes it is."

"And that makes him a suspect." I stated this as a resigned truth, something I'd mastered over the last few years. Resigning myself to all sorts of unsavory truths had become one of my strengths, if you could call it that.

"Your son's name was on that list along with more than a dozen others. He's not a suspect. We're just doing some routine questioning,

13

hoping he might be able to shed some light on who might have done this."

Yes, of course my son's name would be on the list of people who owed a drug dealer money. He had descended just that far since his brother's death. Still, I knew Kurt well enough to know that he did have limits on how low he could go. "Detective Thompson, my son may be an addict, but he is not a murderer."

"I'm sure you're right. There are over a dozen names on the list, and it's highly likely that none of them killed the guy. It could have been a member of a rival gang, another drug dealer, anyone. We're just looking for pieces of the puzzle right now."

Relief flooded me. Of course they didn't suspect Kurt. "Well, sorry I don't have any more information for you."

"Thanks for the water." He pulled a card out of his pocket. "If your son should call or come by in the next few days, would you let me know?"

Would I? I wasn't sure, but I did know that my son would not be calling or coming by. His father had made certain of that some time ago. It was a safe answer. "Of course." I took the card and held open the front door for him. "Uh, Detective Thompson, if you should see him before I do, will you tell him . . ."

He waited for me to finish the sentence. What would I want him to know? That he was ripping my heart out? That I desperately needed to see that he was okay? "Just tell him that his mother loves him."

He nodded and smiled. "You got it."

Two

It wasn't a hard decision to keep quiet about Detective Thompson's visit. Rick wouldn't be by to pick up Caroline for another couple of days, and I saw no reason to call him and tell him any of this before then. Besides, I already knew how he would respond—with a five-minute tirade about how worthless our son had become. Rick had long ago determined that the reason for Kurt's problems was that we had been too soft on him. I'd heard countless renditions of "We just made his life too easy," "He never learned to take responsibility," et cetera, et cetera. It didn't matter how much I reminded him that Kurt had been an honor student and outstanding athlete, that he'd worked part-time to pay for his own used car and performed a couple hundred hours of community service. The answer always came back to soft parenting.

Out of curiosity, I dug through the recycling bin until I found the story of the weekend's murder.

A local man was found beaten to death just outside De La Guerra Plaza early Sunday morning. Due to the severity of the beating, the victim was not easily recognizable, but has since been identified as Rudy Prince.

Mr. Prince was well-known among local authorities as a small-time drug dealer who had been arrested numerous times and convicted on three different occasions for aggravated assault. Police believe the murder weapon was likely Mr. Prince's own Louisville Slugger. According to sources, he used to carve a tally mark in the handle of the bat each time he beat someone with it. The wooden bat is currently missing, and police are urging anyone with information of its whereabouts to please call the toll-free hotline.

My son owed this man money. The man who carried a baseball bat with tally marks. I shuddered when I thought of all the things my son was experiencing that were far too horrible for me to even comprehend. How had that happened?

Just then, Caroline came bounding in from school, her cheeks flushed with excitement. "Hey, Mom, can we get a puppy? Holly Jeter's Mom brought theirs to school today, and he was soooo cute. I really think we need a puppy."

Life is so simple when you're ten; a new puppy solves everything. I kissed her mop of sandy hair and smiled. "What do you think Boots would think of that?"

She looked toward the bundle of sleeping cat, in his usual spot by the heating vent in the corner, then walked over and buried her face in his fur. "You'd like it just fine, wouldn't you, boy? You'd like to have a doggy brother, wouldn't you?"

Boots lifted his head and looked toward Caroline with feline annoyance before stretching, flashing his claws in the process.

"See, Mom, he wouldn't mind. Besides, since Dad's not here anymore, we need some protection. You know, a guard dog sort of thing."

"Yeah right. Now sit down and eat your snack."

As she removed some ice cream from the freezer and took a seat at the kitchen table, I tossed the newspaper back into the bin and thought again how much Caroline looked like a younger, feminine version of Kurt. The two of them were so much alike in so many ways, it almost seemed as though they were twins. Twins with an eleven-year difference in age.

She put a spoonful of ice cream in her mouth, and then another, with no conversation in between. This in and of itself was unusual. Then I noticed she was staring at the front door as if transfixed by the dark stain of the mahogany or polished shine of the brass handles.

I had cleaned off the dirt from earlier but began to wonder if I'd missed a spot. I tried to follow her gaze but couldn't see anything unusual. "What are you looking at?"

"I'm just watching for Kurt." The expression on her face was so matter-of-fact that it broke my heart.

"Why would you be doing that?"

"Last night I dreamed he came back home. Jenny says sometimes dreams tell the future, so I'm just watching."

I was certain that the man she looked for had the same winning smile and easy laugh that had once been such a part of Kurt. She undoubtedly pictured his loose sandy curls swaying in time as he played the air guitar, or felt the tickles in her ribs from former wrestling matches. In her mind he was still healthy, happy, and wonderful—he just wasn't around anymore. Somehow the innocence of childhood seemed to erase her bad memories of the last years before he disappeared completely. The timing of her dream couldn't have been worse, what with the detective's visit today. I was glad she hadn't been home when he came by; at least she'd been spared that.

"Why don't we go for a walk? Maybe we can stop by Holly's house and you can show me her new puppy?"

"Yay! I knew you'd come around." She jumped up and threw her arms around my neck. "Just wait until you see him. You'll want a new puppy, too, I promise you will."

As much as I dreaded the next few weeks of puppy-begging this impromptu outing was bound to cause, it was worth it to get Caroline's hopes off Kurt's arrival. At least she could visit Holly's puppy, pet him, hug him. Something she would never be able to do with Kurt.

Later that night when I tucked her in, I gave her an extra long hug that brought tears to my eyes. She knelt to say her prayers, and began immediately with "Please show us the right puppy for our family. Help Mom to understand how much we need one." When she got to her usual "God bless Kurt," I didn't have the typical mental response that Kurt was too far gone for even God's help. Instead, I found myself pleading right along. *Please, please, please.*

I left her room and sank beside my own bed to pray. "Father, help him. Father, help him." It was as articulate a prayer as I could offer when Kurt was involved.

Three

The next day, I walked across the street to Lacey Satterfield's house for our usual Tuesday morning breakfast and gab session. Lacey was a sixty-something widow who had moved to our sleepy little neighborhood about five years ago and had had everyone talking. Our street was full of fortyish-year-old homes, nice but not fancy, priced considerably higher than houses in similar neighborhoods because we were in the best school district. Why would an older single woman pay extra for that? Besides, she was a retired lawyer—but the rumor on the street was that she hadn't actually retired, she'd been disbarred. No one seemed to have actual substantial details, but few doubted the truth of the rumor, either. I was her one and only friend on the street, and I didn't ask. Having a son who is an addict helps a person understand the principle of leaving private things private.

The exterior of her home had been redone by its previous owner in white and gray minimalist modern, but once inside, it was a return to the Victorian era with lace, linen, and dark wood. Lacey herself was an eclectic mix of just about everything. She always wore sweat suits—I'd never seen her in anything else—and they were always in one shocking shade of neon or another. Today's outfit was lemon yellow, with a matching sequined headband holding back shoulder-length gray hair. "Come on in," she welcomed me. "I just pulled the scones out of the oven, or there's biscotti if you prefer."

I followed her inside and went through all the usual motions of mixing cream in my coffee and putting food on my plate. I sat at the walnut table and offered the only small talk I could think of this morning. "So, what's new? Have you got your spring vegetables planted?" Gardener though I was, I couldn't have cared less. There were more important things to discuss this morning, but I didn't want to jump right in with my real question. Better to work my way into this slowly.

"Nah. I don't think I'm even going to plant this year." Lacey's voice had the gravelly sound of a woman who'd spent most of her life smoking a few packs a day. "My back's too old and stiff for all that. Besides, we can buy perfectly fresh vegetables at the farmer's market every week. What's the point?"

Normally, I would have argued about the sense of accomplishment, breathing the fresh air, working in the sunshine, whatever. Today, my thoughts and energy were moving in other directions. "So, I was just reading my newspaper. Have you seen that story about the drug dealer that was murdered downtown last weekend?" I hoped my tone sounded as casual as I intended.

She nodded once, tilted her head to the side. "Yeah, I saw it."

I fussed with my lace napkin before setting it neatly on my lap. "What do you think about it?"

"What do you mean what do I think?" She coughed once, then continued. "That boy was a thug if ever there was one. He sold drugs to teenagers, he beat no-telling-how-many people with that baseball bat he always carried. I think if the police do find out who killed him, instead of pressing charges they ought to award a medal. Maybe even the keys to Santa Barbara."

Lacey had a strong opinion about many things, but this one surprised me more than most. "Do you really think so?"

"I think you know me well enough to know that I do." She took a bite of the cranberry scone she'd made that morning and nodded. "I find it downright poetic that the killer beat him to death with his own baseball bat. It's almost like an-eye-for-an-eye, you know. I can't think of a more appropriate way for him to die. If our justice system worked a little more like that, we'd all be better off."

I dipped a chocolate macadamia biscotti in my coffee, watching the top layers soften. I held it up but didn't take a bite. "Kurt is one of those 'people of interest' the police keep talking about." I nibbled at the cookie, simply because I needed to do something.

"I wondered as much." Her tone was as matter-of-fact as if I'd told her that the weatherman had predicted fog tomorrow morning.

Why this surprised me I can't say for sure. Lacey had always had more than the average insight. Still, I looked at her faded blue eyes, at the small wrinkles that surrounded her lips, and wondered again if it were a mere mortal that inhabited her worn-out body. "You did? Why?"

"Well, for one thing, it would explain that policeman that came to your door yesterday. He stayed quite a while; it was obvious he had some-thing to say."

"How did you even know he was here?"

"Baby, I live on this street. You know I'm home most of the day."

"But I saw you in the driveway last night. We talked for five minutes and you never mentioned it."

"I don't go poking around in places that aren't my business. Last night you didn't bring it up, so it wasn't my business."

"And now?"

"Now that you've mentioned it, you've made it my business. So I plan to give you my complete and honest opinion. If you want to hear it, that is."

"You know I do." And I truly did. Lacey never spoke fluff; what she said was what she meant. Without exception.

"I didn't know Kurt too long before he cut the strings on his parachute and had his freefall, but I knew him well enough. He's lost his way right now, there's not much doubt about it. But there's not a mean bone in that boy's body, and there's no doubt about that either." She took a sip of coffee. "Kurt's just not the beat-someone-beyond-recognition kind of person. Anyone with half a brain can see that. I don't expect they'll be interested in him for long. But like I said before, whoever did it should be congratulated."

What a relief to know that someone else saw the absolute certainty that Kurt couldn't have

23

done this thing. Still, Lacey and I were not the two opinions that mattered most in this case. "Every time the phone rings, I'm afraid to answer it. I keep thinking it will be the police telling me they've arrested him. I know he didn't do it, but what if the police don't see it that way?"

Her index and middle fingers twitched as if they were holding an invisible cigarette. She raised them to her lips and drummed a slow beat. "Would it really be worse than what you've got now?" She leaned back in her chair and braced her arms against the table. "I mean, no mother wants her son to be accused of murder, but at least you would know where he is. You'd know that he's still alive, for crying out loud, eating three squares, maybe getting some help."

There was some truth in what she was saying. "I can't argue with that. But there's also the other side. It would mean I raised a killer. The well-mannered young man that I raised to hold open doors for women, to say please and thank you, to clean up after himself . . . I thought I was doing everything right." My throat closed, effectively choking further words.

"You were, and are, a great mother. Don't ever doubt that."

I pictured myself walking into the church staff meeting and trying to explain to the governing board that my youngest son was no longer just a prodigal. He was a murderer. I could see their faces, the senior pastor kind but disapproving, the director of missions shaking his head in disbelief, the two secretaries whispering behind uplifted hands. "The hope that Kurt will eventually return, my daughter, my work at church—those are the only things I have left in my life that matter. Nick's death took so much away from us all. If Kurt killed that man, there won't be anything left."

Lacey leaned across and squeezed my hand. "Like I told you, Kurt's not the one who did that. We both know it."

"Sometimes the police get things wrong."

She looked out the window at this statement, but nodded her head oh so slightly. "I'm afraid I've seen too much of this world to argue with that one." She took a sip of her orange juice, which I suspected she occasionally laced with something a little stronger. "You're still a great mother to Caroline, and you would be even if the worst came to pass. Nothing can change that. And I wouldn't expect any of this to affect your church work. The people there, they all know about Kurt, right?"

"Sure, they know he is an addict, they know he started using drugs after Nick's murder, but they all see me as the woman who counsels people in their grief, the one who stands with God through storms and dark times. How can I continue to counsel families who have lost loved ones if they believe my son is out there killing people's loved ones?"

"Never have understood the church crowd, don't expect I'll start now." She stood up and carried her plate to the sink. "I'd give anything for a smoke right now." She tossed the remaining orange juice down the sink. "Seems kind of silly to me that I stopped at my age, especially when the damage is already done." Lacey spent nights, and several hours each day, hooked up to portable oxygen, although she always refused to wear it during our breakfasts together.

"Well, you don't want to do any more damage. Besides, I'm sure it would be dangerous to smoke while you're using oxygen. Wouldn't it explode or something?"

"I don't know, baby, I don't know." She took the plate from my hand and rinsed it in the sink before loading it into the dishwasher. "I just wish that I knew at some point I could once again do the one thing I really want to do. It's not like I'm on a diet and there's hope for a piece of cake after I've lost the appropriate amount of weight. I can never, ever smoke again, and it's all I can think about. There's no hope, and it's maddening."

That would be me if Kurt got arrested. I thought about the strong façade I'd put on for so long. Yes, my oldest son had died in a brutal attack; yes, the grief of that had driven his younger brother into a world of addiction. Still, somehow it would be easier to tell people I had a prodigal than a murderer. All hope fled by simply changing that one word, and hope was all I had to keep me going these days.

The only problem was, I didn't even know what to hope for anymore.

Four

When the phone rang at 8:13 Wednesday morning, I was standing in my recently remodeled bathroom, thinking how the separate *his* and *her* closets had sure turned out to be wasted space under the circumstances. I was hurrying to put on my makeup—in this particular case it was brown eyeliner. I'll never in my life pull out my brown eye pencil again without remembering that exact moment—sort of like most people have triggers that remind them of the day the Berlin Wall came down, or Pearl Harbor, or 9/11. It's amazing how close I came to missing the moment altogether, considering for a long moment just letting the call go to voice mail. I was already running late and the only people who called these days were telemarketers.

But something made me pick it up.

"Mom, it's me."

Kurt's voice was little more than a whisper. Just the sound of it poured over me like the sweetest of symphonies, barely remembered but desperately yearned for.

"Oh, Kurt." The joy of saying his name lasted no longer than the word on my lips. A picture formed in my mind of my son at the police station, getting his one phone call. There was no other reason he would be calling. "Kurt, are you okay? Where are you?" I tried to remember Lacey's words, to convince myself that even if he were arrested, it really could be the best thing for him.

"I'm fine. I'm in Orange County."

"You're where?"

"Mom, I'm in rehab."

Rehab. Oh, the hope that had remained buried beneath the word *prodigal* for so long burst forth like a ray of sunshine after years of rain. "I knew it! I knew it would happen. Oh, Kurt, I am so proud of you. How long have you been there? How are you doing? Can I come see you?"

His laugh sounded weak. "Whoa there, Mom, take it easy." I heard him take a couple of deep breaths, then he continued. "I've been here for a little bit. I've finished the detox process." He gave a low whistle. "That memory'll keep me clean the rest of my life."

"It must have been awful." I'd seen enough about withdrawals and the like to know it had been terrible. I pictured my son shaking, sweating, crying out in pain. Still, a part of me was grateful for it, if the memory of it helped keep him clean.

"It was hard—this call's even harder." I could hear him take another breath. "I'm sorry. For the drugs and the lies, and for going off the deep end at the time when you needed me most. I shouldn't have let you face that alone."

Alone. Kurt didn't even know his father hadn't lived here for the last few months, and yet he'd said the word *alone.* That's how far we must have fallen as a family.

"Oh, Kurt, you're forgiven. When can I see you?"

"They tell me I'll be an in-patient for maybe six or eight more weeks. When I start to get out, I'll give you a call." A muffled voice sounded in the background. "Oh, time's up. I've got to go. Love you, Mom."

"Wait—" But I was too late. The line went dead. He'd hung up the phone before I had the chance to find out where he was, the phone number there, or even a second to voice a response. I stared at the wall trying to ignore the ache in my chest. In spite of everything that had happened, he knew I loved him with all my heart, even if he'd hung up before I could say it. Right?

Almost immediately, I picked it back up and pressed the button for the caller ID. At least I'd know where to call him. The screen lit behind the black lettering of the display.

Private Caller.

I sank onto my bed exhausted, trembling. A few moments with my son was more than I'd had in over a year, but all I wanted now was more. But I had no way of reaching Kurt, of finding out where he was, checking on his progress. In that moment I vowed that this would never happen again. I walked around the house and made sure there was a pen and paper in every room. The next time Kurt called, I would ask for his number and write it down before we talked about anything else. I just hoped there would be a next time.

"Mom, aren't you ready? I'm going to be late for school." Caroline stood in the doorway, her fists pressed against her hips.

I ran to her and threw my arms around her. "Oh, sweetie."

She pushed away and looked up at me. "What's got you acting so weird?"

"Kurt just called. He's getting well."

"Kurt's coming home?" She threw her arms around me and squealed in that high-pitched way only a ten-year-old girl can.

Her immediate assumption that he would be coming home took me aback. Perhaps I shouldn't have said anything to her about this yet, but everything inside of me screamed that she was right. I reached down, picked her up, and swung her in a circle. Together, we began to chant,

"Kurt's coming home, Kurt's coming home." And every time we said the words, I came to believe them just a little more.

Through a miracle of speed, determination, and sheer luck, I managed to drop Caroline at the front of the school with two minutes to spare. I watched her skip toward the door, her blond hair bouncing with each step.

A small voice of worry kept whispering in my head, saying Kurt wouldn't call again, he wouldn't make it through rehab, it wouldn't last long. Maybe I shouldn't have told Caroline anything after all. Who wanted to see her hopes destroyed?

I turned my car toward the church and began to sing "Amazing Grace" at the top of my lungs. Maybe I couldn't stop the internal voice of doubt, but I could at least drown it out.

I found it hard to sit still during the morning staff meeting. The music director told of his plans for a children's summer choir, the children's director revealed plans for vacation Bible school, detail by painstaking detail. All these things were treated with utmost importance—and I knew they were important. Really, I did. Our church was the fastest-growing church on the central coast. We were gaining a lot of notice and it was an honor to be a member of this team. But today, I couldn't think about anything other than my son.

"Alisa, I know the spring women's Bible study is well under way. I've been getting a lot of positive feedback," Ken Maddox, the senior pastor, said as heads nodded in agreement all around the table. "What do you have in the works for the women this summer?"

I shook my head. "I've found that with kids out of school, family vacations, et cetera, it's more frustrating than fruitful to try anything structured. I am planning a weekly meet-at-the-beach event for mothers and their children, and a couple of family movie nights throughout the summer."

Our programs coordinator, Beth Williams, shook her head. "You know, now that our attendance is averaging over a thousand, you might want to reconsider. If not right away, at least by the end of the summer when construction should be complete on the new Family Living Center. I'm thinking we should take full advantage of the facility as soon as possible—use our talents, that sort of thing."

I pretended to write a note on the pad in front of me. "Thanks, I'll keep that in mind, Beth."

Ken Maddox cleared his throat. "There are a couple of other things I'd like to discuss with you. First of all, *American Christian* magazine wants to do a feature on our church, and they want to spotlight you in particular."

I looked at him in shock. "Me? Why?"

"Well, our women's ministry department is

flourishing, and someone on their staff was present at the last Living With Grief seminar we hosted this winter. They were impressed." He looked down at his notes. "Speaking of, I understand you are planning to speak at the upcoming seminar next month." He smiled toward Beth. "And of course, Beth will be there to make sure everything runs smoothly."

She bobbed her head, as if in time to some unseen music. "That's my gift."

I sighed. "Yes, it definitely is."

Organization *was* Beth's gift, there was no doubt about it. But she was so Type A that she was overbearing to work with for any length of time. I tried to avoid doing so as much as possible. I looked toward Ken. "I wonder if we should be looking to feature someone else next month? I could help plan the event."

Beth broke in. "I told her that was completely unacceptable. I can organize these things just fine, but people come from miles around because they want to hear Alisa's story. She does such an amazing job." She looked at me as if God himself had just spoken. Then she began to trace her notebook with her finger and added demurely, "To tell you the truth, though, I wish you would avoid answering the questions about the effect on your family in such detail. Especially the part about Kurt. It just seems so depressing and hopeless, especially after your talk has been so uplifting."

I had come into this room with no intention of telling what was happening with Kurt. But Beth, in her usual way, riled me up enough that I blurted, "Not anymore. I guess I have a new chapter to add to my story."

The room went dead quiet. Everyone at this table knew the story of Nick's death, of Kurt's resulting fall. They'd all been praying for him, just like I had, for the past few years. "This morning I got a call from Kurt. He's in rehab and in the process of turning his life back around. . . ." I blinked the water from my eyes, wanting to see their faces. "Ladies and gentlemen, it would appear that my prodigal is on his way back home."

"Well, hallelujah!" Ken shouted and the others added their own praises, each voice building my joy. We had all been praying for Kurt's return, even though it seemed it would never come. Through the years I'd begun to wonder if we were just wasting our time, praying about something that God couldn't be moved on. In this moment I was so glad that I'd never expressed my doubts to this group, never let them know how much I feared that God was not listening. Now I stood before them and shared their joy, with no spoken words of which to be ashamed. It was a perfect way to end the meeting.

After the meeting, Ken asked me to come into his office and motioned me to take a seat. "This can't top what you've shared, Alisa, but you're doing a wonderful job here. Folks have noticed and the overseers have voted to move your position to full-time, starting this fall. Pay would be significantly more, of course."

"I could use that." I didn't have to say why. He knew Rick and I were separated, our future unclear, but with the way things were headed, I was likely going to need more of an income at some point. "My only concern with going full-time would be needing to be home for Caroline after school. At least when she's not at Rick's."

"Of course. I knew you would feel that way, and I'm sure we could work it out so that you do some of your afternoon work at home."

"Sounds good." I stood up to return to my office, but he waved me back down. "There is one more thing I wanted to talk to you about, but not in front of everyone else."

I dropped back into my chair. "What?"

"You know that editor friend of mine I've been telling you about? Well, I sent him a couple of articles that you've written and a CD of your talks. He's interested in talking to you."

"Really?" I tried to keep my voice steady, but the jolt of excitement that hit me with this news dwarfed the news about going to full-time. Speaking was something others wanted from me. Writing was something I'd always dreamed for myself. A book! Nick had always been such a reader, and to be able to put at least a little of his life on the page forever . . . This day was turning out to be the most wonderful in recent memory.

"Here," Ken continued, handing me a printout, "he gave me a list of things he'd like you to e-mail him. A summary, chapter titles, an opening paragraph, I can't remember what all. I'll be praying that God will lead you in this, as He has in all things."

"Thanks, Ken." I took the paper from him and returned to my office, happier than I'd felt in a long time. As disjointed as my life had been for the last few years, the pieces were finally beginning to fit back together.

I spent the rest of the afternoon thinking about how I would spring the news of Kurt's turn to my husband. Tonight was obviously the right time, since he always picked Caroline up from softball, then ate dinner at the house before loading Caroline and her things into his truck for her three-night stay. We had planned it that way so Caroline could see things were still okay between us, that we didn't hate each other. The one thing we had done right through all of this was to try to make our separation as easy as possible on her, no matter how hard that made it on us.

Should I tell him when he walked through the door? Let him eat first? I ran the various scenarios through my head, and in my fantasy, no matter when I gave the news, his reply was always the same. He always said, "All this time, you were right. I wish I had believed like you did."

A woman could still dream. Couldn't she?

Five

Rick and Caroline made their usual entrance into my kitchen.

Caroline gave me a big hug and sloppy kiss.

"Hi, sweetie. How was softball practice?"

"Good." She looked around the room. "Where's Boots?"

"Asleep on my bed, last time I saw him."

"Great." She dashed from the room, calling, "Kitty, kitty, kitty."

Rick folded his arms across his chest and leaned against the counter, a scowl deepening across his face. He waited until the sound of Caroline's footsteps disappeared up the stairs. "A detective stopped by to see me at the jobsite today." He stared at me so hard, I'm sure he didn't even blink.

I, on the other hand, looked down and began to work the stir-fry in the wok as if it might burn at any moment. So much for planning the right time to break that news. Still, I decided to play dumb and find out what he knew. "Really? What did he want?"

"What do you think he wanted, Alisa?"

The onions and red pepper created a steam that burned my eyes and made me cough. I choked for a good twenty seconds before I looked up at him. "Judging from your tone of voice, I'm sure you're about to tell me."

"That's right, I am." He came to stand so close beside me that I believed the anger burning in him might singe my skin. "He wanted to talk to me about that Prince boy's murder last weekend. But then, you already knew that, didn't you? He told me he stopped by and talked to you on Monday."

I looked full into his face. "You need to back up. You're in my way."

"I really don't care."

"You'll care when the stir-fry chicken burns and we call to order pizza."

He looked at the sizzling wok, then went to lean on the counter, arms folded in front of him. "When were you planning to tell me?"

I turned off the stove top but continued to stir. "Tonight, actually. I didn't see any reason to call you before now. He said all he wanted to do was to talk to Kurt, and it's not like you have known his whereabouts any more than I have for the last year or so. Besides, I knew you would get all upset—kind of like you are now. I just didn't see any reason to go there."

"You didn't see any reason to go there?" He

stared at me drop-jawed. "No reason to go there? He's my son, too, isn't he? You didn't think I had the right to know that my own son killed someone?"

"See, there's the problem right there. I knew you'd expect the worst of him. You didn't say 'suspected of killing someone,' you didn't say 'wanted for questioning,' you said he killed someone. Well, I happen to know that he didn't do anything. I believed that even before I found out some really good news today that proves it." I stared at him in angry triumph. I would win the argument because of the facts I possessed, but this was not how it was supposed to go. Why couldn't we just celebrate rather than try to win these battles? It wasn't healthy, I knew that, but there was nothing healthy left about the way we interacted.

"Oh yeah? Like what?"

"Our son's not even in Santa Barbara right now. He's in Orange County at a rehab facility, turning his life around even as we speak."

He stared at me for the span of a full minute, letting the words work their way through the rapidly dissipating cloud of anger. "Are you sure?" The childlike desperation in his voice made me want to put my arms around him. I didn't.

"He called me this morning. He told me that he was all right, and asked us to forgive him." Okay, I sort of twisted the pronoun from *me* to *us*, but I supposed that's what Kurt really meant to say. No harm done.

Rick pulled out a chair from the kitchen table and sank into it. "Rehab? Really?" He scrubbed his hands across his face, and for just a fleeting second, I saw the high school quarterback my husband once was, the one so full of optimism and ambition, before time had grayed his blond hair and life had crushed his spirit. "I've spent the last couple of hours sick to my stomach at the thought of what my son had become." He rested his forehead against his palm. "Are you sure about the rehab?"

"That's what he told me. He said he'd just come out of detox, and would spend the next six to eight weeks in a residential setting, getting the help he needed."

Rick rocked his head up and down. "Part of me is almost afraid to hope."

I knew how he felt, but Kurt was my son and I was always willing to give him the benefit of the doubt. This time I gave in and put my arms around Rick's shoulders. "I know. But he really is going to make it this time. Just you wait and see."

He made a sound in his throat, which might have been a laugh; I wasn't certain. "That's exactly what you said when I was teaching him to ride his bike. Remember that?"

"I was right then, too." I smiled as I thought back to that warm summer day. It was a Saturday, and we'd walked Kurt's bike over to the school so he could learn on the large, flat blacktop play area. Rick ran behind him, bent at the waist, holding Kurt up as he wobbled and failed over and over again. Finally, Rick stood up and rubbed the small of his back. "My back is killing me. I think we'll have to call it a day."

"Please, Daddy, just one more time." Kurt's eyes were lit with determination.

"Please, Rick, he'll make it this time, just you wait and see."

He rubbed his back and nodded, then proceeded to try again. And again. Not once did he mention his back, and it was an hour later before Kurt finally got the hang of it. Rick spent the next month on muscle relaxers and anti-inflammatories, but with a smile of satisfaction on his face. "It was worth it," was all he ever said. That was the Rick I loved. The one who loved his family so completely.

When he looked at me now, I recognized the torment in his eyes. "Did you tell him . . . about us?"

I shook my head. "I didn't see any reason to add any more to his burdens."

He reached for my hand and squeezed it. For a moment, the last few years of anger and bitterness were overcome by the silent togetherness that far transcended our usual depth of communication. It felt so . . . right. I found myself remembering the smell of burgers on the grill, the sound of laughter in the midst of water fights, and the taste of happy tears after the sun set on another day so perfect I couldn't stand to see it go.

The spell was broken when he pulled his hand away. "I told that detective I'd call him if I had any information about Kurt. I can't believe how relieved I am to call and tell him that Kurt wasn't even in town when that guy was killed." He pulled Detective Thompson's business card from his wallet, picked up the phone, and punched in some numbers.

He held his finger over the last digit. "When did he go into rehab, anyway?"

"I, uh, don't know. He said he'd been there a little bit."

"A little bit? That's all you got?"

"His call caught me off guard. We didn't talk for all that long. There are several things I wish I'd thought to ask, but I didn't." I turned back to the rice in the steamer. "He'd already finished the detox process. That takes several days, right?"

"Which rehab is he in?"

I poured the rice into a large bowl and walked to the bottom of the stairs. "Caroline, time for dinner." I walked back to the kitchen, miserable with my lack of information. "I don't know. He had to get off the phone before I could find out. The caller ID showed private, but I know it's in Orange County somewhere."

Rick smacked the phone back onto the charger.

"A lot of good that'll do us. A phone call from our son, coming from who knows where, claiming that he's in rehab. It could just as easily be a cover-up because he thinks he's in trouble. Until we can prove where he is, and when he got there, this is no help at all. If he ever calls again, you've got to get those details."

"I know, okay? I made a mistake, I get that."

Caroline walked into the kitchen and took her seat. She looked at Rick and smiled. "Isn't it great that Kurt is coming home?"

He cast a disapproving look at me, then squatted directly in front of her and tucked her hair behind her ears. "I hope he does, honey. I sure hope he does."

I just prayed my son would call again soon. With the answers that we all wanted to hear.

Six

I set my alarm extra early and got up to exercise. This was something I'd done routinely before Nick's death, but afterward I couldn't summon the strength to even care. The resulting fifteen-pound weight gain and increasing flab had always bothered me, but only the prospect of my son's return energized me enough to get serious about turning things around. Suddenly, it seemed very important to get back to my former self, the person Kurt would remember.

I had a lot of ground to make up, so this called for serious action. I looked through my assortment of exercise DVDs and pulled out the one I remembered being the most challenging. I was certain I could still do it, and I didn't have time to waste on the easier ones.

A few seconds later, the screen came to life with bone-thin women in tight spandex moving in directions my body simply couldn't follow. Ten minutes into it, a heart attack seemed imminent, and the hard part hadn't even started yet. I pushed the eject button and decided maybe to go for a quick walk around the neighborhood.

I lived on a cul-de-sac of a dozen homes. Well-kept but small lawns fronted two-story family houses, most with garages full of bicycles and hockey gear, and T-ball stands. It was a family neighborhood. As close to Mayberry as you could find in Southern California, at least I'd always thought so. Happy families, happy lives. These days, I felt a bit like the odd woman out, but I still loved this place.

I headed out into the beautiful shades of an orange sunrise, looked toward the sky, and prayed aloud as I walked. "O, Father, thank you that Kurt is in rehab. I *know* that's where he is. I *know* that you've been watching over him all this time. Forgive me for any doubts I had, please give him the strength to get through whatever it is he needs to get through, and please bring my son back home." The cool morning was invigorating, the sunrise beautiful. This had been a terrific idea.

I got home and showered before the time I normally even got out of bed, and to tell the truth, it felt great. I remembered now just how much better I had felt when I was exercising regularly. Today was the first day of a new habit; I was declaring it right now.

By Monday, not only had I lost three pounds, but I noticed I definitely had more patience with Caroline's slow-to-rise morning routine. She apparently noticed this, too, because she said, "Did you get another call from Kurt?"

"What would make you ask that?"

"You're just acting so happy, I thought you must be hiding something."

I reached out and hugged her. "I wouldn't hide good news like that, you know it."

Just then the phone rang and Caroline and I raced toward it. I beat her out by a nose and grabbed up the handset. "Hello."

Caroline jumped up and down in front of me, mouthing the words, "Is it him? Is it him?"

I turned my back so I could give my full attention to the phone.

"Alisa, it's Marsha. I was wondering if you want to get together for dinner tomorrow night. I thought I'd call Carleigh, Tasha, and Sarah, too." Marsha and gang had made a point of being supportive since Rick and I had separated. Normally, nothing would please me more than the thought of an evening out with my friends. This morning, I forced myself to focus on the mundane conversation, trying not to let my disappointment spill over onto Marsha. "Dinner? Sure, sounds great."

Caroline had come around and was once again bouncing in front of me. I petted her softly on the head and shook my head no. It wasn't him.

Over the course of the next days and weeks, the same scene played out over and over again until despair had begun to take root in all of us. He wasn't going to call.

One Tuesday afternoon I answered the phone yet again and stood looking at Caroline's hopeful, bouncing self. "Hello."

"Mrs. Stewart, this is Ray Brooks. Do you remember me?"

I gave the usual disappointed headshake to Caroline, whose shoulders slumped a little as she walked back to her homework on the kitchen table. I turned my attention back to Ray Brooks. The name sounded familiar, and I tried to search through the memories of names and faces that each increasing year seemed to fade a little more. Something deep inside me ached at the sound of his name, and I knew he'd had something to do with one of my sons. "Your name is so familiar. Please remind me."

"I was Kurt's soccer coach back when he was in junior high."

How could I have forgotten? His face came into my memory in vivid detail. A good twenty years older than the average soccer coach, Ray Brooks continued to coach long after his own children had grown up and moved away, simply because of his love for kids and for the game. "Sure, I remember now. Kurt loved that team."

"I'm not sure if you know it or not, but Kurt had been living in a little workman's cabin at one of our orchards." I had a vague recollection that the Brooks family owned a large chunk of the avocado farms in and around Santa Barbara.

"No, I didn't know. We . . . lost touch during the last few years." How would this man, who dedicated so many years of his life taking care of kids who weren't even his own, feel about a mother who lost track of her son? The embarrassment at this admission had its usual effect on me—I chattered. "I did talk to him just a couple of weeks ago, though. He's in rehab and turning his life around." I felt the panic build in my stomach. Was Ray Brooks calling to tell me that Kurt had left rehab, was back in town and causing trouble? Did he want him off his property?

"Yes, so I've heard. I'm really happy for him, and for you. Hey, the reason I'm calling is that our family has sold the lower orchards. The new owner plans to begin work on the property immediately, and first on his list is to demolish the little cabin Kurt was living in. I assume that he will be looking for something a little nicer when he gets out of rehab and gets a full-time job anyway, so I hope that it won't be a problem for him."

"No, he'll probably want to stay with us while he gets on his feet again." At least, that's what I hoped for and what I had planned. I couldn't bear thinking that Kurt would want something different. Rick might vent and rage a little about making him earn his own way back, but this was the last time I would take a call from a former soccer coach that had taken better care of my son than I had. "Thanks for letting me know. I'll be sure to give Kurt a heads-up when I talk to him next."

"Well, the thing is, he still has some of his belongings at the cabin. I think he took some clothes with him when he went in for treatment, but there are still a few things, photos and such, some clothes, that he left behind. I was wondering if you would want me to bring those things by your house? I've got an appointment in Santa Barbara tomorrow afternoon. It's not too much. The kid traveled light."

The tone in his voice said those words like it was a good thing, and I appreciated him for it. The unspoken fact was that a kid who'd spent every single penny he earned, and then some, buying drugs could only afford to travel light.

Still, I thanked him. I couldn't have Kurt yet, but this would be a start.

When I got home from work the next day, an old green pick-up truck sat backed into my driveway. Ray Brooks climbed out as I pulled in, and by the time I parked my car in the garage and got out, he'd lowered the tailgate and picked up the first box. "Where would you like me to put these?"

My plan was to put the things in the back of our storage shed with my Christmas stuff. But there was no need to further inconvenience Ray Brooks, so I said, "Let's just put them on the back porch. I'll take it from there." I stepped toward the truck. "I'll help you unload." It didn't take long before we were finished and Ray Brooks had waved good-bye.

Three boxes. Just three boxes. The sum total of my son's life possessions. The hope for a future now tempered my despair at the past, and I decided right then and there that after these boxes were emptied, I would save them. In a few years I would bring them out and say something like, "Kurt, remember when every one of your possessions fit in these three boxes? Now, look how far you've come." I pictured him graduating from college, getting a nice job, maybe even working with troubled youth in his extra time. He would be exactly the role model those kids needed. Someone who had been there, had gone through the darkness and managed to dig his way out to the light again. I smiled with my dreams as I moved the boxes into the storage shed.

In fact, I was still smiling when I started dinner a half hour later. The doorbell rang, and it seemed to chime in harmony with the tune I'd started humming. I wasn't expecting anyone, but unexpected visits were both common and welcomed around here. I opened the door, wondering which of the neighborhood kids was selling coffee or candy or wrapping paper this week. Instead, I found Detective Thompson.

"Sorry to bother you again, Mrs. Stewart, but I'm still trying to get a line on Kurt. No one on the streets seems to have seen him for a while."

I looked at him with smug satisfaction. I knew exactly what he was thinking—that my son's absence was perhaps a sign of his guilt, like maybe he had killed and then left town. It was time to put an end to all of this. "You would be right about that. No one on the street has seen him in a while because my son is in a residential rehab. He has been for several weeks now."

He looked surprised by this, then nodded and smiled. "Good for him. I've met Kurt on a few occasions, never did think he was a bad kid, just mixed up in the wrong things."

"Well, now he is getting unmixed." I lifted my chin just a little.

He pulled a pen and paper from his pocket and

scribbled some sort of note using the palm of his left hand as a desk. "Which rehab is he in?"

It was just a simple question, which should have had an easy answer. Except that I had no answer to give. "I don't know."

He looked up from his writing at this. "Don't know?"

I ran my hand along the doorframe. "It's in Orange County somewhere, but that's as much as I know. He called me to tell me what he was doing, but before I had time to get the name of the place or the phone number, he had to get off the phone. I haven't heard from him since." I'm no policewoman, but it doesn't take a trained investigator to realize that this might sound like a mother trying to cover for her son. But that's not what this was. I was telling the truth and I wanted him to know it. "He should be calling back soon."

He rubbed the back of his neck and leaned his head from side to side. "Mrs. Stewart, I don't want to be the one to squash your joy here—really I don't—but you're the one who told me you couldn't afford to be blindsided."

"What do you mean?"

"Maybe your son is in rehab and getting all better and life will soon be wonderful. For your sake and Kurt's, I sure hope that's the case. It's just that I've seen a little too much of the other side of this world not to consider a couple of uglier possibilities."

"Such as?"

"Maybe he's lying to you about being in rehab, thinking that's what you're going to tell us, and hoping it might make us hold off looking for him for a few weeks. Or maybe he's in rehab because of a guilty conscience."

I opened my mouth to tell him that he was wrong, that I knew he was wrong. I started to say that I had Kurt's earthly possessions in my storage barn if he wanted to see them, then he could just look through them and be done with it. "I've got . . ." The words shrunk back inside me and I didn't make an effort to retrieve them. Not because of doubt, really. I knew Kurt hadn't killed anyone. But perhaps because the protective maternal instinct had been so extreme over the last few weeks, I just couldn't say it.

"You've got what?"

"To, uh, turn off my stove before my dinner burns."

"Sorry to disturb you. I'll be off." He started down the front porch stairs, then turned as if he'd had an afterthought. Somehow, I knew it was more than that. "Do me a favor. When Kurt checks in next, give me a call with the name of the rehab center. I'm sure it would do us both good if I close his file."

"Sure." I watched Detective Thompson walk to his car, having no idea whether he believed me or was just waiting for me to slip up.

Seven

Between worrying about Kurt, caring for Caroline, praying over the book I'd been asked to think through, and just the day-to-day stress of work, my commutes to and from the church were the only quiet moments I'd had in recent weeks. And most of the time my brain just shifted into autopilot. I'd even managed to pull into my driveway before realizing a truck had been following me for the last few minutes and had pulled up right behind me. For a worrying second I thought it might be the detective again, but then Kevin Marshall stepped out of his car, offering an uncomfortable smile.

"Uh, hi. I was passing through town today, and Chris asked me to bring something by."

He ducked back quickly into his car and reappeared with a small grocery sack. He walked toward me holding it out, and even from a few feet away I noticed his blue eyes—the kind they write romance novels about.

"Chris was, uh, cleaning out some files the other day, and, uh, he found several photos of Nick. We thought you would want to have them." His face turned red, and I realized that right about then he was doubting the wisdom of that decision.

"I'd love to have them." Our hands touched as

I reached out and took the bag from him. For just a moment we looked each other in the eye, a lifetime's worth of sorrow communicating between us. "Do you want to come in for some coffee?"

"Thanks, but I've got to get back."

I also thought his eyes held just a hint of guilt. Was it because he had the son who survived? Or maybe it wasn't guilt at all. Maybe it was my own envy I saw reflected. I pulled the bag away, careful not to look at the contents. "How is Chris coming along?"

"Oh, he's doing fine. Still limps, of course—will for the rest of his life—but he's able to get around and do all the things he needs to do."

"I'm glad." And I was. I'd only met Chris on a few occasions before the tragedy, but he'd been one of Nick's best friends at USC, and one of the two surviving members of the Mardi Gras attack. I wanted him to live the life that Nick was no longer able to.

Kevin nodded and turned. I followed him toward his truck and swung the bag. "Thank Chris for me."

"I will." He cleared his throat. "Just to warn you, I think there are a few pictures from New Orleans in there. We spent a while talking about whether or not we should get rid of those, but Sheila argued that a mother would want to have pictures taken of her son the day before he died. I don't know, but I figured women understood these things better than Chris or I."

"She's right." And she was, but I wondered how I would ever get the courage to open this bag and look into it.

He nodded toward my Ford Escape. "Hey, I noticed as you pulled in, your passenger side brake light is out."

"Yeah, it has been for a few weeks now. I just can't seem to get my act together to take it in and get it fixed."

"That's easy enough to fix. Rick could do that in a minute or two. Tell him to give me a call if he has any questions."

"We're, uh . . ." I looked at the car, then back at Kevin, "separated."

His hand fell from the handle of his truck and he shook his head. "I was trying so hard not to say anything stupid, and now look at what I've done. I'm so sorry."

"No, it's fine. We've been separated a couple of months. Between Nick's death and Kurt's addiction, things just got a little too hard to take around here, you know what I mean?"

"I understand it better than you can imagine." His face was sad as he shook his head, and I remembered Nick telling me about Chris's mom. She'd been somewhat of a plastic surgery addict, until a botched operation left her in constant pain. After that, she'd begun fueling her life with booze and prescription drugs. In Kevin Marshall's face, I could see that nothing had changed for the better in the last few years.

"Well, I've got to be going." He climbed into his truck, and I stood in the driveway and watched him pull away.

A moment later, I stood outside the door to Nick's room, trying to get the courage to open it. His things had remained more or less unchanged since his death, and I had learned early on that spending time in there only opened a sadness that I hadn't yet learned to manage. Avoidance had always been one of my defense mechanisms, and aside from the occasional cleaning, I rarely stepped foot inside.

The room was dark and smelled of dust. I promised myself I'd come clean it in the next week, but not today. Not now. I set the bag of pictures on Nick's denim bedspread, barely glancing at the framed certificates on the wall, the posters of the Dodgers, and the small shelf of trophies, mostly earned in scholastic events rather than sports. I closed the photos in the room with the rest of the memories. I would look at them later. At that moment, I didn't think I had the strength.

Saturday morning, I took the podium at the Living Above Grief seminar. The faces changed from event to event, but the expressions never did. An energy-sapping, mind-numbing grief shrouded this room like fog rolling in off the Pacific. Most of these people were lost so deep in it that sometimes the thought of simply vanishing forever into the emptiness seemed like the only option. I had been there. Truth be told, I was still there, but they didn't need to hear that. They didn't need to know that I still woke up crying, that I dreamed about Nick's murder, that I still wanted to scream and rage and throw a tantrum. No, what they needed to hear was that with God, life could go on.

The PowerPoint presentation was dialed in to perfection. I always started with a few pictures of Nick as a child. "My son Nick wanted to be a missionary from the time he was very small. He used to line up his stuffed animals and tell them all about grace through faith." I flipped to the next slide, which showed him dressed in his favorite costume, his face painted green. "Of course, he also wanted to be a Teenage Mutant Ninja Turtle." There was always a little snigger around the room at this point. Everyone enjoys a cute kid story. I went to the next slide. "This is Nick, repainting the wall in his brother's room." A small murmur of "awww" went around the room before I continued. "Lest any of you be deceived into believing this was public service, he's painting over the words 'Kurt is a stupid head' and several similar comments, which he had applied with oil-based paint. Yes, my son was not only a tagger, but he was a tagger inside his own home."

More stories, more laughter. As we got to the photos from his teenage years, they would look at the gawky, skinny kid who had been my son and smile. I always waited until I had the audience relaxed and loosened up before I moved into the hard part. The last slide I showed was the one from the day we moved Nick into the dorm.

"When my son went away to college, he got involved with a very mission-minded group. So during Mardi Gras, he and a couple of friends took the week off from classes and went to New Orleans. They decided there was no other place in the world more in need of a Savior than the group of people that would be partying on those streets." Here, at this point, I always got choked up. I hated that I did, because I was talking about overcoming, and here I was, four years later, still unable to finish the story. Of course, everyone seemed to understand this, but I considered it a failure. If I was really living in the strength of Christ, I should be able to have the strength to tell this story without crying. Shouldn't I?

"They came upon a group of young men who pretended to be interested in what they were saying. This pretense lasted only long enough to get Nick and his friends to a secluded area where they could rob them. The boys had only about fifty dollars among them, which infuriated their attackers. My son Nick was beaten to death." Each time I told this part, I was grateful for the officer who recommended that I not be the one to identify my son. I still saw him in my mind as the healthy, happy boy I'd always known. "One of his friends was left unconscious but later recovered. The other will never walk without a limp again." For just a flash I saw Kevin Marshall's blue eyes in my mind. It comforted me somehow.

The murmur of sympathy went through the group as it always did. Now was when they were completely on my side. Now was the time I had to deliver the encouragement that would see them through whatever crisis they were facing.

I talked about the day afterward. The trip down to New Orleans to identify Nick's body. I talked about the week and months afterward—the funeral and trial—trying to capture a bit of both the deep sorrows and tender moments of comfort I'd felt. I talked about the comfort some friends offered and the distance that grew between others who'd seemed suddenly afraid of me. I tried to be honest and transparent. They'd know otherwise.

"People always ask me if this makes me angry at God. I won't lie to you—you're all far too valuable for that. Yes, I was angry. Yes, I questioned my beliefs. After all, if God really is able to do anything, why didn't He step in and save my son and his friends? Why did He let them suffer that way?" With each question, the heaviness weighted me more and more, even now.

"And I won't stand up here and insult your intelligence by pretending that I know the answer even now. But the one thing I do know is that He has been there, and more. When I think of what my son experienced just before he died, how it must have hurt him to know that the very people he came to help were the ones who were doing this to him—well, I realize the One who understands that even more than me is Jesus. I wonder at the grief he must have experienced, beaten, abused. And all the while the people He was suffering to save spat at him, called Him names. And it must have been ever so much harder for the Father, who watched the whole thing, felt every bit of the humiliation being heaped upon His Son. He could have stopped it, could have given everyone in the crowd every bit of what they deserved. But He didn't. He loved me enough that He experienced that kind of grief for me, and even for those who scorned His very Son."

I always had to pause here. Even though the words were mostly the same from seminar to seminar, the depth of God's love always struck me anew. I couldn't begin to fathom the love that would allow Him to do that.

Finally, I moved forward with some practical steps toward dealing with grief, my personal experience, and some stories from those I'd counseled.

"I had to learn to accept that He loved me. Period. And let it go. It's exhausting carrying around the weight of grief all the time." Knowing nods all around. "You'll find the burden much lighter if you will allow Him to carry you, rather than trying to do it all yourself." I thought of my son's addiction, my own crumbling marriage, and once again I prayed to God that He would help me through this.

I showed a few more slides at the end, as always, and finished with some from Nick's teenage goofy years to help lighten the mood. Then I opened the floor to questions.

A woman with a flowing skirt and trembling hands stood. "How long did it take you to get to the point where you no longer miss your son?"

Putting on a brave front was one thing, an out-and-out lie was another. I shook my head. "I hope I never reach that time, to be honest. For me, remembering Nick means missing him. And I'll never forget my son. But more and more, the memories come to me with joy rather than just pain. I can laugh when I think about him rather than just fall apart. And the feeling that grows stronger each day is that I can't wait until I get to heaven and see him again. You know, I'm thinking he'll even have his room clean there, which is more than I could say on Earth." Again, a few laughs, but my mind flashed to that bag of pictures still sitting on his bed, just waiting for me to have the courage to open it and look at them. I doubted anything but pain waited for me.

"How did your son's death affect your family?" A voice from the back broke my reverie.

This question always came up, and I hated it. Remembering Beth's earlier comments of the same opinion goaded me into answering. These women needed to know what they were up against. "Nick's brother, just a couple of years younger than him, fell into despair after Nick's death. Drug abuse followed soon thereafter." This admission always caused a soul-deep groan in the room, which shook the place to its core. Today, however, I could add one more layer of hope to my talk. "But I am happy to report that my prodigal has begun rehab and is back on his way to the life he had before." I didn't admit to my separation from Rick. It was temporary. We really would work it out, especially now that Kurt was on the mend.

I saw a raised hand in the back. "Yes, in the back."

"Whatever happened to the boys who killed your son?"

This question usually came, although I always tried to avoid it. The shift of focus from over-coming grief to seeking justice could undo everything I'd just said. "They were convicted and are in jail serving life sentences." I looked through the auditorium. "Anyone else?"

"Do you think it eases your grief, even in a small measure, that the guilty parties are in jail? Would you wish the same thing for other parents of victims of violent crime?" It was the same voice as the previous question, and I recognized it now. Detective Thompson.

I looked into the back row but could not clearly see his face from where I stood. "Nothing done by human hands can ease my grief over the loss of my son. Only God can do that. Does it make me feel better that those men are locked up so that they cannot do the same to someone else's son? Of course it does." If he'd done any homework at all, and I was quite certain he had, then he already knew that the boys who killed my son all had a long record of violent crimes. In fact, the case had become something of a poster child for groups pushing for stiffer penalties, but this was not a conversation I wanted to have at this time.

"Would you say, then, it is the basic right of all parents who've had children die by violence to have the guilty party brought to justice?"

"I don't know about basic rights of all parents. All I know is that my son lived a life that he could be proud of, and in his death, I will honor him by moving forward the way I believe he would want me to. Part of that includes not losing myself in the bitterness of what might have been, or who I can look to blame. Now, are there any other questions?"

There were none. Beth came forward to make a few announcements about the afternoon workshops. As soon as she was done, I hurried down the aisle, determined to demand an explanation from Detective Thompson. How dare he come here and try to undermine what I was doing?

"Mrs. Stewart, may I speak with you a moment?" An elegant-looking African-American woman wearing a stylish suit extended her hand. "My name is Reisha Cinders, and I am the host of the *Christian America Talk Show*. Have you heard our broadcasts?"

As much as I didn't want to talk about broadcasts right now, I did want to be polite. Besides, I knew where I could find Detective Thompson, he'd given me his card. I looked at the woman. "Of course. What do you need?"

"I was wondering if you would like to be a guest on our show."

"Me?"

"I believe your talk could be an inspiration to so many others. And your answers to the questions could have been nothing less than Holy Spirit–inspired. Next month we're having a series on leniency in the justice system. Since I know that is what had previously happened with your son's attackers, I thought you'd be a first-person voice on the topic. Whether you think justice or mercy impacts a life more."

I wondered if she would still think my answers

Holy Spirit–inspired if she knew the questions were asked by the detective investigating my son, and that the answers were given by a mother who would do anything she could to defend him. Still, I took her card. "It sounds like a good program. Let me spend a little time praying about it and I'll get back to you."

She nodded. "I need to know something by early next week."

"I'll be in touch." I walked the rest of the way down the aisle, looking for any sign of Detective Thompson. He was gone.

Eight

Despite my earlier protests, I found that preparing for the conference and delivering my talk, coupled with my excitement for Kurt's U-turn, energized my attempts at writing, as well. I'd chipped away, page by page, on some ideas most nights after Caroline was asleep, and finally after four weeks I had enough to show others for some advice. I knew my friends wouldn't spare me if they thought I was headed down the wrong path.

"Alisa, this is perfect. Absolutely perfect!" Marsha waved the pages in the air as if she were holding up a winning lottery ticket. Thankfully, the sandwich shop we'd decided to meet in after church was noisy and crowded, and no one seemed to notice. "I can't believe it. I'm actually going to be the friend of a famous writer."

"I think you're overshooting just a bit." I really wanted to roll my eyes, but I couldn't help but smile at her enthusiasm.

"No, I am not." She looked offended by the suggestion. "This is exactly what you've been called to do with your life. You've found your place, the place God has been leading you toward all along. Your promised land, you might say."

I looked toward the others. "Okay, now that we've gotten Marsha's optimistic delusions out of the way, what do I need to work on?"

Tasha slid her stack of papers toward me. I could already see red-inked notes in the margin. "This *is* powerful, and I agree with Marsha that you were born for this. I would have to disagree about the perfect part, however. You know how I feel about proper grammar and your lack of it." She smiled and said, "Of course, that's the reason God led me to you, so you wouldn't be left in the wilderness of dangling participles."

"And . . . God led me to you because a few of your chapter titles are a little lacking," Carleigh said. "Some of them are fine, but I think we need to reach for greatness. Don't you? I noted some suggestions." She slid her copy of my manuscript back to me.

"Thanks so much. I don't know how I'd do this without all of you."

"You couldn't." Carleigh laughed, then lifted her glass of iced tea. "To our future writing project."

Glasses clinked all around the table.

Lacey peered at me over the top of her Wedgwood teacup. She took a sip, returned the cup to its saucer, and continued to watch me. Waiting.

There was no reason for me to pretend that nothing was wrong. We'd met too many times over these Tuesday morning breakfasts. "The detective that came to our house, he's showing up other places now."

She looked at me with eyes the palest shade of blue I'd ever seen. "What kind of places?"

"He stopped by Rick's jobsite."

Lacey laughed twice, before it turned into the usual dry cough. She hacked for a few beats, then took a sip of water and a deep breath. She was still grinning when she spoke. "Stopped by his jobsite? I can imagine how well that went over."

Rick had worked his way from carpenter to top construction superintendent in record time, partly due to his impeccable work ethic. He maintained strict rules about what constituted an appropriate time to call or stop by while he was at work. There were very few situations deemed serious enough to be appropriate. "Yeah, I'm sure all the guys wondered what a cop wanted with Rick." I rubbed my index finger along the graceful curve of the teapot's handle. "Come to think of it, I guess they really didn't. They all just assumed it was something about Kurt."

"And they were right enough about that, I suppose. You said 'places,' plural, so where else has he showed up?"

"He came to the seminar last weekend."

"He showed up at your grief seminar?" The wrinkles in her forehead deepened as she pondered this. "Did he make a scene?"

I shook my head. "I didn't even know he was there until the very end of my talk. He sat in the back row, and when I was taking questions he asked me about Nick."

"What'd he ask?"

"If it helped ease my grief knowing the guilty party was in jail, if I thought that all parents whose children were victims of violent offenders wanted to see justice for their child's murderer, or something to that effect."

Lacey stared out her window and nodded slowly. "He's trying to crank up the pressure on you, there's no doubt about that."

"He must think I know something that I'm not telling him." I took a sip of my tea. "I wish I did. I'd give anything to know exactly where Kurt is this very minute, how he's doing." And how I prayed the answer to that question was that my son was truly in rehab. Those were not the kinds of doubts I cared to voice, so I did what I always do, put on an upbeat front. "Besides, if I knew the exact date he checked in and could prove that, it would get Kurt's name taken right off the list. An alibi that would leave no doubt, that's what I want."

"You're right about that. We just have to hope the kid went to rehab before the murder. I still have some friends from my law days, and from what I've heard, the police are grasping at anything they can right now. It sounds like there was no hard evidence left behind. All they have is the list of people who owed the dead guy money. I'm sure they're hoping if they put enough pressure on the usual suspects, eventually someone's going to slip."

"I don't see why he's so intent on talking to Kurt. He said himself he'd met Kurt a few times and thought he was a good kid just messed up in the wrong thing."

"Baby, have you been reading the paper lately? Two gang fights, a stabbing on the east side, and several tourists robbed at gunpoint. Those are the kinds of stories that send the Chamber of Commerce into full-blown panic mode. The businesses are demanding action, the mayor's running scared. This whole city is worked up over the whole violent crime issue right now. There's a lot of pressure on them to find somebody and get him charged. Makes everyone look bad if a killer goes uncaught, even if the city is a better place with the murdered guy dead and gone."

I nodded my head. There was another fear eating away at me, one I'd voiced to no one. Lacey was the safest person to share with, I knew that, and I needed to talk. "I'm starting to wonder if he still is in rehab at all. Wouldn't he be calling home more? Wouldn't they even want us to come down there for some family therapy? What if after a few days he decided it was too hard and has gone back to his old life?"

"He said he'd already made it through the detox process, right? That has to be the hardest part of it all, at least I'd think so. If he were back in Santa Barbara and back in his old habits, the police would have found him by now and your detective friend wouldn't be following you around. No, he's still in treatment."

"Why haven't I heard from him?"

"I'm sure every center has their own protocol about calls home and family therapy. My guess is, you won't hear from him again until he is ready to come home. He'll want to be sure that everything is just perfect before he comes to see you."

"I hope you're right." And I did hope. I was finding it harder by the day to actually believe.

Nine

I passed through the aisles of Vons the next day, pushing my cart with all the determination of a speed walker. I didn't want to be here shopping if this was the moment that Kurt called home. As I rounded the corner of the bread aisle, another cart clanked into the side of mine, forcing my attention back to the here and now. "Oh, sorry. I should have looked first. . . ." When I saw who was driving the other cart, all apologies froze in my throat.

"Well, hello. Fancy meeting you here." From the expression on his face, and the jeans, T-shirt, and Angels baseball cap he was wearing, no one would assume that Detective Thompson was anything other than surprised to be running into an old friend at the grocery store. I, of course, knew better.

"Are you following me?"

He leaned both elbows on the rails of the cart and whispered. "Just doing a little shopping." He gestured toward the chips and salsa in his cart, then smiled up at me. "Why? Should I be following you?"

I remembered what Lacey had said about their not having much evidence to work with. In my head I knew that the guy was just trying to do his job. He wanted to find a killer and silence the public outcry. That all sounded well and good—until my son became part of his doing his job. "You know what? I wish I could tell you something. I wish I knew where my son is. I wish I could tell you the name of the rehab where he's been for the last couple of months and help lighten your load. But I can't. Why don't you go follow some other lead and quit harassing the innocent citizens of Santa Barbara?"

"Hmm, didn't realize that grocery shopping constituted harassment. I do apologize." He tipped the cap and offered a lazy smile. "You know what, though? My gut tells me that someone with nothing to hide shouldn't be so upset about this chance encounter. Are you sure there's nothing you want to tell me?"

I gripped my cart so tight my fingers went numb. "I don't know *anything*. How long is it going to take for you to get that through your head?"

"My head accepts it already; it's just that my gut hasn't quite caught up yet."

"Well, tell your gut to get over it and leave me alone."

"All righty, then. I'll just make my way up the fruit aisle and harass some other citizens for a while. How about that?" He turned his cart the other way and sauntered off, whistling "Yankee Doodle" as he went.

I looked at the couple dozen items still

unmarked on my list and decided we could live another week without most of these things. I hurried to grab the necessary gallon of milk, Caroline's favorite string cheese, and yogurt. Fudgsicles and chicken nuggets would have to wait until the next trip. I wasn't staying in this place with that man for a second longer than necessary.

When I pulled onto my street, I found myself checking the curb for black cars before I pulled into the driveway. There were none. Finally starting to relax, I carried the first couple of grocery bags inside and dropped them on the kitchen counter. As always, I went to the phone and checked it for voice mail. There was one message. I pressed the pass code, held my breath, and waited.

"Hey, it's me. I need to chat with you as soon as you've got a spare minute. Call me. Okay?" My sister's voice carried the same even tone with which she always spoke. You could rarely tell from Jodi's voice, or facial expression for that matter, if she was happy, sad, mad, or afraid. She always came across as . . . for lack of a better word, content.

No message from my son, but of course that didn't stop me from continuing with the second step in my routine—checking my caller ID. Not everyone left messages. Maybe Kurt wouldn't, either. It was a long shot, but it was all I had.

Today's reading told me there were three missed calls. I perused the list. The first was from Lacey; she never left a message. The second was from my sister, the third from a number marked Private Caller. That one set my heart to sputtering.

Every day I received calls marked Private—telemarketers, the local thrift store when they call to say they'll have a truck on the street next week to pick up donations, several of my friends who are particularly uptight about their privacy. None of those things even went through my mind. Logic ceased to exist where my children were concerned. This call was from Kurt, it had to be from Kurt. It wasn't just emotion; there were facts to support it.

When he'd called the first time, the call had been marked private. He told me that he would call me when it was time to be released, probably six to eight weeks. Well, it had been seven weeks and eleven hours, so this call had to be from him. Maybe he was even now on his way home. And that's what I needed, to get a glimpse of my son's face, to see that he was all right, clear eyed, and turning his life around.

What if that was his only chance to call and I had missed it? Would he still come by unannounced, or would he wait for the okay? A discordant clang began somewhere in the deep recesses of my mind, telling me that it couldn't possibly be Kurt because he'd probably left rehab a day or two after calling me, that maybe Detective Thompson was right and he'd never been there at all. I put my hands over my ears to muffle it, but even when I concentrated on staying positive, the negative thoughts pushed their way inside.

I knew one way to win this battle. I would make myself behave as if I believed only the positive. I would prepare Kurt's room for his arrival.

I walked down the hallway and opened the door that had remained closed for far too long. As soon as I switched on the light, I regretted not preparing better for this moment. The bedspread, although clean and tidy, was at least ten years old, and somehow I doubted that multicolored surfboards were age appropriate for a twenty-one-year-old's duvet cover. The blue stripes on the curtain panels looked faded, I'd never noticed that before. Why hadn't I replaced those things while I had the chance? Maybe this room would be too full of bad memories for him. Then again, maybe it would feel more like home—as if his room had just been sitting here waiting for him all this time.

I got the Windex and cleaned the windows, then dusted the furniture and vacuumed the beige carpet. At least it would be clean when he got here.

I opened his mostly empty closet to see if anything needed straightening. An old ski jacket hung in the back—reminiscent of happier times when we actually took family vacations. I hoped those days would return to us now that Kurt was drug free. It would never be the same, of course. Nick was gone and would never be back. Still, better times, even good times, awaited.

The empty closet once filled with things made me think about Kurt's possessions in the back of our storage shed. What if I took his things out, got them all cleaned up, and set them up in his room for him? When he arrived, I could show him that his room was stocked and ready for him, and let him know that he was welcome to stay awhile.

How would Rick feel about that? I was pretty sure he would have issues with it. He held firm to the belief that after children were grown and left the nest, they should not return. Period. Even though he wasn't living here, the house was technically half his. Besides, we'd always tried to work as a team where our kids were concerned. At least until recently.

Surely even he would be willing to make an exception in this case. How could he not see the necessity of doing everything we could possibly do to make certain that our son succeeded in his recovery? A wholesome environment, healthy food, and a safe place to sleep would be paramount at this time.

When the phone rang, I ran into the hallway and

through the kitchen to find the closest handset. I snatched it up, looked at caller ID, and saw Private Caller.

My heart began to pound. "Hello?"

"Mom. It's me."

I sank down onto the bed, tears of joy already clogging my throat. "Kurt, how are you?"

"I'm making progress. Starting tomorrow, I'll be released from the full-time residential program." His voice sounded stronger than it had when he called last. Healthy and happy. Like it used to sound. Before.

"I've just been in your room, getting everything all cleaned and set up for you. So you'll be here tomorrow, then?" I could scarcely grasp the reality of my son finally coming home to me. It had been such a distant dream since he'd left that I'd hardly acknowledged the dream existed. Now I knew that I would do whatever it took to make certain my son stayed sober. Yes, when he got home I would watch him, help him, support him. It would be a long and hard process, perhaps, but a team effort we were all willing to make. I saw the paper and pencil on the bedside table and picked them up. "By the way, what's your phone number there?"

I could hear my son breathing on the other end of the line, so I knew that he was still there. He just didn't speak.

"Kurt?"

"I . . . thought Aunt Jodi would have called you by now."

"Jodi?" I thought about the message she'd left on my phone today. "We've played a little phone tag. She called, left a message. I was just about to call back."

"Did she tell you anything? In the message, I mean?"

"All she's told me is to call her back, that we needed to talk. What were you expecting her to tell me?"

Again, the sound of his breathing on the other end was the only thing that let me know he was still there. Finally, he sighed and continued. "That I'm moving in with them."

A giant tourniquet squeezed the air from my lungs, as if my body wanted to stop the flow of pain into my heart. I couldn't breathe. "Why?" The word croaked out of me.

"The treatment center where I've been staying has a satellite program in Paso Robles, and they've already arranged for me to attend daily sessions. I don't think I can come back to Santa Barbara, where my old friends and old habits are just a phone call away. Besides, Uncle Monte has offered me a job working his olive orchards. Hourly rate plus free room and board as long as I work hard, stay out of trouble, and keep my grades up."

In spite of the ache that filled every bit of my

being, I knew that logically I should be glad that my son was now clean, glad that he was turning his life around. Why did the thought of him choosing to live with my sister over me feel so much like rejection? Like one more level of the failure that had been taunting me through his life for all these years. "Your grades?"

"I'm getting my transcripts together so I can start summer school at Cuesta College. I've been talking to the counselor there, and she believes that if I keep my act together and my grades up, I'll have a good chance of returning to Cal Poly for my junior year."

"It's hard to believe that the same person who lived here, who never planned even a week ahead, has managed to map out the next few years of his life so beautifully." I choked up and stopped talking before I lost it. After a couple of deep breaths, I managed to continue. "I am so proud of you."

"It's been a long time since I've heard those words." His voice was every bit as thick as mine. "From anyone. But no worries, Mom. Things have changed. I've changed. *A lot.*"

The tourniquet loosened with each word. "I've got to see you. At least let me help you move in at Jodi's. Besides, Caroline is going to be a basket case if she can't get her paws on you soon."

He laughed. "How is the munchkin? I bet she's become quite the little lady since I last saw her."

He paused a moment, then continued. "I'll be driving through Santa Barbara tomorrow night on the way up to Templeton. You want to have dinner or something?"

The menu began to form in my mind. Kurt's favorite meal had always been beef stroganoff, even though I refused to cook it very often because of the high fat content and the amount of time it took to do it right. Today, neither thing mattered. "Of course I want to have dinner. You just wait, I'll fix you a meal that'll make you wonder what you ever did without me."

"I know what I did without you, Mom, and it wasn't pretty." Again, his voice choked up. I heard someone in the background telling him that his time was up. "Look, Mom, I've got to go. Would you rather just meet at McDonald's or something? It'll make Short Stuff happy, and I know Dad doesn't want me coming around there. I don't want to cause trouble."

This definitely wasn't the right time to mention the separation. When Kurt came to dinner, I would make certain Rick was here, and we would all pretend that things were just fine. "Of course he wants you coming around here. He was thrilled when I told him that you were in rehab. He will be as excited as I am to see you."

Kurt's resulting laugh had a bitter edge to it. "Okay. I'll call before I leave, just in case you change your mind before tomorrow." He paused for a minute. "Mom, I love you." The phone clicked, signalling the end of our conversation.

"No! I love you, too. I love you, too." The tears poured down my face as the words kept ripping themselves from my very heart and into the phone, over and over and over again. I knew he'd hung up before he ever heard the first word, but I couldn't stop myself. How many years had I spent wanting to say those words to him? Once I started, I just couldn't stop.

Ten

I was still holding the phone in my hand when the doorbell rang. I had no idea how long I'd been sitting there. It could have been a couple of minutes or a couple of hours. Whatever the time, it had passed in daydreams of my son's return.

I shook myself out of my thoughts, set the phone in its cradle, and walked to the door. Only after I opened it and saw the look on Kevin Marshall's face did I realize how I must have looked.

He took a step backward. "I'm sorry. I should have called before I stopped by."

I wiped my eyes and smiled at him. "Oh no, no, it's fine. These are happy tears." I ran my finger tightly under my eyes, hoping I was removing any trace of running mascara rather than smearing it. "Actually, I just got some terrific news."

"That's what I like to hear." His smile warmed me clear through.

"What brings you here?"

"I was at work in the shop yesterday, getting out a couple of bulbs, and it made me think of your brake light issue. Since I had to come to Santa Barbara today anyway, I thought I'd stop by, see if you'd taken care of it."

How long had it been since Rick had gone out of his way to do something for me, simply to be nice? I couldn't even begin to remember a time—the fact that he could probably say the same about me notwithstanding. "No, I've managed to completely neglect it. So that would be wonderful."

"I'll go get my tools and meet you in the garage, okay?"

I raced through the house and smacked the garage door button, then hurried back out to stand beside him as he looked through the toolbox on his truck. "It'll only take a minute or two." He pulled a bulb out and began working on the car. He kept his eyes focused on his hands, but he spoke easily as he worked. "I saw the funniest-looking VW on the street today. It was covered entirely in stone—you know, like builder's stone. It looked like somebody got tired of his sidewalk, rolled it up, and put it on his car. The thing must have weighed a ton."

"Yeah, I've seen it, too. Caroline calls it the Flintstonemobile." I tried to think of something amusing to add to the conversation. The best I could come up with was, "It's pretty clever though, you've got to admit."

"I'll give you that, and if you ask me, what the world needs a little more of right about now is funny. There's been way too much of the other stuff for my liking in the last few years." He looked over his shoulder. "'Course, I'm not one to complain to you."

I shrugged and put on my bravest expression, the same one I put on at all my conferences. "Your problems are no less valid than mine."

"There, all better." He put the plastic cover back over the bulb, then turned his Paul Newman eyes toward me. "You said you got some terrific news. Anything you want to share?"

"Yes, I do, as a matter of fact." I said it absently because what I'd really been thinking was that today, more than any so far, I was glad for the eight or nine pounds I'd lost over the past weeks. The thought was fleeting enough, but I recognized it for the danger that it was. Why should I care whether Kevin Marshall thought I looked good? "Do you remember Nick's younger brother, Kurt?"

He nodded but didn't say anything. And of course he wouldn't. What choice would he have except "Oh yeah, isn't he that kid that went from a straight-A scholar-athlete to a drug addict?"

"Well, he gets out of rehab tomorrow. I just

talked to him, and he's really serious about turning his life around. At least we won't have to live with yet one more tragedy from the attack."

"That's great news." He took a step closer, and for just a moment I thought he might hug me. He didn't. "Chris will be thrilled to hear it. He has always worried about Kurt, and your entire family."

It gave me pause to think of one of Nick's friends still worrying about us. Sometimes in the course of grief I convinced myself I was so alone. It was strange to think about the people who cared that I never even knew about. I felt myself getting choked up and didn't want to go there. I reached out and touched the back light panel on my car. "Well, thanks for this. How much do I owe you?"

"Not a thing. Just one friend helping another."

"It really was a nice thing for a friend to do." I extended my hand and he shook it.

His palm was warm against mine, his grip so firm and assured and safe. I wanted to hold on to that feeling for as long as I could. And he must have felt it, because I'm pretty sure we held on a few seconds longer than necessary. Maybe not— maybe I was just lost in my own fantasy.

I pulled myself out of whatever it was that was messing with my brain and nodded toward his truck. "You tell Chris that we're going to be just fine."

"You can bet I will." He climbed into his truck and drove away.

I watched his truck disappear. Long after he was gone, I stood in my driveway doing nothing. Completely alone.

Eleven

Rick arrived early on Thursday, carrying a bouquet of flowers. "I thought these would look nice on the table."

I stared at the multicolored mixture, too stunned to even react for a moment. "Wow. Thanks." Flowers? From Rick? Even though they were just to make the place look nice for Kurt, I knew the gesture was way out of his comfort zone, and I appreciated them all the more for it. He really was going to try. Once I finally recovered my senses enough to remove the vase from his hands, I went to arrange it on the table, removing the flowers I'd already set there. I placed them on the coffee table in the living room.

"I guess I should have told you I was bringing those, huh? It would have saved you some money and effort."

I flipped my hand dismissively. "A girl can never have too many flowers."

He turned and walked toward the window. "I'm terrified, Alisa. I want this to be for real."

I nodded, knowing exactly what he meant. We

waited then, mostly in silence. It wasn't hostile, or even awkward. I think we were both simply too nervous to make small talk.

When I saw the rusted junker pull into my driveway, a joy pulsed through my veins like I can't begin to describe. I thought of all the times I'd heard the story of the prodigal son, in Sunday school as a kid, then in sermons as I'd gotten older. Looking back, I realized that even as an adult I'd always focused on the son and his journey back, the courage it took to return home defeated. Only in this exact moment did I fully understand the depth of the father's love and pain as he stood watching down the road day after day. I thought of the part where he saw his son coming when he was still far off, and as I looked at the tired red car in my driveway, I understood every bit of his elation at the first glimpse of his son. Tonight, I was certain part of that ancient father's spirit must be with me. The only thing missing here was the fatted calf, but for Kurt, beef stroganoff was probably even better.

My fingers pressed against the handle, prepared to fling the door open, when I felt Rick's hand on mine. "We have to be responsible, Alisa. Do not, under any circumstances, give him money."

His words sucked the joy right out of me. "Why would you say something like that? Our son is back. He's turned his life around. Why would you want to belittle him by making the comment you just made?" I took care to keep my voice soft, for fear that it might carry to the driveway, but everything inside me wanted to scream.

"I know my son. That's how I can say it." His eyes had dulled to that look I'd grown so accustomed to. What had happened to the man I used to know, the same man who had been standing in this living room just moments ago? The one who even dared to hope a little? At that moment, I began to realize we might not be able make it through the evening without Kurt realizing we were separated.

I jerked my hand off the handle and Rick took the hint.

"At least give him a chance."

"I will give him a chance. I'm just not going to give him any money, and I don't want you to give him any, either."

There were plenty of reasons from Kurt's past that made this a valid concern, I knew it. But I was willing to put all those bad things behind us and move toward a new future with the son who had returned to us. I jerked the door open and ran to meet him, never looking back at the man who used to be my husband. "Kurt, oh, sweetie." I threw my arms around him and he hugged me tighter than he'd ever hugged me in his whole life. He didn't let go.

"Oh, Mom, it's so good to see you." He continued to hold me. "I'm so sorry, so sorry."

I held on for as long as I could, before emotion forced me to pull away. The sting of tears was prickling my eyes, and I would not ruin this moment by crying. I didn't want to be a weak female. I wanted to be his strong mother who was here for him and would support him no matter what happened. His hair was closely shorn, his face a bit pale, his body painfully thin. The last four years of hard living made him look older than his twenty-one years, but I had no doubt that he would reclaim his former charm after continuing with a sober life. I intended to do all I could to assist him with that.

"Well, look who we have here." Rick's voice was firm but not unfriendly. He stuck out his hand and Kurt shook it. It was beyond me how men could shake hands at a time like this, even if they were only a step away from estranged. "Good to see you, Kurt."

Kurt nodded. "Good to see you, too, Dad." I wondered if they were both remembering the last time they were together. If Kurt was picturing the hard set of his father's face as he heard he was no longer welcome in this house. If Rick was picturing the pain that dulled Kurt's eyes in spite of the defiant expression. If either remembered Kurt's final words that I sometimes still heard during the darkest of my dreams: *I'd rather die than ever come back here.*

The scene was still so real and vivid to me, it

could make me physically ill if I thought about it for too long. After today, I planned to write it off as simply a bad dream that never really happened. My reality was starting right here, in this very moment.

"Where's Short Stuff?" Kurt looked toward the house as if expecting Caroline to come running out at any moment.

"She's at softball practice. Her friend Jenny's dad will drop her off at the house in about twenty minutes." I didn't tell him how Caroline had cried when she found out she wouldn't be here to greet him. I also didn't tell him that Rick had insisted Caroline not be here in the beginning, until we "check this whole thing out."

Kurt's eyes looked tired, empty almost, as if the spirit had been sucked right out of him. An uneasy sensation gnawed at me as we turned toward the house. What if he turned and ran? Well, I would not let that happen. As we walked through the front door, I linked my arms through his and squeezed tight. I planned to clamp down for dear life if he tried to so much as slow down. It was hard enough to know that he would be leaving here in a few hours to go live with my sister. Only the knowledge that she loved him almost as much as I did made that fact bearable.

Kurt took a step inside the door, then stopped. He looked all around as if seeing his childhood home for the first time, nodded occasionally, and took a few deep breaths. "I'd forgotten how much I missed this place."

I started to say something along the lines of "It hasn't been the same without you," but I didn't want to say anything that he might take as an accusation. Instead, I said the only thing I could think of. "Let's sit in the living room for a little while. I'll bring in some chips and guacamole, and we can spend a few minutes relaxing before dinner."

I heard the sound of a car in the driveway and realized Caroline must have finished practice a little early today. She would be thrilled about that since it would mean more time with Kurt. I walked to the front door and opened it, preparing to call out a thanks to Jenny's father and an offer to pick the girls up from practice next week. Only that's not what happened.

When I saw the black car sitting in my driveway, I gagged on my revulsion. I looked at Rick, who sat in the living room with his son, not one trace of guilt on his face. How could he do that? I knew very well he had set this up. This was why he insisted Caroline go to softball practice. He didn't want her to be here when the police arrived to question her brother.

"Who's here?" Kurt asked.

I turned my gaze from Rick to Kurt, trying to keep my voice and expression calm, although I was nothing even close to it. "It's a detective.

He's been wanting to talk to you for a while."

"Talk to me?" His voice sounded so surprised. So innocent. He looked at his father and nodded, shoulders back. "I guess I better talk to him then." He walked to the front door and met Detective Thompson on the front porch. He extended his hand as if he were applying for a job rather than talking to a detective. "I'm Kurt Stewart. I understand you'd like to talk to me."

Detective Thompson nodded toward me. "I know you're right in the middle of a reunion, so if I could ask a couple of quick questions, that would be great."

Kurt nodded. "Fire away."

"Did you know Rudy Prince?"

Kurt looked at me for a split second before he nodded. "Yeah, I know him."

I noticed the way he used the present tense instead of the past. I hoped that Detective Thompson noticed, too. Kurt obviously didn't even know Rudy Prince was dead, much less have played any part in it.

"Your friend Rudy was beaten to death a while back. We're talking to everyone who was associated with the guy."

"He was no friend of mine, and I didn't *associate* with him. I bought drugs from him. In fact, I'm pretty sure I still owe him some money." His voice was as flat as the look in his eyes. No emotion, no energy. I hoped it was the strain of rehab, not the permanent work of drugs, that had removed the spark from him.

"A little over a thousand dollars, according to his records."

"Yeah, well, is that why you're here—to collect the money? Do I need to pay that to his next of kin now?"

Detective Thompson seemed surprised by the sarcasm. "I'd say you're a lucky man in the debt department. Let's see how well you do in the truth-telling department. I need the name of the rehab facility where you've been, and I need to know the date you entered."

"I stayed at Serenity by the Sea, and I have no idea what date I entered. It was a couple of months ago. I think I went in on a Saturday, but I couldn't say for sure. That time is mostly a fog I'd rather not look back through."

Detective Thompson smiled amiably. "Yeah, I'm sure I understand that. Listen, I don't want to hold up your dinner any longer. I just need an address and a phone number where I can reach you after I check out a few things."

Kurt gave him my sister's address and phone number. "I'm not sure what I can do to help you, but feel free to give me a call." He said it with such conviction, such innocence, I was sure that Detective Thompson now realized he'd wasted his time in coming here.

We walked back into the house, and I glared at

Rick, wishing we were alone right now so I could tell him exactly what I thought about his little stunt. He didn't look at me, and instead sat staring at the carpet. I almost thought I saw a shimmer of liquid in his eyes. Good. Surely now even he saw how wrong he'd been. I turned my attention back to Kurt, determined to salvage this evening. "What would you like to drink?"

Kurt looked at me and his mouth dropped open. Then just as quickly he smiled and shook his head. "Thought you were offering me a martini there for a second, then I realized who it was doing the offering. Oh, Mom, it's been too long." He put his arm around my shoulders and grinned, and as he did I thought I saw a brief spark of his old self. "Do you have any cream soda?"

"It just so happens that I do." Our entire pantry was stocked with every single thing I could remember Kurt ever liking, and cream soda had been his favorite since childhood. It would take weeks for us to eat through the leftovers, but I didn't care. My son had come home.

One cream soda later, just as we seemed to be running out of safe topics to talk about, I heard a car pull into the driveway. This time I went to the door with a bit of trepidation. I reached for the handle, but the door burst open before I could touch it, nearly knocking me down.

"Kurt, Kurt!" Before I even realized what was

happening, Caroline had crossed the room and flung herself into Kurt's lap.

I rubbed my shoulder, took a step out onto the porch, and waved at the retreating car. "I'll pick up Jenny after next practice."

"No problem." Her father waved out the driver's side window as he pulled off.

I walked back into the living room to find Caroline with her arms wrapped around Kurt's neck, murmuring, "I missed you, I missed you," over and over again. Oh, how I envied a child's lack of restraint right now.

Kurt put his arms around her and squeezed, his eyes closed. "I missed you, too, Short Stuff. I've missed you bunches."

He kissed the top of her head. "So, what have you been up to? Have you gotten married or engaged or anything while I've been gone?" His eyes began to twinkle and his voice had regained some its former energy.

"Gross! I'm only ten."

"Ten? Ten? You're kidding me. You look so grown-up I thought you must surely be at least fifteen or sixteen."

She preened with satisfaction at the comment, then leaned back and took his face between her hands. "I'm eleven years younger than you. Remember?"

"No way. That would make me an old man. Like thirty-two or something."

"*Twenty-one. Eleven* plus ten is *twenty-one.*"

"That's right." He rocked her side to side and squeezed her. "I was just making sure you're keeping up with math."

I looked toward Rick, who was watching the exchange. He wiped the back of his hand across his eyes and turned toward me. He looked at me evenly for a few seconds, gave the briefest of nods, then looked toward the floor. I knew that he was struggling not to break down, just like I was.

Caroline put her head on Kurt's shoulder. "Please don't use that word in my presence again."

"What word?"

"M-a-t-h," she spelled it out for him.

"Oh sorry, didn't mean to offend."

"You're forgiven. This time."

With every second of the exchange, more and more of the son I had known emerged from this shell of a broken man. I realized then that it would happen. It might take time, but Kurt was returning to me. To us. Every lost bit of him.

Twelve

"So, what have you been doing with yourself these last few years?"

The fork dropped out of my hand and clanked against the plate, splattering sour cream–laden stroganoff sauce all over the tablecloth and my clean white shirt. I dabbed at a spot on my blouse, not because I was worried about the stain but because I was relatively certain that if I didn't keep my hands busy, I would reach over and try to knock some sense into my husband's dense head. Whether or not he was less optimistic about this reunion than I was, what kind of question was that to ask your formerly drug-addicted son? There was no truthful answer that he could possibly want to tell, and certainly none that we would want to hear.

"You okay, Mom?" Caroline's innocent question came between left-handed bites of egg noodles. "I'm the one who ought to be dropping stuff, since I'm eating left-handed, after all." And she was, in spite of my earlier admonishments. She couldn't eat with her right hand because her right arm remained firmly latched on to her brother. The poor guy could barely move his left arm at all, but given the grin on his face every time he looked down at her, I didn't think he minded so much. Even Rick had let the indiscretion slide.

"I'm fine. Still as clumsy as ever, though." I tried a little fake laugh, which I was certain fooled no one. While I had the floor, though, it was time for yet another of my tactful changes of subject. "So, tell us what your Aunt Jodi and Uncle Monte have planned for you."

I, of course, knew the answer. After my conversation with Kurt yesterday, I'd called Jodi and spent over an hour on the phone, talking with my sister about every single detail.

He shrugged and finished chewing his current bite of stroganoff. "I guess Uncle Monte's decided it's time to quit dabbling and really turn the place into a self-sustaining olive farm. He wants me to clean out the old orchard that was already there, and then we're going to be planting several acres more. Apparently I'll be helping with odds and ends with the gift shop that they're building, too."

Rick shook his head. "I don't get what those two are thinking. Templeton is smack dab in the middle of wine country. People go there to visit the wineries, to taste the wine, to see the vineyards. Who is going to stop at an olive farm in the middle of all that?"

"Aunt Jodi seems to think a lot of people will. She says it's different from the status quo and that works in our favor. Everbody's using olive oil in their cooking now, and apparently the organic thing is huge. She says if we can produce something local and sustainable, folks will jump at the chance. Plus, I think she plans to make soap with some of the oil, too. Maybe some other things."

My heart soared at the longest string of words yet I'd heard from Kurt. And there was a glimmer of his old sharp mind. It was like every passing minute released one link more of the chain holding him.

"Soap." Rick snorted. "Sounds just like her. If ever there was a flower child who just never got over it, it is your Aunt Jodi."

Kurt toyed conspicuously with the noodles on his plate. He glanced up at me, then quickly back down. I was sure he could sense the tension between Rick and me. Add that to the fact that Rick and Kurt had been clashing for the last ten years, long before drugs became the excuse, and that Kurt was about to go live with the family that Rick partially blamed for Nick's death. Let's just say, the tension was thicker than any clichéd phrase you might want to use for it.

I was not going to have it. I was the mother, I was in charge of setting the tone here, and it wasn't going to be set this way. We needed to change the subject to neutral topics for a while. For tonight, I just wanted this evening to end with no explosions of temper, no accusations, and none of the familiar altercations between my husband and son.

I searched my mind frantically for a safe subject. I couldn't bring up any of his old high school friends that I'd seen—most of them were close to graduating from college now, with brilliant lives and careers just waiting for them. There was no need to remind any of us exactly what had been lost here. I couldn't bring up any of his after-high-school friends because many of them were still out there somewhere, just waiting to pull

Kurt right back down into the same pit of addiction they were mired in.

Finally, I asked the obvious question. "Tell me about your time in rehab. What was it like? Did you make any friends there?"

"It was tough. The hardest thing I've ever done in my life." He stabbed a piece of meat with his fork. "Besides losing Nick, that is. But it was good, too. I spent a lot of time dealing with some of the issues that drove me to use drugs in the first place. They taught me that I've got to learn to cope with my insecurities in new ways, and I have to forgive myself for Nick's death."

Insecurity? Kurt had been one of the most popular boys at Ocean Hills High School. Soccer star, gregarious personality, girls were always calling him, even the teachers liked him—which likely had more to do with his passionate studying than his outgoing nature. I wondered how it was possible he could feel in any way lacking. The second comment, though, that one I couldn't let past me. "Why would you need to forgive yourself for Nick's death? You weren't even in the same state where it happened."

Kurt shrugged and seemed to study the tablecloth. "He was always the weaker one. You know?"

I did. Nick may have been two years older, but Kurt had been the stronger of the two in every sense of the word.

"He wanted me to come with them. He kept pestering me about it, how he thought it would be a good thing for me to do, how I needed to 'get serious about my walk' and all that other stuff he started spouting after he went off to college."

It was true that while Nick had always been spiritually minded as kids went, his time at USC really upped his *enthusiasm*, for lack of a better word. I could still remember him sitting at the dinner table and arguing with Rick long into the night. Rick's face would turn bright red, not only from the irritation of having a son who had become a fanatic—his word, not mine—but because, most times, Nick won their arguments.

"Just because you decided not to miss a week of school to go with him, that in no way means you were responsible for anything that happened to him. It just means you weren't there to get robbed and beaten, too."

"If I had been there I could have protected him."

"Or been killed yourself. Kurt, you know that the man who killed Nick was out of his mind on meth. He was going to take down anyone who got in his way of getting the money for the stuff he needed." After I'd said the fully impassioned words, I would have given anything to take them back. I thought of my son's own life of addiction. I thought of Detective Thompson's unending suspicions. Was it possible that Kurt had done something just like the boy who murdered Nick? No, they were different people altogether.

I tried to take a drink of water, but my throat was closed. I looked toward Kurt, wondering if he were having any of the same thoughts I was.

With his right hand, his fork still moved the noodles around on is plate. His left hand now reached up, in spite of Caroline's grip, to rub his forehead as if he had a terrible headache. Finally, he set the fork aside and looked up, directly at Rick. "I didn't 'man up and handle it,' as you would say, Dad. I went off the deep end instead, and pulled everyone else down with me. Well, now I'm clean. Someday, when I see Nick again in heaven, I'm hoping he'll tell me that, with the exception of a few bumpy years, I did okay."

I felt my heart pumping warm like it hadn't in years. It was the same feeling a mother gets on Christmas morning while watching her child delight in the puppy he didn't expect, or scoring his first goal in kindergarten-league soccer, or when he's just won the spelling bee in third grade.

I leaned over and wrapped both arms around my son's shoulders. "I know you'll succeed. I'll do anything in my power to help you." And I meant it. Every word.

Thirteen

I stood in the driveway with Rick and Caroline, waving as Kurt's taillights disappeared down the street. We stood in silence for well over a minute, no one having the heart to attempt conversation. Finally, Rick said, "Well, Caroline, it's time for us to go."

She gave me a hug, then climbed into his truck without saying a word. Tears were already rolling down her cheeks.

"That was beyond anything I hoped for." Rick's voice was choked and barely understandable. He leaned over and kissed me on the cheek. "Thank you."

I didn't trust myself to speak, so I simply nodded. Then, for the second time in only a few minutes, I stood watching taillights as they left my driveway.

The quietness of the house always bothered me most at night. Especially tonight, with my heart still aching from the too-soon departure of Kurt. I needed more time with him. Much more. And to be left only with silence, this night of any—with not even Caroline around to lift my spirits. As much as I'd always moaned about her endless "Come check on me" pleas after climbing into bed, her complaints about homework, the dirty cleats tracking across the carpet, it killed me to be in the house without all that, especially now that Kurt was driving north.

I'd grown to hate the end of the week. Rick took Caroline Wednesday evening through Saturday morning. Sometimes we did dinner, but lately not as much. Mostly I tried to busy myself. And I'd have to do that tonight as well.

I went to my computer and checked my e-mail. This was something I'd started doing obsessively since submitting my proposal to Ken's editor friend after working on it a little more based on the girls' suggestions. That had been a couple of weeks ago, but still nothing. I couldn't understand what could possibly be taking so long for him to respond.

There were a couple of e-mails, one from Sally Spiro, the president of the PTA. I didn't bother opening it, it could wait.

The second was from Reisha Cinders. The name was familiar, but I couldn't remember why. I clicked on the icon.

Dear Mrs. Stewart,

I haven't as yet heard back from you about doing a guest spot on the *Christian America Talk Show*. We have an opening about a month from now, on Monday the 19th, and I'm hoping you're available. The show goes live at 2:00 p.m. We'd probably want you to call into the station around 1:45. If this doesn't work for you, please let me know some other dates when you're available. I will call you next Monday to talk through arrangements.

Blessings,
  Reisha Cinders

I'd always considered helping others with grief a part of my God-given call. It was something I knew I should do. I clicked Respond.

Dear Mrs. Cinders,

That date looks like it will work. I look forward to it and to your call on Monday.

In Him,
  Alisa Stewart

I sent the e-mail, thinking about the newfound hope in my story now that Kurt had returned. It would be so much more uplifting than before. Then I had a flash of brilliance. My new epilogue. The happy ending after the prodigal came home. Two hours later, I had seven pages of what I was certain would be the perfect ending to my book. Without pausing long enough to consider what I was doing, I attached it to an e-mail and sent it on its way to Dennis Mahan at Allenby Publishers Unfortunately, it was only ten o'clock and I was wound too tight to consider sleep. I needed to at least do something to help Kurt. But what? That's when I remembered the storage boxes. I'd been so disappointed when I found out he was moving to Jodi's, I'd completely forgotten about my plan to clean his things up for him. He would be needing those things up in Templeton, too. I could get out all his clothes, wash and fold them. Not only would it be helpful, but it would give me an excuse to drive up and see him this weekend.

I walked out the back door, crossed our California-tiny backyard, and threw open the door to the storage shed. The smell of lawn trimmings and machine oil greeted me with a calming familiarity, even before I threw the light switch. I made my way to the back and pulled out the three boxes. I managed to drag them all into Kurt's room and prepared to begin my task.

The cardboard boxes had a picture of avocados on the side, and the tops were sealed shut with packing tape. Remembering my plan to keep these boxes as a future reminder, I tugged at the tape with care. The first piece peeled back, taking with it only a thin layer of brown fibers. The second piece of tape peeled back with equal ease, and I flipped the top flaps open.

Inside, it was full of clothes, wadded into a giant mess. It looked as though someone had gone into a closet, picked up all the clothes he could find, and dumped them into the box. Which, I suppose, is exactly what did happen.

Seeing the complete disregard with which Kurt's things had been handled made me angry at first. Then, on second thought, it made me extra glad that I had decided to clean all of this before taking it to him. I wouldn't want him to know that his things had been treated with anything but the respect that they—and he—deserved.

Ten minutes later, the first box was empty and three small piles of laundry surrounded me on the floor. Mostly faded jeans and T-shirts, along with three pairs of worn tennis shoes, and one sweat shirt with the words Ocean Hills High School across the chest. The faded navy blue, almost gray now, brought tears to my eyes. I hugged it to my chest and inhaled deeply, looking for any trace of scent that my son might have left behind. I found none. It simply smelled like dust and smoke and mustiness.

I opened the small box next. It had Kurt's personal belongings—the signed soccer ball his tenth grade team had presented him after he scored the game-winning goal during play-offs, an LA Galaxy fleece blanket he'd had since eighth grade, and a trio of framed pictures. I turned the first over. Nick. Smiling for his senior picture. I ran my finger over the glass, stared into the innocent eyes of my firstborn son. Had the thought ever crossed this sweet young man's mind that barely a year after this picture was taken, he would be beaten to death for fifty dollars? Would he still have been able to smile if he'd known how his death would wreck his entire family, that his brother would descend into drugs, that his parents would become distant strangers who eventually moved on with their separate lives? I was glad he didn't know the truth. Glad he'd had those last few months of happiness without being burdened by what was to come. Oh, but I wish I had known then. I would have never allowed the trip to New Orleans to occur. Nick might have been eighteen, an "adult," but I was still his mother. I wouldn't have let him out of my sight.

Something about the surface of the picture seemed wrong. I leaned closer and held it up toward the light. Then I could see that the picture had been crumpled. It looked as though it had been wadded into a ball, then straightened back out after the person thought better of it. I wondered who would have done this. Was it someone Kurt had met during his time away from home? Had Kurt gotten angry about it, ordered the person to leave his sight? I suspected that's exactly what happened, because Kurt had always been Nick's protector. I knew he wouldn't have done this. He may have been younger, but he was stronger in every way—at least we'd thought so.

I turned the second frame over and found a picture of a toddler-sized Caroline standing knee-deep in a mud puddle, her face streaked with grime, a look of complete joy on her face. I remembered when Kurt took this picture for a photo class at school. It made me laugh every time I saw it.

The last picture showed the two boys, maybe eight and ten years old, standing with me in front of the Pacific Ocean, smiling at the camera. This photo had always been in the mix of dozens of photos filling a shelf that ran the length of our hallway. It stunned me to realize that in all this time, I'd never even noticed it was gone. I suppose it shouldn't surprise me that I didn't notice. I'd missed so many things since Nick's death. I'd managed to miss the early signs of Kurt's increasing drug use until it was too late to do anything about it. It was my fault in a lot of ways; I know that. But how could a mother be expected to focus on details when she had just lost her son?

The fog of pain had covered me so completely in that first year—still did at times—it made it all but impossible to see anything beyond the mist that choked and blinded me. It took more energy than I possessed to continue to move, performing like a robot, doing all the usual things—work, carpool, attending Kurt's soccer games. I never woke up on those mornings with any other thought than simply making it through the day before me. Why hadn't I opened my eyes, spent the time to peer through it all to notice that my son had started to self-medicate his own pain? Nick's death had been more or less out of my control, but Kurt's descent, well, I had been there. I should have seen it happening and stopped it.

At least this was the one thing I'd have the chance to do over. This time, when Kurt needed my help, I would be more than certain not to miss it.

I put the items back into the small box, planning to set them up in Kurt's room as soon as I finished unloading the final box, the largest of the three, which I suspected would provide more laundry for my piles. I peeled back the tape and, as expected, found another wad of clothes. I sorted them into the piles, then looked at the remaining items in the box. Toward the bottom there were a few odds and ends. A flyer from a rock concert, some plastic cups and forks, and a tattered gray blanket. I picked it up, planning to add it to the laundry pile. As I lifted it, I heard the thump of something falling from the folds. I put the blanket on the floor and looked into the box. My heart stopped beating when I saw it.

Lying there, perfectly symmetrical across the remaining items in the box, was a Louisville Slugger baseball bat. I squatted down, trying to catch my breath, waiting for reason to overtake the sudden panic that had seized me. And after a few deep breaths, it did.

Louisville Sluggers had to be the most common bats around. Kurt was a very athletic boy; he'd probably joined a softball league or something. Of course that must be it.

When I reached down to pick it up, I wrapped my hand around a shirt first—it wasn't that I was concerned about fingerprints, because I knew there was a reasonable explanation for what I was seeing. I think I'd just watched one too many police shows.

I held the bat up, closer to the overhead light of the room. The grain of the wood was worn, chipped on the end, in fact. Years of playing base-ball would likely do that to a bat. I rolled it over, noting that it looked perfectly normal. Until the very last of the rotation. A couple of darker areas of the wood caught my attention. I grabbed another towel from the laundry pile and rubbed it across the grain, praying that it wouldn't pull away blood red. It didn't. In fact, nothing came off at all. Of course it wasn't blood, just an old stain, for crying out loud. What had even pos-sessed me to think along those lines? It was a little stain—likely mud. If it were blood, then it would be red, instead of this pale dirty brown. No, this was just dirt.

I knew I was blowing this out of proportion, so I looked into the box to see what remained. I pulled up a towel—completely stiff with dirt—and beneath it found a pair of cleats and a deflated basketball. Sports equipment. Of course. Just like the bat was.

But now what? I hesitated and weighed my options. Put it in Kurt's room, leaning in a corner, like it was a treasured memento? Hide it away until I knew for sure? Or should I call Detective Thompson and tell him to come take a look?

After several years of teaching at grief seminars, I knew the official answer I would give to a woman in my position. You call the detective. Now. If there is nothing to this, then you sleep easier that night knowing that you've done the right thing. If this is indeed the murder weapon the police have spent the last couple of months searching for, then your son has some serious explaining to do, and likely some consequences that he rightly needs to pay.

Only the truth would set you free.

But there was no "you" here.

Only me. Only *my son*.

Fourteen

The first thing the next morning, I found myself standing on Lacey's front step. I couldn't help but look over my shoulder as I pressed the doorbell. Illogical as I knew it was, I couldn't shake the feeling that the entire neighborhood knew I was here right now, and they all knew why. I saw no evidence to back this up. Not a single person was outside. But I saw a flash of movement at an upstairs window inside the Coles' house. Someone behind the curtains, perhaps?

"Well, this is a pleasant surprise for a Friday. Come on in."

I startled at the sound of Lacey's voice and spun around. She didn't seem to notice, and I was glad about that. Until I looked at her, anyway.

The circles under her eyes were darker than usual, or was her face simply pale? The hair at the back of her head stood out in all directions as if perhaps she'd been lying in bed.

"I'm sorry. I shouldn't just drop by like this. Were you sleeping?"

"Of course you should just drop by. You know I'm always happy to see you. And no, I wasn't asleep. I was lying in my bed watching some of that daytime trash television. You know, the kind that actually kills brain cells every time you watch it." She coughed a quick laugh. "What's left of my mind thanks you. Now, come in, sit." She turned and walked toward her kitchen, never even looking back to see if I followed. Our friendship was such that she just trusted that I would. "You want something cold to drink? Or some coffee?"

"No thanks. I can't stay long. I just have to ask you about something."

She dropped into a chair at her kitchen table, as if the effort to walk to the front door and back had been overwhelming. "Ask away."

"Well, the good news is, Kurt came for dinner last night and it was wonderful. He looked so much better than he has in a long time. He was happy. He's really determined to make it work."

"Sounds good so far."

"Yeah, that part's great. It's the rest of it that gets a little fuzzy."

She smoothed her hand across the white linen tablecloth. "Let's hear it."

"Kurt's former landlord brought by some of his things a while back. I've been storing them for him. Last night, after he left, I realized he would need the things in those boxes. I decided it would be a good time to go through everything, wash all his clothes, iron and fold them, you know, the mother instinct kicking in."

Lacey leaned back and draped her arm across the empty chair beside her. "Let me guess, you found something you wish you hadn't, and now you're wondering what to do with it." Her eyes locked on me, but otherwise her expression showed no sign of alarm whatsoever. Beneath her fragile shell of a body lived the mind of an incredibly sharp woman.

"How do you do that?"

"It's not that hard to figure out. The boy was an addict who all but lived on the streets for the last couple of years. There's bound to be some skeletons in his closet, and it only makes sense that some of the skeletons would be evident in his personal effects."

I could tell by the flip tone of her voice that she had not followed the path all the way to its true conclusion. She must have assumed I'd found drugs or paraphernalia, and I wasn't ready to correct that assumption yet. "What do you think I should do with what I've found?"

"Get rid of it." She waved a dismissive hand as if the subject wasn't even worth further discussion.

"But isn't that illegal?"

"Listen, there's legal, and there's what's right." She leaned forward on her elbows. "In this case, your son has pulled his life, which was basically a train wreck, back up on the tracks and started it moving in the right direction again. Whatever you found is from his past. That was yesterday, now he's living in today. The thing to do in a case like this is to clear the debris and let him move, leave all the goop from yester-day behind. Get rid of it."

"It just feels so . . . wrong."

"Hey, you're the one with the Christian sensi-bilities, not me. But doesn't the Bible say some-thing about moving our wrongdoings way beyond the east, or something like that?"

"Huh?" I looked at her for a moment, wracking my brain for what she might be talking about. Then it occurred to me. "Well, there is a verse about Him removing our sins as far as the east is from the west."

She pointed at me and nodded. "Bingo. That's the one I'm talking about. Seems to me if God forgives, forgets, and moves on, you ought to be able to do the same thing without much call for conscience. The way I see it, the old Kurt doesn't even exist anymore. Why should his baggage?"

There were a few flaws in her argument, I knew that there were. But she was giving me an answer that I desperately wanted to hear—even throwing in some biblical wisdom. Maybe God was speaking to me through her. I supposed He could speak that way if He chose to.

I wanted to ask more, to keep her talking until she convinced me fully. But I knew that if I did, she would eventually figure out exactly what I'd found. I didn't want Lacey, or anyone else, to know that until I decided for sure what to do with it.

"Thanks, Lacey. I knew you'd have the answer." I stood and hugged her, trying my best to pretend that everything was just fine now.

When I walked back inside my house, I continued to turn all the scenarios over in my mind, as neatly and efficiently as I'd turned the bat in my hand. I went so far as to find the Bible verse in question. I marked the spot in my Bible. It was from Psalm 103:12: *"As far as the east is from the west, so far has he removed our transgressions from us."* Yep, the Bible would back me up. Right? Even Lacey knew that. Finally, I reached my decision.

I tossed a load of Kurt's laundry into the washer, then opened the crawl space to our attic. I climbed the short set of stairs, pulling up with my right hand, holding the bat in my left. Even before I reached the attic space, I felt as if the roof was closing in on me, suffocating me. The entire space was coated with a thick layer of dust that almost obscured the pink rows of foam insulation beneath. I took slow, deep breaths and crawled back across the beams for as far as I dared. When the fear of falling through the ceiling overwhelmed my fear at what I had in my hand, I stopped and pulled back a layer of insulation. I pushed the Louisville Slugger down into the remaining insulation until it lay almost flat, then made sure that it was fully covered when I put the top piece back down. I even used my hand to spread the disturbed dust. Slowly, I retraced my journey and crawled out of the attic.

The obvious best decision was to make no decision at this point. I didn't have all the facts, and I hadn't seen my son in a long time. I needed to know if he really had played a role in Rudy Prince's murder, or if the bat was simply a piece of sports equipment. If I suspected the former, I needed to see how deep and how real a change he had truly made in his life. I promised myself I would put this piece of wood completely out of my mind until some sort of clear answer came to me.

Jana, one of the church secretaries, stood up from her desk the minute I entered the office. "I can't believe you did that."

Logic told me there was no way she knew anything I'd just done, but apparently guilt doesn't listen to logic any better than grief does. "Did what?"

"Called and left a message that you'd be a couple of hours late, without so much as one clue as to what happened. How did dinner go last night? We want to hear everything."

I looked around the empty room and tried to smile. "We?"

She pushed a couple of buttons on her phone and spoke into it, "Carleigh, Beth, Ken—Alisa's here." Then looked up and nodded. "Yes, we."

Beth ran to her desk and sat. The children's ministries director came flying into the room, panting like she'd just run a marathon. She dropped into a wing-backed chair against the far wall and clutched her chest. "Didn't want to miss anything." She looked around, "Where's Ken?"

"I'm here." He leaned against the doorway and offered his usual good-natured smile.

I held up my hands and shrugged, pretending to be as excited as I would have been just twelve hours ago. Before I opened the boxes. I knew that bat was harmless, knew it with all my heart, but an ugly voice deep inside kept telling me otherwise. Now was not the time to listen to it; now was the time for a good appearance. "What can I tell you? He looked great, he's committed to staying clean and sober, and it felt like old times." I paused for a minute and gave a true shrug here. "For the most part."

Beth leaned forward across her desk and reached for my hand. "Was he upset when he found out that Rick and you are separated?"

Rick's and my separation had seemed like such a huge issue just yesterday. This morning . . . it felt insignificant. "Uh, we haven't told him."

"Are you crazy?" Her hand flew away from mine and up to her mouth in a split second.

I flicked my gaze toward Ken Maddox. His face showed neither approval nor disapproval, an expression he had mastered in his years as senior pastor. Maybe that worked well for the average member who needed counseling, but I wanted to know what he thought about this. I made a mental note to ask him later, when I'd regained enough composure to remember why it mattered.

"I am so sorry," Beth said. "You know I didn't mean that like it just came out. It's just that, he's bound to . . . I mean, I just assumed . . . well, I thought you would tell him."

Much of what she was saying was correct and I knew it. But there were other things to consider. "I suppose we probably should have. It's just that we didn't want to mar his homecoming with bad news."

"What if he hears it somewhere else first?"

"That won't happen. I'm going to visit him this weekend up at my sister's. I'll tell him about it then. It'll be easier after he's had a few days to settle into life outside of rehab." I hoped I would have settled into an answer for how to discuss the bat with him by then, too.

Ken Maddox nodded. He looked at me as if he wanted to ask more, but he didn't. We would talk later, and I both looked forward to and dreaded that. He had been the one constant during the storm that had become my family life, and I valued his opinion. Then again, he knew me so well that I was afraid he might realize I wasn't telling him everything. Still, there was no way he would ever guess my secret, I was sure of that.

I realized that everyone was still looking at me, still waiting for me to say more. I knew what they were waiting for. We'd come to the place in the conversation where I was supposed to give God the credit for saving my son. As much as I knew it was true, something about saying the words simply because it was expected felt wrong to me. Especially when I now realized that God may have saved my son a little too late.

Still, I took the cue. "God has blessed us immensely by answering this prayer." The women nodded but continued to look at me as if they expected me to say more. This was a time to bring it all home. "You know that neighbor friend of mine that I talk about? Lacey Satterfield? Well, she's even surprised me by talking about the Bible some because of Kurt's homecoming." Okay, that was a bit of a stretch to the truth, but still, the words themselves as spoken were not a lie.

"Really? What did she say?" Carleigh leaned forward.

"She was asking me about the verse that talks about God removing our sins as far as the east is from the west. It's amazing that God can do that, even for someone with Kurt's past. Isn't it?" Enthusiastic nods all around. Wouldn't that change if they realized the context in which she'd used that verse?

"Well, I think it's time to get back to work,

everyone. We are so happy for you, Alisa." Ken nodded and walked back into his office.

I was thankful for the way the morning had gone. I managed to keep my brave and Christian face here in front of my co-workers, and that's what was required of me now. The time for questions, doubts, and otherwise stumbling about was for my private prayer time alone.

When I walked into my office, there was a bouquet of a couple dozen roses sitting on my desk. I turned and looked at Jana, who was smiling broadly. "What are these?"

She shrugged. "They were delivered about an hour ago." I walked slowly to the desk and opened the card.

As you said, a girl can never have too many flowers.
Dinner last night was wonderful. Thanks for being the voice of hope, for giving us all a reason to believe again.
Love,
Rick

Fifteen

On Saturday afternoon, Caroline and I drove north a couple of hours to the little town of Templeton. Once pastoral and open, it had been steadily growing more developed, with new houses and restaurants popping up all over the place. Its proximity to Paso Robles and its ideal climate for cultivating vineyards had made it a popular spot for wealthy outsiders to buy land and try their hands at opening a winery. Many such places dotted the beautiful hillsides here.

I had thought briefly about waiting a little longer before taking this trip, make it look like I was certain that everyone there had it all handled. But two days was as long as I could hold off without seeing everything for myself. I needed to know what was happening with my son, and besides, he needed his clothes.

I pulled up the long gravel driveway that led to the hundred-year-old farmhouse. When Jodi and Monte bought the place three years ago, we all thought they were crazy. Now, after three years of Jodi's touch, the once dilapidated pile of rotting boards and peeling white paint was a cute little yellow and white farmhouse, with white shutters and a screened-in porch. I hoped that she would be able to help my son continue with his own interior renovations, and to be honest, I knew that there was no one more qualified than my sister. If ever a woman possessed strength of spirit that was contagious, it was Jodi.

I slowed my car and looked beyond the house at the thirty-five picturesque acres of rolling hills, olive trees, and a winding, usually dry creek. I paid special attention to the rows of olive trees, searching for the slightest hint of movement, hoping to catch just a glimpse of my son's tall, thin frame. I saw nothing but green.

Jodi was out the door and waving from the front porch before I came to a stop. She wore her usual combination of long flowing skirt, Birkenstock sandals, and scoop-necked T-shirt. Her long ponytail, gray for the last ten years, hung loosely across her right shoulder and fluttered with her vigorous waving.

Caroline raced from the car and launched herself into Jodi's arms. "Aunt Jodi!" She wrapped her arms around my sister's neck and squeezed. "I've missed you."

"I've missed you, too. How is fifth grade?"

Caroline leaned back and rolled her eyes. "Boring."

Jodi laughed and looked over Caroline's shoulder toward me. "You're just in time. I've been trying a few new recipes and I need a taste tester."

"New recipes?" Caroline licked her lips and looked toward the house.

"Yes, I'm thinking I might print a *Stevens Farm Olive Oil Cookbook* for the gift shop. I mean, if people are going to buy our olive oil, they need to know what to do with it. Right?"

"Right." Caroline's voice had definitely lost some enthusiasm. "Any cookies you need me to test?"

"Well, I haven't thought of any cookie recipes

yet, but I've made some dipping spices for bread, and pesto, and some oven-baked French fries that will help your taste buds soar, even if I do say so myself."

"Ummm, where are Kurt and Monte?" Aside from the fact that Caroline was dying to see her brother, her taste in non-cookie food was limited to plain pasta, cheeseburgers, and perhaps the occasional banana. Just the mention of Jodi's olive treats was enough to send her fleeing.

Jodi pointed toward an all-terrain vehicle parked out by the trees. "See the quad sitting way out there at the back of the old orchards? Monte and Kurt are out there thinning trees. You can walk on out if you'd like. I'm sure they'd love it if you gave them a hand."

"Thanks." Caroline tore off across the dirt path without a backward glance. Her blond curls bounced in time with the dirt puffs her running feet liberated from the dry ground.

"Monte's been feeding his brain on the proper methods of olive farming. Apparently, there's a lot more to doing it right than just giving the trees water and fertilizer."

"Who knew?" I looked at my sister and laughed. "I still can't believe you two did this. When you sold everything and moved up here, I figured it would last a year or two. And now look at you, making it all work in spite of the fact that I still think you were crazy to do it."

She shrugged. "We felt led, that's all I can say."

I'd been involved in the church for all my life, I'd believed in God, His Word—all of it—for as long as I could remember. But I had no memory of ever having such a conviction that He was speaking to me about something that I would set aside everything I'd ever known or planned. Even my writing. I loved it, but if I was called to it, why had it taken an editor's voice and not God's for me to get started? Had I ever moved into the unknown, just because I "felt led"? Not that I could remember. Did Monte and Jodi have more faith than I had, or was Rick right when he said they simply had less common sense? Whichever was true, today I found myself beholden to both of them for the decision they'd made.

This was the perfect place for Kurt to get back on his feet and reestablish himself as a productive person. Here, he was close to family, and Monte and Jodi would give him the best of guidance. He was also far enough removed from his old friends to keep him away from trouble. At least, that's what I kept telling myself.

"You know what, before I tempt your palate with all sorts of delicious yummies, why don't I give you a quick tour of the beginning of the gift shop?"

"Sounds great." Besides, I was hoping our tour would lead me close to where Kurt and Monte were working. More than anything I wanted to see him.

Jodi loaded me in her Prius and drove me to where the work had already begun on the foundation for her planned gift shop. "I'll have a small storage area here." She pointed at one of the corners. "Then this will be the main gift shop," she said as she made a sweeping gesture that covered an entire half. "This corner will have a little sampling area, and I'm thinking of a small stove for cooking demonstrations." She stared at the corner for a moment, and from the look on her face I knew that she was no longer seeing the bare concrete that I saw. She was already visualizing hardwood floors, shelves bursting with merchandise, and the crowds of people she was certain would soon fill the place.

"It looks wonderful." It wasn't a complete lie, just an inaccuracy. To me, it didn't look like anything other than a rectangle of concrete on the ground, but it did *sound* wonderful. I supposed that was close enough. I walked around the frame and waited until I thought an acceptable amount of time had passed to ask the question that I really wanted answered. "How is Kurt doing?"

As I knew she would, Jodi stared into space and thought through every bit of what she was about to answer. "He's working hard, of course. Kurt always was a worker. He's spent a lot of time talking to Monte about what he wants to do with his life, how he wants to stay clean and move on." She twisted a strand of her long gray hair around a finger.

"But?"

She looked at me and cocked her head to the side. "What makes you so sure there's a but?"

"You're my sister. I know you."

"Yes, you do." She reached out and took my arm. "Come, let's walk toward the orchard while we talk."

"Sounds good." I congratulated myself on how normal my voice came out.

Jodi shielded her eyes against the late afternoon sun. "Maybe we'll catch a glimpse of our men at work." She giggled and said, "I'll bet by now, Caroline's got them all straightened out."

"I'm sure." I continued to walk toward the trees, listening for any sound of work in the orchards, and waiting for my sister to continue. I'd begun to think she wasn't going to.

"The thing that concerns me—concerns both Monte and me—is that something about him just doesn't . . . I don't even know how to express it fully. Something about him just doesn't *feel* right. We've spent some time talking about it, and we both sense the same kind of disturbed vibe from him. It seems like there is something he is wrestling with, something he can't quite harmonize with his spirit. I know Monte's been spending some extra time with him, trying to gain his trust so that Kurt will eventually talk to him about whatever it is."

"Maybe it's just guilt or embarrassment at his wasted years."

She nodded, a little too slowly to be true agreement. "It could be. But . . . I wasn't going to tell you this part."

"Tell me what?"

"Last night he disappeared for several hours. It was after he'd finished up his work, and he was back by around ten. I mean, he's not a youngster; he can come and go as he pleases. But there have also been a few hushed phone conversations, and it just all feels a little secretive."

"Have you . . . I mean, after he disappeared, did he come in smelling like smoke? Look glassy-eyed?"

"No, not at all, and believe you me, we've made it a point to look for those things. Maybe it's just me overanalyzing, but if there's something that's eating at him on the inside, well . . . drugs would offer a quick way to dull the ache from whatever's bothering him." She shielded her eyes from the sun and pointed toward the orchard. "There they are."

I could see feet sticking out from under an olive tree that twisted toward the sky like a proud elder statesman. "What are they doing on their backs?"

"Something about pruning. You lie on your back and look up. I don't really understand it all, but apparently the two of them do, so I leave them to it."

The branches on the tree above them moved with more gusto than the light breeze should have produced. I looked toward the rustling limbs and realized that Caroline had climbed up into it. I heard her voice then. "This one right here, I think it's a problem."

I made it a point not to laugh as we walked over to the tree. I didn't want to hurt Caroline's feelings and I didn't want the guys to hear our approach. When I got close enough, I nudged Kurt's foot with my own. "Hey there, Farmer Kurt, how's it going?"

Kurt slid out from under the tree, wiping dirt and bits of wood chips off his arms before locking me in a hug. "Well, it's totally rocking now that Farmer Caroline is here. She's climbing up into the trees and scouting out rogue limbs for us, saving us all kinds of time and effort."

Monte laughed and stood up. "Yeah, I'm thinking I maybe ought to hire her, too."

"Please, Mama, can I?" Caroline's voice resonated with such earnestness it made me smile.

"Maybe you can come up here this summer after school gets out. Maybe we'll both come up for a day or two."

"It's not the same. I want to stay up here with Uncle Monte and Kurt."

"Trust me, Short Stuff, you're better off at

home." He pulled away and nodded at me. "You guys are earlier than I expected."

He'd maybe gained a couple of pounds, and it seemed as though some of the paleness had already begun to wash out of his cheeks. Maybe it was just from working in the sun, but I preferred to believe it was the restored health of a restored family that gave him a better color. "I wanted to get here in time to see you at work. You know, to make certain your Uncle Monte wasn't sitting back in an easy chair reading a magazine while you did all the labor. I know how he is."

Monte nodded. "That's exactly what I was doing until I saw your car coming into the driveway. Watching my afternoon soap operas and eating bonbons is what I do all day. 'Course, I figure somebody's got to be the supervisor." His salt-and-pepper short-trimmed beard had wood chips in it from whatever it was they'd been up to, and his ruddy face was flushed with exertion. "Truth is, that boy of yours is about to send me to an early grave. My macho pride demands that I try to keep up with him, but I'm just too old and too out of shape." He patted his belly, which had gained a nice roundness in the last decade. "Tell you what, Kurt, since your mother's here already, why don't we knock off a little early, go wash up, and have an early dinner. I know she doesn't want to make the long drive home after it gets too late."

"Slacker." Kurt smiled at Monte and nodded.

"I'll just finish pruning this tree we were on and be right in. *Somebody's* got to do some work around here."

Jodi had made a Mediterranean pita dish, which looked a lot like pizza except that it was covered in spinach, olives, and feta cheese. I couldn't help but compare the healthy entrée with whatever it was my son had been eating the last couple of years. I became more and more thankful for Monte and Jodi's choice to be here.

I watched Kurt, searching for any sign of the agitation that Jodi had mentioned earlier. Of course, the Louisville Slugger's presence in my attic gave a strong indication of what might be bothering him, if indeed it was *the* Louisville Slugger. In the last few days I'd thought of little else, and had started to suppose that the bat was truly nothing, or just at his place by coincidence, or maybe he had taken it to hide it for the guilty party. That would have him wrestling inside himself, right? Over the course of time I'd started to convince myself that he hadn't done anything at all, that it was as harmless as the basketball and the cleats and the soccer ball I'd also found in his things. Jodi's comments seemed to contradict that, but maybe Jodi and Monte were simply reading him wrong. I had decided not to bring up the subject of the bat with Kurt, but now I wondered if I should.

It was amazing the kinds of scenarios a mother

could concoct in her mind to protect her children. Thinking about all these made me more than realize why Kurt had been able to hide his drug abuse for so long. I was willing to believe most anything—so long as it meant I didn't have to believe the worst.

After dinner was over, I looked at Kurt. "Coach Brooks brought by all your things while you were in rehab. I've got them loaded in the back of my car. Why don't you come out and help me carry them in?"

I watched him very closely for any sign of a reaction at this news. His face didn't change at all, but for just a split second,

I thought I saw the light of panic in his eyes. Maybe I just imagined it. He stood and walked out the door with me, and as we started down the drive, he said, "Did you go over to the cabin and load up the stuff yourself, or did he?"

The question could have been innocent enough, but I was afraid I knew why he asked. It was the same question that troubled me. "He had the ranch foreman load everything in some boxes, then he brought them to me."

I turned to look at his profile in the fading sun. His eyes blinked faster than normal. "Oh, right. Juan Miguel." He rubbed the back of his neck and seemed to exhale a vast amount of air. "He's a great guy. I think he's probably an illegal immigrant, but you talk about a hard worker. The guy doesn't speak more than a dozen words of English, but 'work hard' are two that he does know and live by. I could never keep up with him."

This conversation relieved me more than a little. On the off chance that it truly was Rudy Prince's bat, one of the many things that had concerned me about all this was who had put the bat in the box and would he eventually tell? If that person didn't speak English, he likely wasn't watching the six o'clock news. Even better if he were an illegal. He certainly wouldn't be waltzing into the police station to talk about evidence. It was the best possible situation. No, that wasn't true. The best possible scenario would be if the bat had never existed in the first place.

I opened the rear hatch of my Escape and pointed toward all the clothes, neatly lined on hangers. "They probably got a little wrinkled on the ride up, but I washed them all and pressed everything. You shouldn't have to worry about wardrobe for a while."

He nodded absently and began to sift through the remaining box of odds and ends. After a moment he looked up, and I wasn't sure if he was panicked or relieved. "Is this all there was?"

I looked at him for a few seconds and gave it serious thought before I responded. "Is there something else you were looking for?"

He shook his head. "No."

"Good, because that's all there was."

Sixteen

Monday morning I awoke having decided, though still uneasy about it. I'd given myself all of Sunday to think it over. I'd even prayed about it—though perhaps not with my usual degree of absolute seeking. Mostly I sought peace for what I already planned to do. At least I'd given myself that extra day, not wanting to do anything impulsively that I would regret later. But why would I regret it? A mother does what's best for her son, that's what a mother is supposed to do, and that was the end of it.

I somehow managed to go through my morning routine as if everything was the same. I got Caroline up and dressed for school, packed her lunch, and stood smiling and waving at the door, just like always. "Have a good day at school," I called in my too-cheerful, get-her-off-to-school voice.

She turned around and rolled her eyes. "Yeah, like that's going to happen." Then she went skipping down the street, her backpack shifting with each hop.

Once again I amazed myself at the show I could put on. From the exterior, it seemed like a perfectly happy normal day, the complete opposite of the truth. Something about that thought made me shudder, but it did not change my resolve.

I walked back inside, careful to lock the door behind me. Then, oh so casually, I walked to the other doors and confirmed that they, too, were locked before I went to sit on the hearth, stretching out my legs and yawning. I'm not sure whom this show of casual normalcy was supposed to fool. There was no one here but me, and I certainly knew better.

I waited just a few minutes, took a deep breath, then turned and wadded some newspaper into balls. After I piled the kindling over it in a rough rendition of the Boy Scout teepee Nick had learned so many years ago, I removed the box of matches from their place on the mantel. I held the box in my hand and simply looked at its rectangular shape, felt its lightness in my hands. Such an insignificant little piece of cardboard, but once I opened it, once I dragged the red tip of the match over the striking surface, there would be no turning back for me.

Time to cross the line and move on.

The flame moved from match to paper to wood in a matter of seconds. One tiny little wooden stick had the power to destroy so many things—things that by appearance were so much stronger. After the kindling was fully engulfed, I threw a couple of small pieces of firewood onto the top and watched the slow movement of the fire as it found its next piece of fuel. I added a larger piece of wood. This needed to be good and hot. I didn't want to take the chance of leaving any traces behind.

As the fire began to grow into a flaming mountain, I felt sufficiently satisfied with my work to leave it to its course for a moment. I let myself into the attic and looked around at row after row of dusty pink insulation, all exactly the same. Panic engulfed me, like the flames had swallowed the newspaper. What if I couldn't find it?

I crawled from board to board in the general direction of where I knew the bat was hidden. When the fear of falling through the ceiling became almost unbearable, I shoved my hand between board and insulation and peeled it back. Absolutely nothing. I leaned across to the next row and repeated the same, with the same result. Ten minutes later, I was flat on my belly across the supporting boards, pushing my hands into the center of the fluffy pinkness, feeling around for anything unusual.

The roof seemed to be closing in on me and the attic space was getting hotter by the minute. The heat coming from the chimney at the far end of the house couldn't be helping. Finally, my hand pushed against something hard. I peeled back the padding and finally found what I'd sought. Tears welled up in my eyes then, both from the relief at having found it and from the fear of what it might stand for. I picked it up with my bare hands, wiped it clear of any remaining insulation, then descended the stairs.

I sat on my hearth and held the piece of carved wood in my hands, considering what I was about to do. If this was truly nothing, I was destroying, for no reason, something that had belonged to my son. If it *wasn't* nothing, if it was *something*, well, I was about to do something so outside of the law that there wasn't even a gray area to it. I was destroying evidence. Of a murder.

I spent a minute holding it, making certain my convictions didn't waver. They didn't. Everything would be better if I just got rid of it. It wouldn't matter anymore. I could put the whole question out of my mind and get on with life. I spun the bat around in my hands, picturing home runs and strikeouts, certain that was the truth behind this bat. A rough spot on the handle pricked at my finger and I pulled it up for a closer look. What I saw removed all doubts. Tally marks. Forty-two tally marks to be exact.

I remembered the story in the paper, Rudy Prince's beating tally. Forty-two people. Forty-two. Did my son account for any of those marks? What had he, and forty-one others like him, endured at the end of this bat? The man who did this deserved what he got. Lacey was right about that. There was no comparison between the two lives: a man so proud of hurting others he kept count, and my son who was working in Monte's orchard, preparing to go to school, beginning a productive life. Those notches felt like forty-two heads nodding at me. For a second, I found my peace.

I looked at the wooden bat, at the fire roaring in my fireplace, and then up toward the ceiling. "God, I am willing to take the consequences for this action, but surely you will not ask that of me. I gave you my first son; He died trying to serve you. Now, you've brought my second boy home, just like the prodigal son ran to his father so many years ago. That father held him close and celebrated his return. He didn't spend time revisiting the son's past sins, though they, too, must have been awful. Kurt has turned his life around. Surely you would not ask me to take that away from him, to send him to prison with the kind of person that he once was? Even you, in all your holiness, would not ask that. Would you?"

There was no answer. But to be perfectly honest, even if I'd heard a booming voice from heaven say, "Keep the bat; turn him over to the authorities," I just don't know if I could have done it. How could any mother? I had the chance to save my son who had been all but unsavable over the course of the last few years.

Maybe Rudy Prince was the person who sold Kurt his very first crack, the one who turned him into the kind of person that could kill him. I knew

Kurt must have been high to have ever been able to do this, and wasn't there some sort of justice in the fact that the man's own drugs crazed my son enough to kill him? Wouldn't that fall somewhere into the eye-for-an-eye category? He poisoned their minds with drugs. Why wouldn't one of those poisoned minds keep him from doing it anymore?

I tossed the bat into the fire and watched the flames dance around its edges. Slowly at first, and then tongues of fire began to lick up from the bottom all around it. I tossed another piece of firewood on top just for good measure. I wanted this thing to burn completely and fast.

Kurt would have his chance. I'd just seen to it.

It didn't surprise me that I couldn't sleep. I sat in my king-sized bed with several pages of my manuscript scattered around me, unable to focus long enough to read any of them. I couldn't write this book—what kind of hypocrite would that make me? Even though no one would ever know, I would know. I needed to e-mail Dennis Mahan and tell him to withdraw my proposal because I'd reconsidered. Tomorrow that's what I'd do. Not tonight. I didn't have the energy.

I finally picked up the remote and aimed it at the small flat screen mounted on the far wall, then scanned through all eighty channels at least twice. Eventually I settled on a reality show about a group of parents trying to get their kids into some special dance program, not caring one bit about who they hurt in the course of helping their child.

Suddenly, I was helping Kurt get onto the show. But something was wrong; he didn't sing. That's when I saw the bat in his hand. I saw him swinging it at a man in the crowd. I ran forward to stop him, until I realized he was hitting Lonnie Vandever. I started screaming, "Hit him again, Kurt, hit him again." I jerked awake, covered in sweat.

I turned off the television and walked down the hallway. I looked into Caroline's room and saw her sleeping soundly in the bottom bunk, covers mussed into a big pile in the middle of her bed. One small foot hung over the right edge of the bed, and her head was pressed against the wall on the left—she always thrashed in her sleep. I closed the door and walked down the stairs, where I opened the door to Kurt's room. Too many troubling thoughts assaulted me to stand there for too long, so I walked out and crossed to Nick's door, hesitating for a long moment before I turned the knob and went inside.

I had put all thoughts of Chris Marshall's pictures out of my mind, but now I saw the bag lying on my son's pillow like an old friend. I picked it up and went back upstairs to my room. I climbed under the covers and gently pulled the top edges

140

of the bag apart. There looked to be about a dozen photos inside.

I pulled them out, placed them in a neat stack on what had once been Rick's side of the bed, and dared to look at the first one. It showed Nick, Chris, and a half dozen other kids their age, cheeks painted with the red letters USC, the crowd of the Coliseum in the background. They were pumping their fists in victory, so I assumed the Trojans had won this particular football game.

There were several more pictures of the boys around the dorms, at football games, and clowning around. Then came the photo that took my breath.

Nick was standing on a street corner, his finger pointing down the street behind him. I could tell from the French look of the buildings that this photo had been shot in New Orleans. I looked down the street in the direction Nick pointed and scanned the crowd, wondering if Nick's killer was standing somewhere in the middle of it.

His name was Lonnie Vandever. When I had seen him, during the long weeks of the trial, he had been short-haired and clean-shaven. That's not the man that Nick had seen. I searched the photo for the black hair and scraggly beard I'd seen in his mug shot and in many of my nightmares, long before tonight's dream added Kurt and a baseball bat. I couldn't make out anyone clearly. Besides, what happened to the boys happened away from all the crowds. Lonnie Vandever wasn't anywhere near this place.

Another picture showed people on the street with eyes and cheeks as red as flames, their necks stacked high with brightly colored beads. These were the people my son wanted to reach. It was because of them that he was dead. I wished there was some way I could track down the people in this photo, these very ones, and ask them if they realized what had been suffered because of them. I wanted to ask if they were living lives worthy of the sacrifice made on their behalf. Something inside of me stirred at the thought. I sounded like a preacher talking about Jesus, and how we needed to live worthy of the sacrifice He'd made for us. Tonight, more than ever before, I had the realization that I didn't even come close.

Seventeen

"All I can say, baby, is you must be even more cold-blooded than I am."

For a second I froze. *She couldn't know.* Then, confused even further, I looked down at the short-sleeved shirt I was wearing and then back up at Lacey. "Huh?"

"Well, to see the smoke pouring from your chimney yesterday, a day when it was easily sixty-five degrees outside, well, I just figured you must be having cold flashes instead of hot flashes, or something."

The smoke! How could I not even consider the fact that it would blow like a beacon? My mind started clicking off the names of all the neighbors who might have been home yesterday morning to have seen it. Maybe Margaret across the street or the Holts.

Lacey reached across the table and squeezed my hand. "Well, to see the look on your face, I don't have to wonder what it was all about." She snorted. "I wish I'd known for sure that's what was going on. I would have walked outside, taken a few deep breaths, and seen if I couldn't get a secondhand high."

"Oh, Lacey, you would not." I laughed, although I was in no mood for laughter. I shook my head and started to cry in spite of the brave front I was trying to put on. "How stupid could I have been?"

"Last I heard, there's nothing illegal about having a fire in your fireplace."

"Well, it's pretty obvious there wasn't a need for a fire yesterday." I couldn't voice aloud the thought that troubled me most. What if Detective Thompson had just happened to come by yesterday? Lacey thought I had destroyed drugs. I certainly didn't want to say anything that would clue her in otherwise.

"Actually, I'm proud to death of you."

"Proud of me? Whatever for?"

"Most people would just flush the stuff down the toilet. Not the kind of stuff you want to have flowing to our ocean and getting into the groundwater supply. Know what I mean? Yeah, a fire was a much better choice."

A picture flashed through my mind of trying to flush a bat. The thought almost made me laugh. But it didn't.

"I understand that you're planning to send Caroline up to Monte and Jodi's this summer." It was the first thing out of Rick's mouth on Wednesday when he arrived to pick up Caroline, and it was an out-and-out accusation.

I was still on edge from Monday's fire and didn't have the strength or the desire to draw my sword and have a sparring match with my husband. "Oh, come on, Rick, you know better than that."

"I do? All I know is what my daughter tells me. You certainly haven't mentioned it."

"I haven't mentioned it because it's not true."

"So Caroline is lying then? Should we call her down here right now and make her apologize?"

Honestly, the man could be so unpredictable and infuriating sometimes. I thought back to our days as homecoming king and queen and wondered what had ever possessed me to marry him. "She was helping Kurt and Monte prune the trees, and Monte made a joke about hiring her. She thought he was serious and got all worked up about it, as Caroline is known for doing. I finally told her that maybe this summer we would go up there and stay a few days while she helped out."

"So she is going."

"A few days, with her mother, to see her aunt and uncle. I don't see anything wrong with that. Do you?"

"I'll tell you what's wrong with it. If it weren't for Monte's mind-poisoning, we'd still have Nick here with us right now. Now he's getting his hands on Kurt, too, which I'd forbid if it weren't for the fact that Kurt's twenty-one and there's nothing I can do about it. But Caroline's only ten. I'm telling you right now, I'm not letting Monte and Jodi sink their claws into Caroline."

"Rick, Monte didn't poison Nick's mind, and he's not poisoning Kurt's. What would make you even suggest such a thing?"

"It's all his Jesus-love-and-rainbows stuff that put Nick on the streets of New Orleans, right in the middle of the biggest party in the world, walking unarmed through streets most cops would think twice about. Tell you the truth, I'm scared to death that after Kurt's been up there a few months he'll be shaving his head and chanting in an airport somewhere. What if Caroline does the same thing in a couple of years? There are worse things that can happen to her than just being beaten to death. I won't have her up there being exposed to all that."

"Nick's decision to go to New Orleans had nothing to do with Monte and you know that. It was his own idea—his and his friends. In fact, it's the friends he made at USC that helped talk him into it. You insisted that he go to a large secular school instead of the small Christian college where he wanted to go, because you wanted him exposed to more of the world. That's where his influence came from."

"That's not where it started. I don't have a problem with you taking the kids to church— good morals are important to instill young. But there's a limit, and I think it's time that we start making some rules where Caroline is concerned. Maybe I should get her Sunday through Wednesday, and we just take the whole church thing right off the table. That way there's no problem."

I closed my eyes, unsure what I felt more, anger or sadness. I knew Rick was never going to be a perfect church husband. But to hear the disgust in his voice over what was so important to me. And Nick. Calmly as I could, I said, "There is a problem, Rick. I want Caroline raised in the Christian home that she's grown up in. We agreed when she was born that she would be raised with Christian beliefs."

"Yeah, well, that was before I realized how off-the-wall all this stuff was going to get. I didn't know that Nick would go over the edge. Even you can't argue that. It was his fanaticism that got him killed. I think we should be fairly unified on the fact that we don't want to see that happen with Caroline."

"It wasn't Nick's beliefs that got him killed. It was a man on the streets, who had absolutely no belief in anything other than his own needs, that got Nick killed. If someone had raised that boy with Christian values, we never would have lost our son."

"I can stop that argument right here and now. You raised Kurt with those values, and it sure didn't help him, did it?" His voice dripped with the same sarcasm that clouded his face.

This was not the first time he'd thrown similar words at me. Still, they never failed to sting. I heard my voice begin to rise. "I'll agree that no matter how you raise a child, there's no guarantee that he will turn out perfect. But once again, Kurt's problem was caused by the same boy who killed Nick. Kurt was just fine before that. And"—I looked at him, happy that I had the little jab that would help me win this argument—"it was Kurt's faith that helped bring him back."

"Says you. I had lunch with Bruce Thompson yesterday; he tells me that Kurt showed up at rehab the very day after Rudy Prince's murder. It seems more than a little fishy to me, wouldn't you say? It's almost like he was looking for an alibi."

"You had lunch with Detective Thompson?" Something like betrayal twisted in my gut.

"Yes, Bruce and I have met a couple of times now. He's a nice guy. You know, I don't know why you're so afraid to talk to him. I would think that someone with your beliefs more than most people would want to get to the truth of what part our son played in Rudy Prince's death."

"That's because I know he didn't play a part." I stood up. "If you don't have anything good to say about your son—the one who has made great strides in turning his life around—then get out of my house."

He leaned back against his chair and smirked. "This house is just as much mine as it is yours, in case you've forgotten. Just like Kurt is just as much my son as he is yours. I'm not saying he had anything to do with that boy's death. But if he did, or if he knows anything about it at all, he needs to man up and accept the consequences. That's been the problem with both our boys. They spent so much time with you, they never understood some of the principles of being a man."

I wanted to ask him exactly whose fault that was. I was never the one who demanded the ski boat, the Jet Skis, and the cabin at Lake San Antonio. He was always the one who wanted all the toys and all the accessories, and he was prepared to sacrifice time with his family to get it. I finally let it go as, "Yeah, well, funny, I never heard them saying they really hoped Dad would work again this weekend because they sure wanted to hang around me so they could get soft."

"You've enjoyed the fruit of my labor every bit as much as I have. The girls' trips to the spa, the nice clothes, the SUV we paid cash for."

"I never asked for those."

"But I never had to force you to take them just the same."

"It was my 'consolation prize' for having a husband that cared more about the boss's opinion than his wife's—or his children's." I glared at him, letting every bit of my anger blaze through my eyes.

"Watch yourself. I would hate to see this all turn ugly." He stood and called, "Come on, Caroline, time to go." Then he stalked out the front door and out of sight.

Long after he left, I thought about what he'd said. The conversation had already gone way past the point of ugly. He had been talking about something else, I was sure of it.

Eighteen

When I walked into work the next morning, Detective Thompson was waiting in the church office. If it weren't for the fact that Jana sat right there, I would have told him to get out. Now I would be forced to be a bit more tactful, but I intended to get the message across just the same.

"What are you doing here?"

Jana glanced up from her desk and frowned at my lack of polite preamble. She had no idea how much worse it would have been if I'd said what I wanted to.

"I have an appointment with Pastor Maddox." He smirked as he looked me directly in the eye. "I had a question about a couple of Scriptures I've been reading, and I've heard that this is a Bible-based church. I figured if anyone could help me, then he could."

I crossed my arms and looked down at him. "Oh really? What Scriptures might those be?"

He pulled out a piece of paper and unfolded it. "Well, the one that's really been on my mind lately is this one from Proverbs. It says, 'A truthful witness does not deceive, but a false witness pours out lies.' I've been spending a lot of time thinking about this verse, and I wonder if a false witness might also be someone who knows the truth but doesn't come forward. What do you think?"

To an outside observer, it would appear that he was watching me with detached interest, simply wanting my opinion on a topic. I knew better. What I didn't know was whether he was fishing or whether he knew something. Maybe he had seen the smoke from my chimney after all. Jana looked up at this exchange, clearly intrigued by the conversation.

I picked up my mail from the sorter and shrugged. "I'm sure that's a question for Pastor Maddox, not me. He's more the theologian than I am."

"But surely you must have an opinion on this. What do you think?"

"I suppose it would depend on the circumstances. I also think there are a few verses in the surrounding chapters about false witnesses who make up things just because it suits them—you know, like they want the public to think they are doing a great job solving cases, so they badger people into saying things that aren't really true—those kinds of things. Why don't you ask Pastor Maddox about that?"

Just then the door to Ken's office opened and Ken came walking out to greet his next appointment. Detective Thompson smiled at me. "Maybe I'll just do that." He shook the pastor's hand and the two of them disappeared into the office.

When Caroline walked through the door after school on Monday, I could tell by the droop of her shoulders that it had been a hard day. She was sensitive to a fault, and these kinds of days were not altogether uncommon. Still, I played dumb, thinking I could get more information that way. "Hi, sweetie, how was your day?"

"Fine." She hung her backpack on its usual hook and started for the kitchen and her daily bowl of ice cream. Usually, this entire scene was played out with much more exuberance and gusto. Something was clearly wrong.

I followed her into the kitchen and watched as she put a heaping scoop of double fudge brownie in the bowl. "Everything okay?"

She ignored the question for the length of time it took to sit at the table and take a bite of ice cream, then she looked up at me. "What does custody mean?" She put another spoonful in her mouth, but her gaze never left my face.

I sat down beside her. "Was Susie upset today?" I had known that sooner or later the Whitakers' ugly divorce would spill over onto Susie, and from there into Caroline's group of friends at school. I thought about my words before I answered, because I wanted to answer truthfully, but in a tactful way, too. I could never be certain what might be repeated back to the group tomorrow during recess. "Well, it means to be in control of something or someone. For instance, you have custody of Boots the cat. He stays at your house, and you're in charge of seeing that he is cared for and safe."

Caroline nodded and looked toward the cat's bowl, which sat empty in the corner of the kitchen. "Yeah, that's kind of what I thought." She continued to stare at the bowl, her eyes sad.

Then I had what I considered a flash of brilliance, and I continued. "It doesn't mean that other people can't spend time with Boots, and even love him. It just means that he stays with you and you take care of him. So if Susie's mother gets custody of her, it doesn't mean that her daddy doesn't still love her, or that she can't love him back. It just means she'll be living with her mom."

Before I could finish giving myself the big congratulatory pat on the back, Caroline dropped her spoon in her bowl and threw herself into my lap. Her sticky chocolate face smeared ice cream on my shirt, but at times like this those things just don't matter. "So even if Daddy gets custody of me, you'll still love me?"

This question almost knocked me out of my chair. "Caroline, what would even make you think to ask that question? Daddy and I are just spending some time away from each other. We're not getting divorced like Susie's parents are. We both still have custody of you."

"Yeah, but I heard Daddy talking to someone on the phone. I heard him say that maybe the only way to keep me from getting into trouble like Kurt did was for him to get full custody of me. I thought that sounded like I might never get to see you again."

"Of course not, sweetie." As I kissed the top of her head, my mind reeled. Custody? Full custody?

I couldn't believe that Rick would even think that, much less say it. His threat about things getting uglier came back to me. I realized I had only begun to see how deep it could go. At that moment I was grateful that I hadn't yet e-mailed Dennis Mahan about not writing the book, because now I realized if he was willing to publish it, I might very well need the money.

Nineteen

"Hey, Mom, what's shaking?"

I couldn't believe my son was here, standing at my front door. "Kurt!" I threw my arms around him and hugged him tight, relishing the thrill of the unexpected visit. Until . . . the dark possibilities of what such an unexpected visit could mean. "Is something wrong?" I sniffed the air for any telltale sign of alcohol or smoke. Only the fragrance of the jasmine climbing the side of my garage met my nose. I studied his face for any hints and saw that his eyes looked clear and bright.

He reached down, picked me up, and swung me around in a circle. "I wish you wouldn't worry so much. Everything is fine." His laughter was as clear and bright as the sound of children playing at the beach on a warm summer's day. "Monte gave me the day off, and I thought I'd drive down and see how you're doing. Where's the rest of the herd?"

Now was obviously the right time to tell him about Rick and me being separated, but I just couldn't ruin this moment. It could wait just a little longer. "Your father and Caroline are out and about. They should be here a little after four."

He nodded. "Tight. I'm needing a Caroline fix. Nobody latches on quite like that girl does."

I laughed as I remembered watching her try to eat with both her arms wrapped tightly around his. "You say that now, but if you stick around long enough, you'll either change your mind, or you both might die of starvation."

"Speaking of which, how 'bout we partake in a little mother-son snack? What do you say?" He put his arm around my shoulder and led me inside as if this were the home he'd never left.

I grinned up at him, enjoying the moment for what it was worth. "What kind of snack are you thinking about?"

"Have a seat right here, and I'll figure it out." He deposited me at the kitchen table, then stuck his head in the refrigerator a split second later. "There is a shocking lack of food in here, I've got to tell you."

Well, the timing wasn't going to get any better than this. It was time to come clean. "That's because I'm only shopping for one and a half these days."

"Huh?" He closed the refrigerator, a block of

cheddar cheese in his hand, and came to sit beside me at the table. "What's up?"

"Your father and I have been separated for a couple of months now."

He flopped back against his chair in a way that would have earned him a lecture about good posture just a few carefree years ago. Somehow, things like posture didn't matter so much anymore. "But . . . the other night at dinner. He was here, you were here. Everybody was here."

I reached over and put my hand on his slumped shoulder. "Of course everybody was here. We all wanted to see you. Your father still has dinner here every Wednesday, when he comes to pick up Caroline. Sometimes he stays for dinner on Saturday after he drops her off, too. I'm sure since you're here, he'll stay tonight."

"Are you getting divorced?"

The question would have drawn an immediate "no" just a few days ago. After Caroline's revelation of Rick talking custody, I wasn't so sure anymore, but I wasn't ready to admit that aloud. "We just needed some time away from each other. We've been having a rough go for quite a while now."

"Yeah, like after one son died and the other became a worthless bum." He shook his head slowly side to side. "This is all my fault. Every bit of it."

I heard that sadness in his voice again, the

exhausted frustration that tinged his words in the weeks after Nick's death. Nothing good could come of that, and I needed to snap him out of it.

"Kurt. Look at me. Do you remember anything about your father before you left?"

He raised his eyes to mine, surprised, I supposed, by my change in tone. Then we both started laughing. Rick had always had a quick temper, long before the tragedy, but he had also had a great heart. It was only in the aftermath, with the increasing pressure of constant pain, that the eruption of his temper seemed to bury the good heart under too much debris to still see it.

"We're going to work things out, I'm sure of it."

"Are you going to counseling?"

I looked at him and smiled. "You really don't remember your father, do you?"

"Yeah, he never did believe in shrinks, did he?" He flipped the block of cheese over in his hands.

There was no reason to deny the obvious. "Not so much."

"He must have freaked out when he found out I was in rehab. You spend most of your time there in therapy. I'll bet he yapped plenty about that."

"Actually, I think you just may be the thing that changes his mind about a lot of things. Especially now that he can see the turn your life has made. See there, it might be you alone that gets us moving in the right direction to save our marriage."

He nodded, his expression focused elsewhere. Was he thinking about drug dealers and baseball bats? I knew I would lose my sanity if I didn't block this thought, and block it quickly. "How about I get us some crackers to go with that cheese?"

"Hmm? Oh yeah, sounds good to me."

I went to the pantry and pulled out the box of saltines, then reached below and got a couple of cans of cream soda. "I guess we'll need some ice for these. If I'd known you were coming, I would have had some in the fridge."

"Not another word. I'll take care of it." He swept past me and filled a couple of glasses with ice, then poured each full with fizzing cream soda. He held up his glass. "To new beginnings."

As I brought my glass up to clink it with his, our eyes locked. I continued to hold his gaze as I said, "For all of us."

"Kurt, what are you doing here?" Rick's question sounded a bit more accusatory than I supposed he'd meant it. At least, I hoped he didn't mean it the way it sounded.

Kurt laughed. "Well gee, Dad, it's good to see you, too."

A slight hint of color went across Rick's cheeks. He actually leaned over then and gave Kurt a distant kind of embrace. "Didn't mean it that way."

" 'Course not." Kurt returned the brief hug and

said, "I hope you're hanging around for dinner."

I realized that every ounce of me hoped he wouldn't. I knew it was wrong, definitely not biblical, but having Rick around would ramp up the tension. And frankly, there'd been more than enough tension around here lately. But I looked at him and nodded. "There's plenty."

"Well, uh, well, I guess so."

"Yay, Daddy!" Caroline, who had remained silently wrapped around Kurt's leg during the exchange, actually disentangled herself long enough to jump up and down. "I knew it, I just knew it."

"What did you know, Short Stuff?" Kurt shoved her playfully.

"Now that you're okay, we're all going to be one big happy family again."

I looked at Rick, thought about his custody conversations, and realized that I had been hoping that, too. As far wrong as things had gone between us, I had always hoped and believed things would someday work out. Only, now that they should be improving, things actually seemed to be slipping farther away. And I might just have to accept that some things could be too broken to ever be fixed.

Dinner didn't answer that question one way or another, and a few hours later, I walked Kurt out to his car.

"Are you sure you can't spend the night? You

could come to church with us tomorrow. There are tons of people there who would love to see you. Mr. Wall, your old Sunday school teacher. Mrs. Marston, the children's choir director. They both ask about you all the time. So do a lot of people."

"Hmmm, I don't think I'm quite there yet. All those people have a pretty good idea of how I've spent the last few years. Embarrassing, you know?"

I reached up and stroked his cheek. Just a slight hint of stubble tickled my palm. "It shouldn't be. Everyone there is saved by grace. We've all been forgiven by God for our sins. Maybe your sins were a little more noticeable than some others, but a sin is a sin. Right?" I needed to hear these words, probably more than Kurt needed me to say them.

"That's what Uncle Monte says, too. And maybe in God's eyes it's true, but I'm not so sure all the good churchgoing folk would agree. And to tell you the truth, it's still a little hard for me to accept that God can just forgive me for everything. You just don't know, Mom." He looked past the driveway in the general direction of downtown, and I wondered if he was thinking about Rudy Prince.

God could forgive anything, I knew that. God would want my son to live a productive life, the one he'd been intended to live all along. "Your sins have been removed as far as the east is from the west, never forget that." I reached out and hugged him.

"Maybe next time I'll stay."

He opened the door to the old beater Datsun he'd acquired at some point in his past. I wondered what had happened to the blue sports car he once owned. He'd spent years saving up his money, and the day he turned sixteen he went to the used car lot and found the car of his dreams—well, the car of his dreams in the under-ten-thousand-dollar category, anyway. Had it been stolen? Wrecked? Had he sold it to pay off a drug debt?

It hurt to think about all the things my son had gone through, but I was determined to stay positive right now. I put my hand on a large patch of rust. "You know, one thing you can say about this car, at least the red blends nicely with the large bouquet of rust."

He laughed. "A bouquet of rust. It sounds ever so much better than the reality, doesn't it?" He sat in the driver's seat but didn't close the door. "Mom, there's something I need to ask you, but I really don't want to."

Was he going to ask me directly if I'd found a bat in his things? I wasn't sure I could play that off as easily as the last time when he'd asked if I'd found anything else. I braced myself for it but tried to appear calm and relaxed. "You know you can ask me anything. That's what mothers are for."

"Well, you've more than fulfilled your quota of mother-required help for me at this point. It's just that . . . I need some money. When I found out you and Dad were separated, I promised myself I wouldn't ask, but here I am being a selfish pig and asking anyway."

"How much do you need?" I looked at his car and realized that whether or not Monte was paying him a decent wage, he probably did need more to help get him back on his feet again.

"A couple thousand."

Thousand? A couple *thousand*? I had been expecting a few hundred at the most. He stared at his steering wheel, unable to even lift his head to look at me, and I knew that it was killing him to ask for this. The right thing to do would be to ask what he needed the money for. What kind of parent would give two thousand dollars to a kid who, until a few months ago, was a hard-drug addict? Was I just foolishly ignoring all the signs again?

No. I'd been fooled once, but the Kurt who ate with us tonight was a new person. Someone who, more than anything, needed to feel trusted, and I didn't want my son to think that I didn't have full faith in him.

"I don't keep that kind of money at the house. I could have some for you the next time you stop by. How soon do you need it?"

"As soon as possible. Maybe I'll drive back down next Saturday."

"Is everything all right?" The question gave him the wide-open opportunity to ease my mind with what he planned to do with the loan.

He chose not to take it. "Fine. Just needing a little help right now, that's all."

Needing a little help right now? Would that help take the form of white powder up my son's nose? Little rolled smokes? Or injections that I didn't even want to think about? With all my heart I believed that was not the case, but if I needed to trust him, he also needed to trust me. The question would stay in no longer. "Kurt, what are you planning to do with the money?"

"It's not for drugs, Mom." He smacked his hands softly against the dashboard. "I knew that's what you'd think."

"That's not what I think, but two thousand dollars is a lot of money to hand to someone, anyone, without some idea of what it's for."

"I still owe the rehab place. I have upcoming tuition bills." He turned and put his hands on the steering wheel. "Keeping this hunk of metal rolling. It's taking a lot of money to get back on my feet, but I'm clean and I'm staying clean." He pulled at his eyelashes, a habit so familiar from his childhood.

Shame poured over me like scalding water. I was starting to sound more and more like Rick. "I didn't mean it that way." We both knew that wasn't the complete truth, but I think he understood I at least regretted asking the question. "I can have it for you by next Saturday."

"Thanks, Mom."

As he drove away I stared after him, still hearing Rick's warning in my mind, *"Don't you dare give him money."* Well, I *was* going to give him money, quite a lot of it. I only hoped and prayed that he was telling the truth about where it was going to go.

Monday morning I was still agonizing over Kurt's request. For every five signs I could list showing how he'd changed, part of me just knew he was holding back something. I was pretty sure I would still give him the money, but the whole process made me squirm. And that wasn't helping at work any, as Monday was the day the magazine came in to profile our church.

"Hold still," Marsha chided me. "Do you want to be perfect in your photo or not?"

I looked at her reflection in the mirror. "Honey, there's not enough makeup in the world."

"Never underestimate me." She took my chin in her fingertips and turned it side to side. "A tad more color on the left cheek."

"I don't know why you're making such a big deal out of this."

"Because it is a big deal. A spread in *American Christian* magazine, complete with photos, is a big deal. Besides, you're the only really pretty one on staff. We've got to play up your assets, because that makes us all look good."

"That is so not true. Carleigh is beautiful, and so are Jana and Beth."

"Carleigh is pretty enough in her outdoorsy sort of way. If she'd do something with her hair and makeup she'd look a lot better. As for Jana and Beth, well . . . they are beautiful on the inside and that's what counts. It just doesn't translate well onto film." Marsha's tone was matter-of-fact as she applied dark brown eye shadow to her brush. "Now close your eyes and hold still."

I did as I was told, thinking about her comment about Beth and Jana being beautiful on the inside. The same could no longer be said about me. Even though I'd more or less come to terms with what I'd done, the fact that there were Louisville Slugger ashes in a trash can in my side yard burned a gaping hole in anything of beauty that might have been there. I was certain of it.

Twenty

"Hey, Mom, since it's Saturday, Uncle Monte let us knock off work early, and I thought I'd head down there in a few hours. Maybe around dinner. You game for a little mother-son bonding?"

"I can't think of anything better." I still found myself amazed each time I heard my son's voice like this. Clear, even, and happy. After so many years of slurring, stammering, and miserable, I had begun to wonder if I would ever live to hear this again. I had made the right decision that morning at the fireplace, I became more certain with each passing day. "But Caroline's already here, so we'll have to make it mother-son-and-daughter bonding."

"Even better." His voice sounded so upbeat. It reminded me of something or someone, but I couldn't quite put my finger on it.

"I'll be there around four o'clock. That work?"

"Perfectly."

After we got off the phone I hummed as I made a quick grocery list. Spaghetti had always been high on both Kurt's and Caroline's list, some salad and rolls, and maybe for tonight a pineapple upside-down cake. I hadn't baked one in years, but Kurt had always loved them. I'd have to get some ice cream as a concession to Caroline, who hated anything that wasn't chocolate.

As I drove toward the store, my enthusiasm wavered. Saturday. He wasn't just coming down for bonding. This was the day he'd wanted the money.

I checked my watch. The banks would be open only another hour or two. Should I stop at the bank? Pretend I got there just after they closed? These questions turned over and over in my mind, but no clear answers came. "God, won't you please tell me what I should do here?"

I've never been one of those people who hears the voice of God. But sometimes after I said a prayer like that, I'd get a little feeling, a niggling inside. Usually I attributed it to God's quiet voice, although sometimes maybe it was just the answer I wanted to hear. No matter, because this time I heard nothing. Not a single tiny stirring inside me that pointed in either direction. Nada.

Before I had time to think better of it, I turned into the bank and pulled open the door. The young blonde behind the counter arched her eyebrow when she saw the check I'd written for cash. Two thousand dollars' worth of cash. "I need some ID, please." Her pink V-neck was cut a few inches lower than I considered decent, and she wore a large cocktail ring on each hand of white plastic fingernails.

I handed her my driver's license, which she looked over carefully. She finally handed it back. "Two thousand dollars is a lot of money."

The explanation that it was for my son made it as far as my tongue, but stopped before it crossed my lips. It was none of her business. "Yes, it is. Now, if you don't mind, I'm in a hurry."

She took her time counting out the money, stopping occasionally to straighten the gaudy orange-stoned ring on her right hand, looking up every couple hundred dollars. I'm not sure what she expected to see, but I had the distinct feeling that whatever it was, it would make me look guilty.

Maybe she expected to see my accomplice, and hoped that somehow she'd be rewarded for stopping this evil withdrawal scheme. I don't know, but it bothered me. Even though I was simply withdrawing my own money from my bank, I squirmed at her obvious doubt of my innocence.

How many times would someone look at Kurt and misjudge him because of his past? Someone whose judgment would truly matter to him, like teachers, employers, friends. That thought alone began to weight the decision in favor of giving him the cash. Still, I wouldn't do it right away. I'd take my time and hold on to it for a little while, just to be certain.

Caroline was out the door and had wrapped herself around her brother's legs before I even realized he was in the driveway. I ran down the steps two at a time, but there was no reason to have hurried. It was obvious by this point I was going to have to wait my turn. "Kurt, Kurt, Kurt." She squeezed his legs and put her cheeks against his knees. "I'm so glad you're here."

He almost fell as he leaned over to try to return the hug. "Tell you what, Short Stuff, if you'll let go of my legs and stand up, I'll be able to give you a hug, too."

She squeezed tight for a couple more seconds as if afraid that if she released him he would disappear. I understood exactly how she felt. Finally, she climbed to her feet and he picked her up and hugged her tight. This lasted only a few seconds until he said, "Wow, when did you get so big? I used to be able to carry you around all day. Now I'm thinking you're heavier than all those gigantic tree limbs I'm dragging around for Uncle Monte."

"It's all that good ice cream that makes me grow so big." She drew her arms so tightly around his neck I was afraid he couldn't breathe.

He did manage to choke out a laugh. "Ice cream?"

She leaned back and smiled at him. "Yeah, mom tries to tell me it's the broccoli she keeps putting on my plate, but you and me, we know better."

"You and I," I corrected out of sheer habit.

Kurt smiled over Caroline's shoulder at me. "Well, there's the eat-your-vegetables monster right there."

He leaned forward to put Caroline down, but she wasn't having any of it. She held on tight and dangled from his neck, even after he let go and had bent forward at a ninety-degree angle. "You're not getting rid of me that easy."

"You're going to put me in the hospital with a thrown-out back if you don't let go."

"At least then I could come see you every day."

Kurt straightened up at this comment. He looked down at her, then back at me, a shimmer of liquid at the bottom of his eyes. "Well, I guess if you're willing to sacrifice my health to keep me around, I'll just have to carry you up the stairs and into the house."

She giggled. "That's right."

He carried her into the living room, and with one smooth motion managed to pull her arms free and launch her flying across the room and onto the couch. "There's more than one way to get rid of parasites, you know."

"I'm not a parasite." She launched herself back at him, and before I could stop it, the two of them were wrestling on the floor. Arms and legs were flailing everywhere, and Caroline's hysterical laughter could have been heard for at least a mile away.

"Okay, you two, knock it off before the police show up."

The words were a joke, one I'd used dozens of times when the boys were being rowdy. A common joke in many households probably. Only at that moment, it wasn't funny. I swallowed back the gasp that rose to my throat, and when I looked at Kurt, I could see the words pained him, too. Only Caroline remained oblivious and continued to thrash around like nothing had changed.

Kurt sat up and held out his arm to deflect the latest attack from his sister. "Okay, kiddo, that's enough for now." He stood up and looked at me, then drew me into a hug. "There now, it's Mom's turn for some Kurt love."

"Me too." Caroline threw her arms around both mine and Kurt's waists. "Group hug."

"Group hug it is." Kurt and I both lowered our arms to include her.

After we were all hugged out, I looked down at Caroline. "I believe you have a little homework to finish up, don't you?"

"Aw, Mom, Kurt's here. I don't want to do homework."

"Well, I'll be here for a while, so get it done now and I'll take you on in a game of Battleship after dinner."

"You're on, except I want to play Guitar Hero."

"Guitar Hero? I'm not sure I remember how to play."

"Don't worry, you'll do fine." She bounded up the stairs two at a time. I knew I would have to double-check the homework she was about to do, because in her haste, accuracy wouldn't even be a consideration.

"So, come sit down. Tell me how things are going."

He went to the refrigerator and pulled out a cream soda. "You want anything?"

"No thanks."

"Things are good." He pulled a glass out of the cupboard, filled it with ice, then came to sit at the kitchen table. He took a long sip, then looked at me. "It's hard work up there. In fact, I'd say that working on a farm like that could convince a lot of kids who think they don't want to go to college that maybe they do."

"Yeah, I'll just bet." Of course, Kurt had always been college bound before he started using. Just like Nick. His grades maybe hadn't been quite as high, but they were still exceptional. "Are your transcripts coming together?"

He nodded. "I should be able to start classes part-time next semester."

"Why only part-time? Don't you want to buckle down and get it done?"

"Sure, I'd like to, but you know that money is an issue for me right now. I can't afford not to work full-time."

I thought back to our plans for our boys. The deal had always been that as long as they were in school full-time, we would pay tuition, room, and board. I couldn't think of any reason that would change now. The only thing different was that it had been delayed by a few years. I pulled the envelope out of my purse. "Well, here's a start."

He hugged me. "Thanks, Mom. You have no idea how much it means to me that you believe in me."

"Of course I believe in you. I love you."

"I love you, too. And you are the greatest mother ever." He reached over and squeezed my hand.

"Maybe your father and I could help a little with tuition."

"No, that wouldn't be right. But . . . while we're on the subject anyway . . ." He patted the envelope. "This is great, and I know it's asking a lot, but I could use just a little more money."

"How much more?"

He looked up at me, then back down. "Another grand."

"Kurt, that's not a *little* more money."

"I know, and this will be the last time I ask. I'm just about to get everything squared away. Hopefully, after I get a couple of paychecks ahead, I can get a car I don't have to put so much into. All these repair bills." He was pulling at his eyelashes again.

I looked at my son, the one who had returned to me after years of being away. I thought of the future that would be his if I hadn't destroyed that bat, and I realized I was just glad to have him here with me.

"Okay, I'll see if I can get some money out of one of the CDs." I knew there would likely be a penalty for early withdrawal, but I would figure it out somehow.

It wasn't until long after Kurt left that night, when I was tossing and turning in my king-sized bed, that something dawned on me. Him pulling his eyelashes. I'd noticed it both times when he asked for money and remembered him doing it as a boy. But until now I had forgotten when he'd done it. It used to be an almost certain sign that he wasn't telling the complete truth. And the tone in his voice when he said I was the greatest mother in the world. I knew that sound. The sound of a used car salesman—the kind that will tell you anything to make the sale. Is that what my son had become?

Twenty-One

Rick's truck pulled into my driveway late Thursday afternoon, making me wonder what treasure Caroline needed from her room. Whatever it was, I hoped Rick would wait for her in the truck. I just didn't want to deal with him tonight.

As if reading my mind, he climbed out of his truck and started toward the door, a bouquet of flowers in his hand. That man always had a singular ability to find the one thing I didn't want him to do and then do it. With a flourish.

Caroline bounded up to me and gave me a hug. "Dad said he would take us both out to dinner tonight. Isn't that the best?" She bounced up and down and clapped her hands, effectively ending any argument that I wanted to raise. "He said that you could choose the restaurant. Anywhere you want to go!"

I looked at the flowers in his hand, then cocked my eyebrow. "What's the occasion?"

"Do I have to have an occasion to bring my wife flowers and to take my family out for a nice dinner?"

"Let's just say, it happens with an infrequency that lends suspicion to this generous offer." I knew I was being rude, but I couldn't seem to stop myself.

"Caroline, why don't you go change into something nice for dinner, okay?" He watched until she disappeared into the house before he said, "Actually, I come bearing good news." He held out the flowers and I took them.

"What kind of good news?"

"Kurt is no longer a suspect in the murder of Rudy Prince." He actually looked down as he said this, a rare show of humility.

"How do you know this?"

"Bruce Thompson. He called me just a couple of hours ago and said they've got the guy in custody."

"Someone else was arrested? I hadn't heard that."

"Of course not. I'm sure they haven't officially announced it yet."

"Then, why would he tell you something like that, before it was official?"

"I think we've spent enough time talking about it all that he knew I'd been eaten up over it." He looked at the ground again. "He called me this afternoon to let me know."

Part of me wanted to be thrilled over this news. To believe with all my heart that the guilty party was in jail and all our troubles were over. Maybe Kurt really was innocent.

The other part felt sick. The bat I'd burned was too deeply connected to the murder not to mean something.

I thought of Detective Thompson at the grocery store and at my grief seminar and even at church the other day. I thought about the fear his presence struck in my heart. "When will it be made public?" What I really wanted to know was, when would it be in the paper or on the news? I needed details, lots of them, but I couldn't ask for them now without being obvious.

"I'm guessing tomorrow morning's paper, but what do I know about it?" He shrugged. "That's enough of that depressing talk." He put his arm around my shoulder. It was the first time we'd touched in a long time. I pulled away.

"Where were you thinking of going to dinner?"

"Like Caroline said, you get to pick. Let's see, as I recall Chuck's was always your favorite place."

"Chuck's is too nice a place to take Caroline." I thought of the years that he'd been so frugal about anywhere we took the kids for dinner. Chili's was as nice as it ever got, and even that was rare. Besides, I was certain at this point that I wouldn't be able to eat a bite, not until I knew the full details of the arrest.

"It would be good for her. A chance to practice her big-girl manners."

"Caroline and big-girl manners in the same sentence?" We both laughed.

"She's got to start learning sometime." This was a huge concession for him to make, and I knew that he truly was trying to make amends. I supposed the least I could do was accept the gift.

"You've been right all along, Alisa," he said. "I'm starting to realize that, because I'm not even listening to myself anymore."

"What do you mean?"

"Remember when I told you not to give him any money? Well, I loaned him three thousand dollars last week. He needed to have some work done on his car, some things like that. I told him it was a loan, but I don't think I'll let him pay me back. I think I'll tell him just to apply the money toward school." He stood looking at me, and I knew that he was waiting for me to say something positive, about his taking the right step.

What I really wanted to do was throw up. Instead I managed to say, "Well, I'm glad. That you've come to believe in him, I mean." How I managed to say the words, I'll never know.

He looked puzzled by the lack of enthusiasm in my answer, and I knew that he was. I certainly wasn't going to explain it to him, though.

Kurt had been getting money to "fix his car"

from both of us. I thought of the used car salesman voice, I thought of this new piece of information, and then my imagination went completely overboard picturing all the possibilities of what my son might be up to.

"So, as I was saying, dinner?"

"Sounds great." I said it even though I didn't want dinner. I wanted to confront my son and find out what he was really up to. And I wanted to find out what was happening with Rudy Prince's murder investigation.

A good meal can be its own distraction, and Chuck's desserts never fail to grab my attention. But by the time the last bite of cheesecake disappeared and our surprising evening was over, my mind went again to the information Rick had passed on. I was distracted when I said goodnight to Rick and Caroline. Distracted as I sat down with the mail I hadn't managed to open earlier. Finally, I knew I couldn't wait any longer. I had to go online and try to find some answers. But of course there was no news to be found yet. The police hadn't made their official announcement about the arrest.

Still needing to kill more time before another pointless attempt at sleep, I opened my e-mail. There was only one item in the inbox. The subject line said simply Book Proposal Response.

My heart pounded as I considered what I might

see when I opened this, and what I was prepared to do about it. If he was offering a contract, how could I possibly take it now? Then again, how could I possibly not take it?

I finally mustered the courage to left-click on the mouse.

Mrs. Stewart,

Thank you very much for your recent submission. I found your writing voice fresh and interesting, and obviously your personal experience and training qualify you in a unique way to write this book.

Unfortunately, however, at this time I am going to have to pass on this project. Grief books are an over-published niche at the moment, and while your speaking platform is developing, you aren't able to bring a national profile we feel a new grief book would need. As well, there were concerns from several on our editorial team that the recent epilogue felt unrealistic and perhaps too new to be used.

Your writing does show promise, and I would encourage you to continue to build your platform and work toward publication. I wish you the best in your career.

Dennis Mahan
Senior Acquisitions Editor

I closed the e-mail, relief and devastation warring inside me. With what I'd learned tonight, I couldn't write the book, I knew that. But it meant more than just one more dream crushed. It also meant one less source of income if Rick and I divorced, adding worries to an already overwhelming load.

It occurred to me then, if editors who didn't even know me or this situation could see the falseness in my "happy ending," how could I continue trying to fool myself into believing it? Everything was a lie, and even perfect strangers could see that.

Twenty-Two

ARREST MADE IN BEATING DEATH OF LOCAL DRUG DEALER

The Friday morning headline in the paper confirmed what I already knew. What I both feared and craved.

The arrest would take the pressure off Kurt,

and maybe it proved what I'd hoped all along—
that he really was innocent. One less pressure
point would mean one less thing that might
drive him back to his old habits. If he were no
longer a suspect, then there was one issue of his
life taken care of.

Except . . .

Someone else was in jail right now. Someone
who might very well be innocent. Or maybe
not? I had to read the article.

His name was Gary Singer. He was twenty-five
years old and had been a hard drug user since
his mid-teens. He had an impressive list of
previous arrests, everything from drug-related
issues to breaking and entering, theft, and assault.
I read the story.

This type of violence is apparently nothing
new to Mr. Singer. He was arrested on assault
charges last year. Allegedly, he saw his girlfriend talking to another man and flew into a
rage. He beat the man unconscious and his
girlfriend sustained three broken ribs before
police arrived to break up the carnage.
Witnesses at the scene were quoted as saying he "was like a crazed animal."

A Santa Barbara couple took Mr. Singer
into their home two years ago, attempting
to help him begin a new life. Within the
week, he left the home, taking over $10,000

worth of valuables with him and leaving the man with a concussion.

He was suspended twice during his tenure at Santa Barbara High School. One of these episodes involved beating another student with a hockey stick.

I thought of the contrast between this boy and my Kurt. Much like the contrast between Rudy Prince and Kurt, there was no comparison. Kurt had turned his life around, looked forward to a productive future, and was finally overcoming the tragic past that had weighed him down for so long. Gary Singer had lived a life that showed nothing worthwhile. Not only was society better off with him behind bars, but you could even say he was better off, as well. They'd help him get clean, perhaps teach him a trade.

I had one person who might help me get some perspective on this, and thankfully we hadn't met on Tuesday morning as usual. Lacey had rescheduled for this morning, and I was more than grateful. She was the one person who didn't judge me on my status as women's ministry director or busy PTA mom or all the other usual tags I was constantly trying to live up to. Lacey simply took me for who I was, without all the tags, without all the expectation of perfection.

As I walked up her driveway, a debate warred inside me. I desperately wanted to unload all this on someone, someone who wouldn't imme-diately send me packing to the police station, someone who could look through all the angles. But if I told her and she didn't step forward, that would make her guilty, too. I couldn't lay that kind of burden on her.

"Are you just going to stand there all day, or are you coming in?"

I'd been so engrossed in my internal debate, I hadn't even noticed that she'd opened the door. I wondered how long she had been standing there, waiting. "Sorry. Lost in thought."

From her expression it would be impossible to tell if she was annoyed or amused. The twinkle in her eyes was the only giveaway. "Obviously." She opened the door a little wider in invitation.

I followed her inside, sat at the table, and poured us both some coffee while she removed the scones from the oven. "Smells like apple today."

"Cinnamon raisin."

"I guess it was the cinnamon that threw me off, since you put it in your apple, too." My mouth had switched into overdrive, just like it did after Nick's death. For months I carried on scads of perfectly normal-sounding conversations with dozens of people. Each of them probably went home amazed at how well I seemed to be doing. What none of them seemed to recognize was that, while my lips might have been speaking, my mind was nowhere in the vicinity, and my heart . . . well, my heart was obliterated. Amazing how the feeling changed so little from one life trauma to the next.

"So, you gonna tell me what's eating you, or are we just going to sit here and indulge and pretend like everything's status quo? Just let me know, because I'm content either way."

I folded my arms on the table and laid my head on it. "I don't know if I can."

"If you can what?"

"Oh, Lacey, if I unload all this on you, then it will be your burden, too. You're too good a friend for me to do that."

"Sounds to me like you and I have different ideas about exactly what a friend does. I've always thought friends carried one another's burdens and that's what made them friends."

"Yeah, well, this is different."

She stirred her coffee with a small spoon. "I see." She continued to stir, the metal of the spoon clinking against the white bone china. "What shall we discuss, then?" She drummed her fingers across her chin in mock concentration. "I know, the weatherman says that we'll likely be in the low seventies all week, with the possibility of early morning fog. There's something we can discuss." She pulled the spoon from her cup and set it across her saucer as prim as you please.

I started to cry. Just a few tears at first, until the entire Pacific Ocean seemed to spew from somewhere inside me. Somewhere during the deluge, I felt the gentle pressure of a hand on my shoulder. "It's okay, baby, it's okay."

At some point I finally calmed myself enough to raise my head. I wiped my eyes on my napkin, then looked at her and shrugged. "I can't tell you. It wouldn't be right."

"You know," she said, pulling her chair directly over by mine, "I *am* a lawyer. You could hire me."

I looked at her, even more confused than I had been before. "Huh?"

"That's right. There's this thing called lawyer-client privilege. You give me a retainer, I become your lawyer, and then anything you say to me would have to be held in strictest of confidence. It's the way our system works."

I looked at her and once again wondered at her ability to read me so completely. "I don't have any money with me."

She walked across the kitchen, picked up her purse, and removed a five-dollar bill from her leather wallet. "Here, I'll let you borrow this." She put the money in my hand, then took it away again, looking at it as if she was surprised. "Are you kidding me? You want to retain a lawyer of my caliber for only five dollars?"

"Well, I . . . I could go get more."

"You sure drive a hard bargain, that's all I've got to say. Five dollars it is, but don't you dare spread the word. It's highway robbery." She smiled at me then and put her hand on top of mine. "Now, my newest and cheapest client, tell me what's on your mind."

"I'm not sure where to start."

"Well, I can't tell you that, either, but I'll bet it ends somewhere with this morning's paper. Do you want to start there and go backward?"

"How do you know?"

"Honey, any second grader could work that puzzle. After Kurt came back you told me you'd found something from his past and weren't sure what to do with it. Not long ago, there was a blazing inferno in your chimney, in which there was obviously something you never wanted found. Now, another boy has been arrested for the murder that Kurt was once suspected of, and you come over here all teary. I'm thinking, if what you found earlier was only drugs or something like that, you'd be coming over here today all ecstatic. The guilty party is in jail, and the police will finally be getting off your back for good, and Kurt can go on with his life. Instead, you show up looking like someone just kicked the hope right out of you. I'm thinking there's no way that all these things are not related."

Somehow, knowing that she already knew, maybe not the details, but the heart of the truth, made the confession slide right out. "It was the bat. The thing I found, it was the bat."

She nodded her head. "And I'm guessing there are Louisville Slugger ashes in your fireplace right about now?"

"Not exactly." I looked at the white lace of the placemat. "The ashes got picked up with the trash a few weeks ago."

"I see." She nodded and stared off into the distance. "Does Kurt know you found the bat?"

"No. When I brought all his things from the cabin up to Templeton, he looked through it and asked, 'Is this all?' I wanted to hear what he had to say, so I said, 'Yes, there was nothing else.'"

I looked at Lacey and saw her studying me closely, no trace of judgment or condemnation on her face. "Had you already destroyed the bat by this point?"

"No. After I found it, I hid it in the attic because I couldn't decide what to do at first. But when I saw how hard he was working and how much he had changed already, I came home and built a fire." I twisted the lace between my fingers. "I don't know, I guess I've kind of convinced myself that he didn't do it. I mean, maybe someone else put it there. And you know, maybe this guy they've arrested really is the killer."

"And Kurt, how's he doing? Is he staying on track?"

"Yes. He's getting his transcripts together to get

back in college. My brother-in-law keeps telling me how hard he's working."

"Let me do some checking around. I know some people who usually have a good idea what's going on. I'll find out what I can about this other boy that's been arrested, what kind of evidence they have, things like that. We'll have a better idea of what we're dealing with when we have a few more of the facts, not just what they're telling us in the news."

"Thanks, Lacey."

"That's what friends are for."

"You're not my friend anymore. You're my lawyer."

She smiled. "That's right. I knew I couldn't stay in mothballs forever. I'll shake them off and we'll get down to the truth in no time."

I think that's what I was afraid of.

Twenty-Three

After breakfast, I spent an unproductive day at work before saying my good-byes just after lunch. The best thing about my part-time hours was their flexibility as long as I was efficient, but today I was in for the longest two hours of my life as I headed to Templeton.

I thought about what I would say to my son and worried about how he would react. I had lied to him, trying to reassure him. Now, I was going to drop the truth on him with all of its inherent baggage, including an innocent man locked up in the Santa Barbara county jail. I wanted to know the truth about his involvement, and I needed to know it now.

Would this send him straight to the arms of drugs for relief? Is that what he'd been doing with the money he'd been borrowing from both Rick and me anyway? Were there signs of the glossy cover-up of semi-permanent change, or had he really had the true, cell-level life change that I had believed? Yes, his change was real, I knew it was. Jodi's intuitive nature would have sensed if it were otherwise, and I couldn't imagine that Monte wouldn't notice anything as they worked side by side every day.

Today when I drove up the driveway, I bypassed the house altogether. If I stopped and talked to Jodi for too long, I might lose my resolve. I needed to go through with this before I changed my mind.

I was certain Kurt and Monte would be out in the orchards somewhere, so I drove as far as my car would take me in that direction. I took a deep breath and walked toward the orchards, while everything inside me screamed to get back in my car and go home before I wrecked Kurt's life. And Caroline's. And mine.

I heard the sound of their voices coming from the middle of the trees. Kurt said something I couldn't quite make out, followed by Monte's rumbling laugh. The sound of scraping and cracking led me in the general direction. I finally saw them between a couple of trees, covered with dirt from head to toe, dragging loose branches into a pile. They looked up as I approached and smiled in greeting. I didn't return it. I nodded at Monte. "I need to talk to Kurt for a minute."

He nodded. " 'Course you do. I was just about to take the quad up the hill anyway. I'll leave you guys to your privacy." Without another word, or even a readable expression, he walked over to the ATV that was parked a few feet away and climbed aboard. The motor roared to life and he disappeared behind a trail of dust.

"What's wrong?" Kurt's voice seemed deeper than usual.

I knew that things would only get worse from here. The weight of this visit would drag everything down, until his voice would be the least of my worries. I reached out and touched his cheek, so warm and soft, with the grainy texture of dirt and bits of wood chips clinging to the mix. I looked into his eyes, searching for any sign that drugs had been part of the reason he was borrowing money. They looked clear. My hand fell away and I turned my back on him, wrapping my arms around myself. "I'm not sure where to start."

"Why don't you start with what's bothering you?"

"Kurt, did you play any part in what happened to Rudy Prince?"

The question hung in the air between us, taking all the oxygen with it. Somewhere in the distance, I heard birds chirping a happy song, completely out of tune with the deepening tension so nearby.

"I don't know, Mom. I don't think so."

This was not the answer I wanted. I wanted to hear "No, nothing at all." Or just the truth, straight and plain. I was tired of wondering, exhausted with vague.

"You don't *think* so? I wouldn't think that would be the kind of thing you would forget."

"Well, if I did something, I don't remember it. But I keep having these dreams."

"What kind of dreams?"

"When I was in rehab, I kept dreaming about waking up back at my cabin with a baseball bat in the bed beside me." His voice trailed off, leaving no sound but the horses neighing from the next property over. Or maybe it was the blood rushing through my ears.

His "dream" was bringing me face-to-face with a truth I did not want to know. "A baseball bat?" Still, to this day, I have no idea how I managed to squeak that question out of me.

"Yeah. A Louisville Slugger, and a bloody one at that." He turned to face me, but he kept his eyes focused on the ground. "Rudy Prince always carried a Louisville Slugger with him—

he used it to hurt anyone who crossed him, and intimidate everyone else. Anyway, the night before I left, I either dreamed he came to me—or maybe he did, I'm still not sure which—wanting some of the money I owed him. Of course I didn't have any."

"Did you dream that, or did it really happen?" Hysteria was descending on me.

"When I first started having the dream, I thought it was just that because it always morphed into Rudy beating some homeless guy, and me getting so angry I was somehow beating Rudy instead. But when it kept coming back, I started to wonder if maybe there was something to it. I . . . uh . . . well, I'd been really wasted the night before, and sometimes after a night of partying I used to have memory blackouts, so I wasn't sure what to believe. The day I got out of rehab, I stopped by my old place before I even came to your house. I wanted to see if the bat was there, so I would know for sure." He shrugged. "They had already bulldozed the thing and there was nothing left. I had assumed all my stuff had gone with it, and in a way I was relieved. I figured that if I had done something stupid, but the evidence was gone, I could leave it buried in my past."

This was the part where I was supposed to tell him about the bat, about Gary Singer's arrest, but there was more of a reason I'd come here. Something else I needed to ask, and I wanted the answer now. "Kurt, there's one more thing I need to ask you, and I want an honest answer."

"Okay." He sounded unsure.

"Why have you been borrowing money? From your father *and* me?"

He linked his hands and cracked his knuckles. The same boyish grin I'd always loved crept across his face. "I wondered when you two would bust me for that one."

"Well, you're busted. Now, what are you doing?"

"I didn't want to tell you about it yet, but there's this girl. We were together for a while, and I found out that she's pregnant."

"Pregnant?" That knocked the wind right from my lungs. "Is it . . ." I stopped myself at the use of the word *it* and corrected, "Are you the father?"

He shrugged. "According to her I am."

"But you don't know for sure?"

"I know a few things for sure, like that we were together for a couple of months last fall. She's now six months pregnant, so the timing is right."

"And the money is for?" A picture flashed across my mind of a white coat in a dark room, latex gloves, and a disembodied voice, "This will all be over in just a minute." I tried to shake free from the nausea of the images that followed.

"To help her out, of course."

"Help her out with what?"

"Taking care of herself. You know, medical checkups, food, some medicine they've got her taking. I guess she's had a few problems."

"So, she's not . . . I mean, she plans to keep the baby?"

"She's planning to put it up for adoption." He rubbed at a particularly dirty spot on his hand. "She went to this place called Life Network a couple of weeks ago. They said they can help her, put her up with a clean place to live, help her find a nice family to adopt the baby—if that's what she decides to do."

A grandchild. This certainly was not the way I'd dreamed of someday hearing such news. In fact, at this point, the thought had never even occurred to me. An unmarried son, a woman I'd never met, who probably was using drugs just like my son was at the time of conception. How was I supposed to feel? I'm not sure, but something about the thought of putting him up for adoption, of never seeing him, it just hurt.

Then all sorts of ugly possibilities began to fill my mind. This woman had likely had several sexual partners in the last six months. Had she found Kurt an easy target for money since he was the only clean one of the bunch? Considering the large amounts of money he'd already given her, doubt shook flags on every pole in my brain. "What if the baby's not yours?"

He shrugged his shoulders. "It's not like I'm

paying child support or anything. But the fact is, we were together and now she's in trouble. I don't want to leave her to face that alone. The least I can do is help her out."

I put my arms around him. He'd grown up so much. His willingness to take responsibility for this woman's child that he didn't even know was his, it made me want to cry. This was a person who deserved the chance at a new life. I pulled back so I could look him in the eye, although his face blurred beneath my tears. "You know those dreams, the ones about the bat?"

"What about them?"

I squeezed him until I thought he must surely be suffocating. "You've started a new life now. You need to quit thinking about your past life and leave yesterday and its nightmares behind. Become the man you were intended to be."

"That's what I want to do. More than anything."

"Then do it."

At that moment, with the promise of a grand-child—even if I would never know her—and the potential for the man my son had become, I real-ized I had made my decision. There would be no turning back.

Jodi was waiting for me when I left the orchard. She stood in the middle of the driveway and didn't budge until I came to a stop. She walked around to the driver's side and motioned for me to roll down the window. "You are not leaving here until I take you to coffee. You may have driven all this way to talk to your son, but your sister demands her share of time before you go."

She didn't ask a single question, and she didn't do her usual, "Come inside and I'll fix us something to eat." No, she must have known that I needed to get away from the house. I swear, my sister would have been burned at the stake a couple of centuries ago for reading minds, or whatever it was they called it back in those days.

I put the car in park and got out. "Sounds good." And it did. I wanted to talk to her, but I couldn't tell her the things I so badly needed to say.

Could I?

"I'm so glad you're here." She put her arms around me and hugged. It was the hug of love and support no matter what. I recognized it well. "So, I was just sketching out some designs for the interior of the shop. Do you want to come take a look-see, or are you ready to go?"

"I'd love to see them." I wasn't sure what I was or wasn't going to tell her, and it was best to start with just some friendly conversation as a warm-up.

"I did have a row of shelves right here." She pointed at the drawing of what was now an over-sized bay window. "But I just couldn't stand the thought of hiding the beautiful hillside views

from that side of the building. It would completely wreck the innate rhythm I want to create.
I decided to make the window extra wide, so it's
actually a little bench seat, for anyone who might
want to rest awhile, enjoy the views, and take
another sample."

"I think it's perfect."

"Well, probably not perfect, but it's as close as
I can get to it."

If ever there was a human, aside from a God-
incarnate human, who could put the word *perfect*
beside her name, it was my sister. It amazed me
that she didn't see it like that. I thought of my
own mistakes, always plenty, but lately who
could even begin to count them? What would she
think of me if she knew the whole truth?
Somehow, I didn't want to know. "You ready to
go? I'll take us to that new place in Paso Robles
that has everyone talking. I've heard the chef is
down from San Francisco."

We climbed into my car and started down the
rural street that led away from Jodi's house. Oak
trees towered above the road, with moss hanging from the branches like garland from a
Christmas tree. Vineyards filled a good portion of
the hillsides, most of them neat and tidy rows
of vines, each trunk supported by a pole, each
branch held in place by two rows of wire that
ran the length of the row. We drove past one large
vineyard that looked different from the rest. It

looked more like shrubs than vines, and there were no wires, no support poles. "What's the difference between this vineyard and the others? A different kind of grape?" I asked the question mostly to make small talk.

"These grapes are dry farmed. They're not on an irrigation system like the other kind."

I knew that summers here were very hot and dry. I couldn't imagine anything besides tumbleweeds growing without irrigation. "Does that work?"

"Quite well, apparently. The yield per vine is much smaller due to the lack of water and less pruning, but supposedly when you take into account the extra cost for the water and labor, the cost per ton of grapes is about the same. So you can spend more time and money and produce more, or spend less time and money and produce less."

"Interesting."

"It always reminds me about the first verses of John 15, 'I am the true vine, and my Father is the gardener. He cuts off every branch in me that bears no fruit, while every branch that does bear fruit he prunes so that it will be even more fruitful.' You know, it's not enough for Him to put minimal effort into us. He gives us all that He has so that we can be all that we're supposed to be. Sometimes the pruning is painful, but it's ultimately because that's what needs to happen."

I thought of myself as a grapevine and didn't like the image. I could almost picture the hand of God coming after me, and I suspected he might be holding a machete instead of shears at this point. I wondered what I needed to do to get moved to God's dry farming list.

Twenty-Four

"So, how was your time with Kurt last Friday? Anything you want us to pray for?" Pastor Ken asked, leaning in the doorway of my small office Monday morning. Behind him, I knew that both Jana and Beth had stopped what they were doing so they'd be sure to hear my reply.

"He's just fine." I think I smiled as I wrangled the words from inside, but I'm not sure.

"It's not very often in today's world that you get to see a real-life prodigal make such a complete turnaround. Although, I have to admit, I've always thought Kurt had the hand of God on him in a special way. Even back when I first came here, it was so apparent he was gifted with leadership. The other kids all looked up to him, listened to him."

I cringed when I thought of it. Nick was the one with God's hand on him. Kurt's leadership had very little to do with being led by the Spirit. I managed a grin, on the outside anyway, and said, "Yeah, leadership if you mean putting shaving cream on the junior high director's car, letting a live king snake loose in the girls' tent at Lake San Antonio, and other equally divine measures."

He laughed. "Hey, I didn't say that God made him a perfect adult at the age of fourteen. But leadership is leadership. Besides, he never did anything mean; it was all harmless childhood pranks."

"Try explaining that one to Rufus Milner. Remember the allergic reaction he had to the stink bomb the boys set off in the Sunday school wing?"

"Well, it wasn't deliberate. Even Rufus knows that. Of course, he was mad enough that he chose to overlook that part for a while, but he eventually got over it. I think even he would laugh about it now. And I know he would be so happy to hear how Kurt is getting a fresh start, just like the prodigal."

I wondered what Ken would think if he knew about the bat. And the fact that I'd burned it. And the fact that I still wasn't saying anything, even though another boy was locked in jail right now. As happy as he was about Kurt's change, would he think it was a reasonable thing to do? No, that was a lie, I didn't wonder. I knew it was on the far side of the line he would not be willing to step over.

The rest of the day I spent working and hiding in my office. It amazed me how much you could accomplish when you skipped talking with people. I was just thinking I might get through the day without further complications when an Outlook reminder popped up on my calendar. My phone call with Reisha Cinders was in fifteen minutes.

"You've got to be kidding me." I said the words aloud, although there was no one in my office to hear them.

If I had remembered this at all, I would have come up with some excuse and cancelled it several days ago. Now it was too late. I had no choice but to go through with it, even though the last thing I felt like was being called a role model for anything. Still, it was something I had been called to do.

Called to do.

This thought slapped me back into the reality of what I'd done. Usually before a conference, or any kind of appearance, I spent a great deal of time in prayer about it, asking for the right words when I spoke, the right answers for people's questions, for God to be glorified. Today, not only had I forgotten all about this engagement, but it had never even occurred to me to pray about it.

"God, please use this show for your glory." It was the only thing I could come up with, although I doubted very much He was listening to me at this point. There was no time to sit and ponder this; it was time to make the call.

A few minutes later, I was on a national radio talk show, talking about grief. At one point Reisha Cinders said, "I understand that the man who killed your son had been arrested several times before for violent crimes, yet he was once again out on parole and free to hurt again. Do you feel that our legal system has gotten too soft on criminals?"

This was the reason she had me on the show, I knew that; but how was I supposed to answer this question? The entire country would expect me to feel that our justice system had indeed been too soft on Nick's killer, but the entire country had no idea what I'd burned in my fireplace. "Well, I . . . I mean, of course I wish that Lonnie Vandever and the others had never been released from prison the last time, had not been free to attack my son. But I don't want to start a nationwide policy based on one particular case. I think each case should be judged on its own merit, and each defendant, as well." By the time I finished giving the answer, a fine sweat had broken across my forehead. I didn't want to talk about these kinds of issues anymore, so I took the offensive. "I find that God has been sufficient for my grief, and I believe that focusing on what might have been works against that healing."

"Hmm. I suppose you have a point there. Don't you agree, though, that our government needs to do what it can to protect our citizens?"

"Definitely." I thought of Detective Thompson and his gut feelings. "But at the same time, we need to remember that the government can make mistakes. The system needs to work for everyone. The police aren't perfect."

Silence filled the airwaves for at least ten seconds. This might not sound like a long time, but when you were on a live national broadcast, it seemed eternal.

"Why don't we talk about processing grief. You teach seminars on this, correct?"

I exhaled my relief. Reisha Cinders wasn't going to risk any more answers that didn't promote her agenda, so she was going to change the subject. I was all for it.

By the time I finally hung up the phone, I had a stomachache that no amount of antacid could control.

Twenty-Five

"Well, best I can tell, it's all circumstantial evidence."

Over quiche and juice at our weekly Tuesday breakfast, Lacey's throaty voice brought the news I'd expected.

Somewhere inside me, far beneath any conscious thought or logic, I had been hoping there was direct evidence linking this other boy to the murder. Absolute proof, even. Then I could know that my son was truly innocent, in spite of what

I'd found, in spite of what he'd told me. Since this was not the reality, I could at least find relief in knowing the other boy would not be convicted. "That means they'll have to let him go. Right?"

"No. It's circumstantial, but still pretty compelling. And the DA has been getting a lot of pressure from the mayor, so I expect this will go all the way to trial."

"Compelling stuff like what?"

"As you already know, his name was on the pay-owe—that's the same list Kurt's name was on. He was also seen in the downtown Santa Barbara area on the night of the murder, but I'm guessing so were several other people on the list. There's a partial fingerprint that appears to be his, but it appears as though the masterstroke of evidence against him came from the fool's stupidity."

"What do you mean?"

"A piece of the puzzle that they've never made public was that it appeared as though Rudy Prince had been robbed after he was murdered. One thing they've been on the lookout for was a gold medallion that he always wore on a gold chain around his neck. It was custom-made. I don't know all the details of it, but it was one of a kind. Anyway, Gary Singer apparently pawned the medallion and chain down in Oxnard."

This was the kind of information that could lead

me to hope again. "So is it possible that Gary Singer really did rob and kill him? Maybe Kurt ended up with the bat some other way?"

Lacey reached over and squeezed my hand. "Baby, we both wish that were true, but let's not lie to ourselves. Okay?"

"Then, how else did Gary Singer get the medallion?"

"The story he's telling is that he came upon Rudy Prince's body. He claims he didn't know the guy was dead, just thought he was unconscious. Being such a fine, upstanding citizen, he then rifled Rudy's pockets and says he found a bag of cocaine and some money, both of which he took. I suppose that would explain the fingerprint. Then he took the gold chain and medallion. According to him, he figured when Rudy got out of the hospital, he'd be able to sell it back to him for what remained of his drug debt."

"Nice fellow."

"That's what I'm telling you. There's no comparison between this kid and Kurt. Kurt is useful to society, Gary Singer is just trouble."

"If he pawned it in Oxnard, how did the police in Santa Barbara even know about it?"

"They've been on the lookout for it from day one, and pawn shops are always on their watch list." She shook her head, which made the large fuchsia flower on today's headband wobble back and forth. "Greed got him. If he'd just tossed that thing in the trash, he would still be a free man today."

"So, like you said, it's all circumstantial stuff. I mean, a jury would see that and know that there's nothing concrete, right? What do you think will happen to him?"

"You want my honest answer?"

"You know I do." I said it with a confidence that I certainly didn't possess. In fact, I was pretty sure I didn't want to know the answer.

"Baby, he's going down. With his record, no one's going to believe a word he says. No matter what the truth is."

The answer sank to the ground with what was left of my heart. An innocent man was going to prison for a crime my son had committed. A crime I'd helped cover up. I looked at Lacey with all the courage I could muster. "I've got to tell, don't I?"

"If you go forward now, there's more to it than just Kurt. You've destroyed evidence in a capital offense."

I hadn't even considered that part. "Lacey, would I go to jail?"

"I practiced civil law, not criminal, but I know that destruction of evidence is a misdemeanor in the penal code." She tapped her fingers against her lips, and I could almost see her mind perusing the legal library of information she'd learned over the years. She pulled her hands away. "They could also claim obstruction of justice and accessory after the fact, and they're both felonies. I don't think they would send you to jail, but we both know you'd lose your job, all your church friends, everything."

I thought about the people I'd worshiped beside for the last twenty years and wanted to argue. But I couldn't. "Maybe."

"And if Rick starts talking custody for real, you've got to know that this would be the thing that tips the scales. Are you willing to lose both Kurt *and* Caroline to save a self-serving drug addict who would just as quickly turn around and rob you? Remember, that's what happened to the last people who tried to help him."

"I don't know what to do."

"Well, you better be certain of that answer before you do anything you'll regret. My counsel as your lawyer is to stay quiet. My advice as your friend is the same. Prison is where this guy belongs anyway. Just let justice run its course."

Twenty-Six

Lacey's advice followed me to work at the church, making it nearly impossible to focus and even harder to follow a conversation. As preoccupied as I'd been these last weeks, it was amazing nobody ever mentioned it. I finished the minimum I needed to get done for the day and left the church just after noon. I needed to be home when Caroline got out of school at three, but I had no intention of going anywhere near my house until that time. Busy, and away from my thoughts, was where I needed to be. I suppose I told myself I was going to pray, but ever since I laid eyes on that bat, prayer had almost ceased to exist for me. And seemed to be farther away with every passing day. Prayer is part listening, and I was pretty sure I didn't want to hear what God might have to say.

I turned the radio up full blast and started driving down the coast. At first, I thought I might stop at the Beach Grill on Padaro, order a crab salad, and enjoy the ocean and the beautiful day. But when I got to the exit, as much as I planned to turn, my car kept going straight.

I reached the outskirts of Ventura, wondering what I was doing there. It would have been a nice time to stop by Caroline's favorite store in the mall and pick her up a new pair of shorts since she had outgrown most of last year's. That didn't happen, either.

The direction I found myself heading was the one place I knew I had no business going. Still, somehow I found myself in the parking lot of Kevin Marshall's garage. A couple of cars were up on lifts, the high whine of hydraulics pierced the air in regular bursts, and the smell of oil and hot engines was almost overwhelming. I quickly realized the stupidity in driving here. I pulled to the far edge of the parking lot and began the process of making a three-point turn.

As I completed the reverse portion and put the car into drive, I saw movement out of the corner of my eye. Kevin was jogging toward me, his face lit with concern. He came right up to the driver's window. "Alisa? I thought that looked like your car. What's going on?"

What are the odds? It was a busy garage, mechanics everywhere. What would make him look up at the very instant I pulled into the parking lot? I rolled down my window. "Hi, Kevin. I'm fine, just out for a little drive and realized I needed an oil change. Decided to stop by spur of the moment, but I can see that you're busy. I'll just be on my way."

"Whoa. Just slow down there a minute. Joey just got back from lunch and isn't working on anything yet. I'll have him fit you in. Why don't you come into my office and we can talk while you wait?"

"No, that's okay. I can see that you're busy."

"I'm never too busy for a friend. He pulled open my door. "Leave the keys and I'll pull it around. We got coffee inside or I could get you a soda."

Door open, I didn't see myself getting out of this easily. And the situation was progressing toward embarrassing as mechanics began looking up from their work to see what was happening. "I'll pull it over. Which bay did you say?"

"Left." He shut my door and then paced beside the car while I parked it in the appropriate spot. "Hey, Joey, can you do an oil change for me ASAP?"

"Sure thing."

Stepping from the car, I looked and saw a twentysomething tip his hat in our general direction.

I nodded back at him and wondered if after he got under the hood, he would be able to tell that I'd had my oil changed about a thousand miles ago. Probably. Hopefully he would keep his mouth shut and not come blabbing into Kevin's office about how that was the biggest waste of time ever. I could just picture it now.

I felt the pressure of Kevin's hand on my elbow. "Back here." He led me to a small office in the corner. He shut the door behind us, and I wondered just what kind of reaction that would get from the guys out in the shop. Some crazed lady pulls into the shop, the boss practically drags her out of the car, and now they're going into the office and closing the door.

"Now, have a seat and tell me what's going on." He removed a couple of magazines from a worn tweed chair and stacked them on a much larger pile on his desk.

The bare walls closed tight around us, and there was barely room for the desk and my chair, but somehow it felt homey, not confined. "Nothing really. I was just having a bad day, went for a drive, and somehow I ended up in Ventura. Next thing I knew, I was in your parking lot." The heat from my cheeks could have warmed a small country.

"What made your day so bad?"

I didn't look at him. "I'm sure the last thing you need is some whiny female in here talking about her problems."

"You're the farthest thing possible from a whiny female, and we both know it. Now tell me what it was that made you so upset you drove all the way to Ventura."

"I don't know. It's a lot of things, and they all just seem to be adding up right now. Rick was talking custody a few weeks ago—not to me, mind you. Our ten-year-old is the one who over-heard it. He hasn't said a word to me about filing for anything. And then, our son Kurt . . ." I stopped there. I didn't want to ruin this moment by telling a lie, or even a half-truth, but I certainly wasn't going to tell the complete truth. "Well, let's just say, Rick suddenly decided that he'd been wrong about some things, and now all of a sudden, he's coming by with flowers."

"And that bothers you because?"

"The man was talking custody two weeks ago. Behind my back. I can't confront him because that would put Caroline in an awkward position."

He scooted his chair right up against mine and put his arms around me. I cried on his shoulder until the navy work shirt had a dark wet spot on it. I settled myself down, but he didn't let go, and I didn't pull away. I suspected he needed this unconditional embrace every bit as much as I did. It felt so warm and so safe. No angry accusations, only acceptance and support. He probably wondered why I cried so much over my husband bringing flowers, or maybe he understood that there was much more I wasn't saying. I'd like to believe that someone could actually understand me that well. We were good for each other.

When I realized just how far my thoughts had strayed down the path, I did pull away, although he kept his hands on my shoulders. He was a married man. I was at least technically still a married woman. "I'm sorry. I didn't mean to break down like that."

"Of course you didn't, but it's what you needed." He wiped his thumbs across my wet cheeks. We looked into each other's eyes for a split second longer than necessary, then he drew back, too.

I stood up and gathered my purse. "I'll just go wait out front for my car. I know you've got other things to be doing." I wiped my fingers hard under my eyes, trying to clear the telltale signs of smudged makeup.

He handed me a tissue from a box on his desk.

"I'll be in Santa Barbara next week on business. I'll try to stop by and check on you then."

"You don't have to."

"I know I don't. I want to."

His answer was the thing I hoped for most.

Twenty-Seven

Another Saturday. Another gathering to help those paralyzed by grief. Only, grief seemed to be the farthest thing from my mind at the moment. I could lead an entire conference myself on dealing with guilt. But grief? Still I presented and still the audience applauded generously as I concluded my talk. Many were wiping their eyes when I asked for questions.

The first came from a red-eyed woman on the front row. "How long did it take you before you got over your son's death?"

"Of course, you never really get over losing a child. I will remember and miss and love Nick until the day I die. However, with God's help, I've been able to smile again, to get on with my life, and to live each day because it is worthwhile." It was what they wanted to hear, what they needed to hear, but lately anything to do with God had gotten harder and harder for me to say. And some tiny part of me nearly shattered when I realized how long it had been since I'd last really thought about Nick.

I pointed toward a hand in the back. "In the last row."

"Do you believe that every life has equal value, or do you think that some people are more deserving of life—and even justice?"

Fury seized me. How dare Detective Thompson show his face at another of these events? I focused on keeping a neutral expression, an upbeat tone, but my whole body shook with anger. "I believe that Jesus died for everyone, I believe that He forgives those who come to Him and ask Him to do so, I believe none of us deserve His love and grace. So in one way, I'd say we're all unworthy." I heard a few mumbled amens in the crowd. This would be a good way to end it and get out of here before Detective Thompson had a chance to ask anymore questions. "I've enjoyed being with you all and sharing my story tonight. I pray that the God of all comfort will give you peace."

I walked from the podium and straight toward the back. I saw him slipping from his seat and heading toward the door, but this time I followed him. When we got outside, I said, "Do you mind telling me exactly what that was about? Why are you still following me around? You've already arrested the guilty man."

He came to a stop and looked at me. "Just a hunch. Gary Singer is crying about his innocence all over the station, and call me sentimental, but something about it rings true to me. While, on the other hand, something about your son's story still smells a little bit like last week's trout."

"Does it bother you so much to see someone no longer under your control that you have to try to make him guilty, just so you'll still have something meaningful to do?"

"Oh, I've got plenty to do, and part of that is making certain I'm not sending an innocent man to prison. You just said that you believe every life has equal value. So you would agree with me, then, that it is just as important that Gary Singer not go to jail if he's innocent as it is for your son. That's right, isn't it?"

No, I really didn't think so. I'd seen the paper. Gary Singer's life had nowhere near the value my son's did. Especially now. Still, I wasn't going to admit that to Detective Thompson. It would only add to his suspicions. "Sure it is. But since my son is innocent, your point is, well . . . pointless."

"See, that's where we disagree. My gut keeps telling me there's more to Kurt's story than I'm hearing. It's also telling me that you know more than you're telling."

"Well, your gut has a large imagination. Now, if you'll excuse me, I need to go inside and talk to anyone who needs my help."

"Have a nice evening." He nodded at me and walked away.

Twenty-Eight

"Wow, that's a cool car. Who is that?" Caroline looked out the front window then back at me.

I peeked over her shoulder at a bright yellow two-seat convertible in our driveway. "No idea. Likely someone at the wrong house. Now quit stalling and let's get back to your homework."

I had already turned my attention back to Caroline's math when the doorbell rang. I opened the door to see a bone-thin woman with tanning-bed dark skin and bottle-blond hair that was roughly the texture of straw. The semi-vacant expression in her eyes and the sandpaper texture of her face made her look like one of the homeless I might see in downtown Santa Barbara, except this woman was driving a nice convertible. "Can I help you?"

"You don't remember me, do you?" Her voice was just a tad slurred.

I didn't remember her, but after she asked the question, there did seem to be a hint of something familiar. I noticed then that she had a plate of chocolate chip cookies in her hands, and deduced that she must have been at one of the recent seminars. "I'm sorry, I'm terrible with names and faces. Would you remind me?" I still wasn't fully convinced that this lady didn't have the wrong house, but I wanted to be at least polite, just in case.

"I'm Sheila Marshall. You know, Chris's mother and . . . *Kevin's wife.*"

Did I just imagine it, or did she say those last two words with a bit of added volume? "Oh, Sheila, hi. I'm sorry I didn't recognize you. It's been a long time."

"Yes, it has. And how are you, young lady?"

I looked down to see Caroline standing right behind me, curiously watching this scene. "Caroline, get back to your homework." Whatever it was that had brought Sheila Marshall here, I was pretty sure I didn't want Caroline to be any part of it.

"Aw, Mom."

"Wait just a second, young lady. If you're going to study, you need to keep up your energy. Here, why don't you take these?"

Caroline's eyes locked on the tray of chocolate chip cookies. "Wow, thanks!"

I looked at Sheila Marshall, still concerned as to what this visit was all about. "Caroline, go put those on the counter in the kitchen for now."

"Can I have just one?"

"Not until after dinner."

"Come on, I didn't have my usual treat after school."

There was no way I was going to let my child eat anything from this woman's hand until I found out exactly what was going on. "Caroline, I'm not going to argue with you about this. Put them on the counter for now and we'll talk about it later."

Caroline walked away mumbling under her breath. There would be time to deal with her attitude later. For now, I needed to find out what was going on. "Thank you so much for the cookies. As you can see, you've made my daughter's day." I smiled at her and waited, hoping that she would explain exactly why she had done this.

She seemed to sway a little on her feet. "When Chris pulled out those pictures, I just realized that we haven't done enough for you after what happened to the boys. We should have been more supportive. I told Kevin just that very thing this morning." She looked directly at me, and even though her eyes were obviously a little unfocused, I wondered if I saw something like anger or defiance in there. I couldn't be sure.

I suppose the polite thing to do would have been to invite her in, but I wanted to be just polite enough to not offend, while getting her out of there as quickly as possible. "I'm just glad that Chris is all right."

"If you consider walking like a cripple all right, then yeah, I guess he is." She shook her head once as if to clear the cobwebs. "Sorry, I know we should be grateful. Life is just so hard sometimes."

A jingling sound came from somewhere inside her purse. "Just a minute." She reached inside and pulled out a cell phone, which she flipped open and stuck to her ear. "Hey." I could hear a man's voice muffling from the receiver, but I couldn't hear what he said. She made a face, then smiled up at me, sweetly. "Funny you should ask, because I'm in Santa Barbara. In fact, right now I'm standing on the front porch of Alisa Stewart's house. I thought maybe I'd do something nice for her, too."

The muffled voice was louder now and it sounded angry, but I still couldn't make out the words. I looked toward Caroline, who was making no pretense of doing homework. She was sitting on the floor, her books opened on the coffee table, eyes locked on what was unfolding at the door.

"Yeah, I'm on my way home right now." She stabbed the power button on her phone. "I've got to go. I just wanted to let you know that I'm thinking of you, that's all." She sauntered to her car, hopped in, and disappeared down the road.

"What was that all about?" Caroline asked.

"I really have no idea. Now, let's get back to homework."

A few minutes later I made up an excuse to go into the kitchen. I picked up the plate of cookies and threw them in the trash. I wasn't sure what Sheila Marshall was or wasn't up to, but I wasn't taking any chances with my family.

I thought about what poor Kevin must live with

on a normal basis. He worked so hard; it must be awful to come home to someone so unstable. Somewhere during the course of the evening my thoughts turned to how nice it would be to spend time with someone like him. Sheila had no idea how good she had it. I wondered if Kevin thought the same thing about Rick. Did he think Rick should appreciate me more?

I tried to stop the train of thoughts, but they just kept barreling down the track. He said he'd stop by this week. I'd never before spent any serious time thinking about any man other than Rick. I'd always stopped those kinds of thoughts when they started. It occurred to me then that over the course of the last few weeks, deception had begun to get easier than it used to be.

An hour later, when the phone rang, I was right in the middle of chopping veggies for a salad. I decided to let it go to voice mail, but I looked at the caller ID just in case.

Kevin Marshall.

I scooped the phone off the counter while little white pieces of onion dropped from my hands to the floor. "Hello?"

"Hey, it's Kevin."

"How are you?"

"I'm fine, but I called to tell you how sorry I am about Sheila's visit."

What was I supposed to say to this? That I appreciated the cookies that she made? That I understood now more than ever why he could relate with my grief so well? I finally decided to go with, "No problem. It was good to see her again."

"Yeah, I'll just bet. Anyway, she's pretty stirred up about some things right now, including the fact that I've been through Santa Barbara a couple of times recently. And one of the guys at the garage mentioned the fact that you got your oil changed. She's a little fired up about it."

I started to say that it was all innocent and I would talk to her, but it would have been a lie and we both knew it. "I'm sorry that my visit caused you so much trouble."

"Your visit was great, and Sheila is always looking for some kind of trouble or other. The only thing is, I'd told you I'd probably stop by to check on you this week, and I didn't want you to think I was lying to you. It's just that . . . I probably need to stay close to home for a few days."

"I understand. No problem."

"I'm hoping to make it up there next week. If I do, I'll call you."

"Great. Hope to see you then."

I hung up the phone, half of me torn with sadness that I wouldn't get to see one of the few remaining bright spots in my life right now. The other part, the part riddled with guilt, told me that Sheila may have just saved me from doing something I'd regret the rest of my life.

Twenty-Nine

Thursday, just as I started making lunch after work, the phone rang.

"Hey, Mom, I was wondering . . . man . . . maybe this was a bad idea." Kurt's voice grew softer with every syllable, until I was pressing the phone hard against my ear just trying to understand him.

"Kurt?"

"Well, I'm driving down to Santa Barbara this afternoon to see Pamela. I thought you might want to come meet her."

"Pamela?"

"The baby's mother."

"Oh." It only now occurred to me that I'd never before thought to ask her name. In fact, I hadn't asked anything about her at all. And suddenly I realized that, yes, I did want to meet her. And yet I didn't. At least as long as there was doubt involved, I could pretend that she was using Kurt's money for a decent place to live and good medical care. Knowing the reality might just be one more dark spot in my life. "I would love to meet her."

"Good, I'll be by at four o'clock."

I pretended to do yard work while I waited for him to arrive, glancing up every few seconds. As it turned out, that was completely unnecessary, because I heard the creaking from the old hunk of

222

metal before I actually saw the thing. I walked over to the opened driver's side window. "Are you sure Pamela doesn't mind if I come with you?"

He nodded. "I told her I was bringing you. Back when we were together, I used to talk about you a lot. I think she's looking forward to meeting you."

I wondered what Kurt might have said about me during his time away from home. Did he tell her that his own mother had given up on him? Did he tell her that I'd been so self-absorbed after his brother's death that I forgot to notice that he wasn't doing so well? "And she still wants to meet me?" I sort of half-laughed at this, like it was a joke, but it wasn't.

"Of course. I told her you were the best mother in the world."

"Best mother in the world seems a bit much. How about just best mom in Santa Barbara?"

"Nah, California at least." He nodded toward the passenger seat. "Now climb aboard and we'll be off."

I looked at the black peeling vinyl and the sagging cushions of my intended location. "Hmm, why don't we take my car?"

"Oh, come on, Mom, where's your sense of adventure?" Even as he said the words, he turned off the ignition.

"There's nothing wrong with my sense of adventure. It's my backside I'm a little more concerned about."

A few minutes later, I was pulling out of the driveway. When I got to the end of our street, I turned to him. "It suddenly occurs to me, I have no idea where we are going."

"Oh right, I didn't tell you that part, did I? Cottage Hospital."

I kept my foot on the brake. "Cottage Hospital? Has she had the baby? I thought she was only about six months along."

"She is, but I think I told you she's had some medical issues. Her blood sugar has been out of whack, and I guess now they're getting concerned about her blood pressure. I'm not really sure what all is going on, but that's what we're about to go find out, isn't it?"

I drove toward the hospital growing more and more concerned about what I would find when I arrived. I knew that gestational diabetes was fairly common. I wasn't so sure about the blood pressure. Was this because she'd been on drugs? Had she been using drugs when she was pregnant?

We rode an elevator up to the maternity ward and found her room. The head of her bed was slightly elevated, her long black hair fanned across the pillow, but her eyes were closed. I glanced at the television set on the wall, where the women from *The View* were arguing about whether six-year-olds should be allowed to bring their cell phones to school. I turned my attention back to Pamela. She was a beautiful girl. Fine cheekbones, smooth skin—skin that was definitely a bit pale, but she was in the hospital, after all.

"Pamela, we're here." Kurt touched her gently on her shoulder and she opened her eyes. She blinked a couple of times, then smiled up at him.

"Hey." Then she looked toward me and straightened on her pillow. "Oh, hello."

"Hi." I started to extend my hand but wasn't sure what protocol would be in the situation. Instead, I stayed planted at a close but safe distance and nodded. "Hello. I'm Alisa, Kurt's mother."

She smiled at me and nodded. "You're just as beautiful as Kurt always said you were."

I felt my cheeks grow hot; I don't know why. But it was uncomfortable enough that I wanted to change the subject. "He's always had the gift of overstatement."

"Nuh-uh. Not when it comes to my mama." He squeezed my shoulder, then went to sit on the edge of the bed. "What are the doctors saying?"

"I should get out of here first thing in the morning. Everything is stabilized, but I have to take it easy for the next few months. Not quite bed rest, but almost."

"What are you going to do?"

"I already talked to my host family. They were

great about it. I couldn't believe it. Susie told me not to worry about it, that she would help me out as much as I needed helping."

Kurt looked toward me. "Life Network set her up with a host family. She's living with them until the baby is born."

I looked at the girl on the bed and hoped that her host family would give her some of the guidance she needed. "Sounds like you found a nice family."

She nodded. "The best." She pointed toward a packet on the beside table. "Get that for me, will you, Kurt?"

He handed her the manila envelope, and she removed a few pieces of paper stapled together. She handed them to him and nodded toward me. "This is the family I think I've decided on. What do you think?"

I went to look at the smiling couple on the first page and gasped before I could stop myself.

Kurt looked at me. "What's up?"

"That is Lori Radcliff's daughter and her husband. I can't think of their names." I looked at the sheet of paper. "Oh yes, Rachel and Stefan Tuttle, that's right. I know they've been struggling with infertility for years, but I wasn't aware that they had begun looking for a child to adopt."

Pamela looked at me, a hint of desperation in her eyes. "Are they nice people?"

I knew she needed the comfort of knowing that

her child would be safe. I needed to know that, too, and while I didn't know the couple very well, I knew the family. "I can't think of any nicer. They would be a great choice."

"Good." She sat back and closed her eyes in relief, or exhaustion, I wasn't sure.

Just then, a nurse in pink scrubs came walking into the room. "Time for your medicine." She carried a white paper cup of pills in her hand.

Kurt stood. "We'll be going. I just wanted to see that you were okay, and to let you meet my mother."

Pamela opened her eyes and smiled up at me. "I'm so glad to have met you. Take good care of Kurt."

Spontaneously, I reached down and squeezed her hand. "I will. You take good care of yourself."

She squeezed back. "I plan to."

As Kurt and I walked down the hallway toward the car, my mind was twisting in all sorts of new directions. "She could stay at our house. I could help her while she's on bed rest."

"Whoa there, easy, Mom." He put his hands on both my shoulders and pulled back as if he were reining a horse.

"No, really." I was already picturing the setup. "It would work. We could do this."

He shook his head, his face suddenly serious. "I knew you'd say something like this, but that's not where this is headed. Pamela and I, we aren't . . .

I'm just trying to do the right thing for her. As soon as the baby comes, Pamela plans to go back to Florida and live with her family, finish school, get a job. If she came to live with you, it would be that much harder to give the baby up for adoption, for all of us. It would not be the best decision for any of us."

I knew that in many ways he was right, but there was plenty of argument left inside me. I'd wait and think it through before I stated my case again, though. "I'm so proud of you." And I was. So proud. And at times like this, it was so obvious to me that I had done the right thing on the night I struck that match.

Thirty

A MOTHER'S HEART BROKEN

The headline in Monday's Life section of the newspaper caught my eye, as I suppose it would any mother's. The picture beneath it showed a woman I'd guess to be my age, soft in the face and with eyes that could only be described as tortured. She held two eight-by-ten photographs in her hands, both of clean-cut young boys wearing the forced smiles of school photos. The caption beneath read, *Theresa Singer holds photos of her two sons. Joe, pictured right, died of leukemia when he was twelve years old. Gary, pictured in happier times, is currently awaiting trial for the murder of Rudy Prince.*

That sat me back in my seat. This was the boy who had been arrested for murdering Rudy Prince? Even if the picture was from a few years ago, this innocent-looking child couldn't possibly be the drug-addicted maniac that I'd been picturing in that prison cell. It didn't look much like the hollow-eyed man I'd seen in the booking photos, either.

I picked up the paper, carried it outside, and put it in the recycle bin. I didn't want to see any more.

"Mom, where are my tennis shoes? I know I left them right here." Caroline pointed at the bottom stair. "They're not here anymore. I've got to have them for PE today. We're running the mile."

"Caroline, if you left them right there, then right there's where they would be. I haven't moved them."

"Well, somebody moved them, because I left them right here."

"Did you look in your closet?"

"Yes."

"How about the car? Did you take them off in the car on the way home from your father's?"

She cocked her head to the side. "You know what, maybe I did." She disappeared out the door into the garage and returned a minute later, tennis shoes in hand.

I went over and patted the bottom stair. "Sure glad you left them right here, aren't you?"

"Well, that's where I usually leave them." She pulled the long pink laces together and tied the first of a double bow. "So, did you pack my lunch? Today's menu is that mixture of cardboard and rubber the school has the nerve to call pizza."

"Yes, I packed your lunch. It's in your backpack." I pointed toward the bulging blue camouflage bag. "Now, you need to get moving or you're not going to make it in time for a game of handball before the bell rings."

"Mo-om, nobody plays handball anymore."

"Since when?"

"Last week, when we decided that handball was lame. Now we do cartwheels out on the lawn." There was a wistful tone to her voice.

"Who decided?"

She shrugged. "You know, the group."

"But you love to play handball." And besides that, I knew that she hated cartwheels.

"Mom, it's lame. Now, I gotta go." She pulled her backpack strap over her right shoulder and opened the front door. I watched her disappear down the sidewalk and thought about how much I hated what peer pressure did to our kids.

I climbed into my car and drove to work, listening to the radio as usual. Reid and Sam, the morning hosts, were discussing the morning's news. This was fine until Reid brought up the article about Gary Singer's mother.

"Can you believe that? She lost her youngest son to leukemia when he was just twelve years old. She says right here . . . Wait, let me find it. Yes, here it is. 'I spent so much of my energy dealing with Joe's illness, I just didn't have anything left for Gary. I saw what was happening but couldn't stop it. It's all my fault. If I had forced myself to deal with it then, my son wouldn't be an addict now. It should be me facing jail time, not my son. I will never be able to forgive myself.' End of quote. Can you believe the burden that poor woman carries?"

I flipped off the radio, pulled my car to the side of the road, and cried on the steering wheel. I'd never thought of the other mother, of the other family that maybe was very much like my own. The death of one child followed by the addiction of the second, which went down and down from there. This was the woman I was letting take the pain for what my son had done. As much as I'd managed to convince myself that the dream was totally a coincidence, that the bat had been planted—in this moment, I had to acknowledge that I knew better.

But what could I do about it? Going forward meant losing Kurt all over again. And he was doing so well. College waited for him. And, like Lacey said, I was going to be in trouble if I went forward, too. What if I went to jail for destroying the evidence? What would happen to Caroline then?

I knew the answer. Her father would get full custody, and I wouldn't be able to see her. I couldn't face that. I'd lost too much already. "God, surely you wouldn't ask that of me!" I wailed at the sky. "How could you even think of asking that from me? It's too much, too much."

At some point I started my car and drove toward work. As I pulled into the church parking lot, I saw Carleigh in the driveway. She smiled and walked over to me, her brown curls dancing happily in the spring breeze. I put on my best church face and smiled back.

"Isn't it a blessed morning?" she asked.

"Yes, it certainly is." I smiled back at her and thought of Caroline, handball, and cartwheels. I realized then that grown-ups aren't so different from kids after all.

"Lacey, I don't think I can do this anymore."

It was only Tuesday. I hadn't even had breakfast yet and I already felt exhausted. I couldn't imagine making it through the week. I laid my head on her kitchen table and slapped my palm against the walnut surface.

"As soon as I saw that article in the paper yesterday, I knew you'd start having doubts. Alisa, you need to think this through."

"What is there to think through? There is an innocent boy locked up in jail right now for a crime that my son committed."

"Yes, and that innocent boy has a rap sheet longer than this street."

"But he's still innocent."

"This time. All you're doing by letting him out is prolonging the inevitable. He will eventually end up in prison, I can guarantee it."

I didn't doubt at all what she was saying, but my justifications for what I'd done were feeling thinner and thinner "I know that's probably true." And Kurt was clean, he was good, he was living a worthwhile life now. "But is it fair for him to go to prison for someone else's crime?"

"Our legal system's not about being fair. It's about society's version of justice. If you ask me, society would be better served by having Gary Singer locked up, and having Kurt Stewart doing well in college and making something useful of his life." She put her hand on the back of my head. "Are you willing to face charges yourself for this?"

Just the thought made me want to cower in fear. "I don't know. You know I don't want to, but I don't think I can live with myself, knowing what that mother is going through. I don't know what else to do."

"That's a decision you're going to have to make for yourself. But I can tell you, I don't think substituting Kurt, and the life he is building, for that Singer boy's life is a fair trade. I'm sorry that his mom has had such a rough time of it, but you had your own, too. It wasn't a bit fair that either one of you lost a son the way you did, but the fact is, Kurt has turned his life around and that Singer boy has not."

The words made so much sense when she said them. But as much as they were exactly what I wanted to hear, this time they didn't offer the release I'd hoped they would.

"You read the article. That poor mother is blaming herself," I said. "I know what that's like, because I did the same thing. At least I did until I destroyed the evidence and somehow managed to convince myself that nothing really happened. Well, now there's no denying the fact that something did happen. How can I allow that poor woman to live with any more sorrow than she already has?"

"Baby, you do what you've got to do. I'm not going to talk you into something that will eat you alive, but I am going to make sure you think about every aspect of this before you do anything. What do you see happening if the truth comes out?"

I shrugged. "Not much doubt I'd have to step down from my job at the church. They were going to move me to full-time, but obviously that won't happen. If Rick and I are going to get divorced, I'll need to find something that can pay the bills. As for my friends at church . . ." The words that rose to their defense died somewhere before they reached my lips. I wanted to believe they would be there for me, and I knew that a few of my closest friends would be. The others, well, I tried not to think about what would be whispered as I walked down the aisle to my usual seat.

"They would crucify you and you know it."

"Probably some of them would." I sat up and rested my forehead in my hands.

"Of course they would. I'm guessing that from the sheer volume of the backlash you'd have to leave there altogether. Not only the job, but the church."

I was the Christian here. She was the friend I was supposed to influence for the better. I wanted to argue with her, tell her that these people would still love me and support me no matter what. The problem was, I wasn't so sure that would be the case.

That afternoon, after a quick trip to the grocery, I found Kevin Marshall standing at my front door, looking at me with his deep blue eyes.

"Hey," he said, with a smile I could barely resist.

I wanted to reach out and hug him, tell him thank-you for taking time out of his day to come see me, for distracting me from the things that haunted me. Instead, I settled for, "Hey, yourself."

"Well, I told you I would be in town this week, and here I am. I guess if I'm going to keep popping by like this, I need to call first and give you a little warning."

He stood there, looking like everything I so badly wanted at this point in my life. But there were so many things going wrong, I knew that if I didn't stop this, and stop it right now, it would only make the disaster that much worse. I took care to keep my voice casual. "There's no need for old friends to call each other when they are going to stop by."

He smiled. "I'm glad to hear you feel that way. I was wondering if maybe you'd like to go grab some dinner? We could talk about how things are going. There's a new place in Solvang I've been wanting to try."

It sounded so wonderful. A nice dinner, conversation with an interesting man, at least a few hours' distraction from the things weighting my life. But when two married people start talking about going out of town to eat dinner, there's really no other reason for it than they feel guilty. I had more than enough guilt in my life right now; I knew that I couldn't stand even a little bit more.

"Kevin . . ." I looked at him, not wanting to hurt him, but knowing I could go no further with this. We were fast approaching the point of no return, the same point an addict crosses when the drugs become more important than doing the right thing. I would not put my family through that kind of aftermath again. "I'd love to, really I would. It's just that . . . I can't. . . . I mean, you're so wonderful, and I love spending time with you, and I want to spend time with you, a lot of time. But, separated or not, I'm still married to Rick. It just doesn't seem right. . . . No, that's not true, it's more than that. I know what I'm feeling is wrong."

He put his fingers against my lips. "You don't have to say another word. I understand." His face turned a light shade of pink, and I knew that he did.

I couldn't look into his eyes anymore and let my head drop. "I think we both understand each other, a little too well."

"Yeah, I think you're right." He gave my shoulder a quick squeeze and let go. "I'm going to miss our visits. It was one of the few things I looked forward to."

I knew exactly how he felt. "Me too."

"Well, I better get going." He turned and walked down the steps, got into his truck, and drove away for the last time.

It felt good to have done the right thing. A really hard thing, something I would rather not have done, but something that was right.

There was something else I needed to make right, and I needed to do it while I still had the courage.

Thirty-One

For the entirety of the two-hour drive to Templeton that Friday, I thought about Kurt, I thought about Pamela, and I thought about the baby who would soon be born. Put up for adoption or not, I didn't want my grandchild knowing that his real father went to prison. Still, Theresa Singer's words were plastered like wallpaper in my mind. I couldn't shut them out, no matter how hard I tried to think of other things. And the part of my conscience that seemed to have gone numb through all of this, well, it was suddenly awake, kicking and screaming. You can only stifle God's Spirit so long. This was not a gray area. This was black. Dark black.

Once again, I drove past Jodi's house and straight out to the orchards. Once again, I followed the sound of the men at work. They saw me coming before I got there and stood watching my approach.

Monte smiled. "The last time you turned up here unexpectedly, we found out you were about to be a grandmother. I'm wondering what news today's visit might bring."

As much as I wanted to laugh, or at least smile, I couldn't bring myself to do it. Instead, I started to cry.

"I'll, uh, I've got a couple of things to take care

of in the barn." Monte disappeared on the quad, leaving me alone with my son.

"What's wrong, Mom? Are you still thinking about the adoption?"

"No, Kurt, I'm not. I wish that were what this is about, but it's not."

"What then?"

"I haven't been completely honest with you. In fact, I downright lied."

"About?"

"You asked me if there was anything else in your stuff when I unpacked it. I said no, but that's not true. There was one more thing." I looked at him through my tears. "There was a Louisville Slugger there, too."

His head drooped. "I guess I'm not surprised. The memory flashes are coming more often now, and they're getting more intense. I've tried to convince myself all that was just a nightmare, but deep inside I know better. I think I've always known. It was real." He rubbed the back of his neck. "Why didn't you tell me before?"

"I was never going to tell you. I was going to let you get on with your life without ever knowing for sure."

"What made you change your mind?"

I wanted to stop right there, never continue the conversation. But I did. "Someone else has been arrested for the murder."

His head jerked up. "Who?"

"His name is Gary Singer."

He gave a half snort as he looked down and began to study his own foot as it plowed a track in the dirt. "I guess that doesn't surprise me. If it weren't for the fact that I know he didn't do it, I'd have written him in as the most likely candidate."

Once again I thought of the unfairness of trading the already reformed citizen standing before me for a man that even a former addict considered less-than. I began to doubt my resolve, but then I saw Gary Singer's mother's face.

"I've tried to convince myself that he doesn't matter, that it's okay for him to be in jail because he probably deserves it for some other crime he never got caught for. But, Kurt, I can't let his mother spend the rest of her life believing that she is the cause for all this."

He nodded. "I know you're right. It's just . . ." He looked at the land around him. "I really thought I was going to make it."

I grabbed him by the face. "And you still can. Get out of here. Now. Head to Mexico or Canada or wherever it is they won't find you." This idea came from somewhere deep inside me, and was spoken before I'd even realized I'd actually thought it. But I liked the idea. A lot. It left us with hope. "I'll go to the police on Monday. That will give you two full days to get to somewhere else besides here. I want you to make something of the life you've just started to build, and you can't do that if you're locked up in a prison cell."

He looked me in the eye for the space of ten seconds, then slowly started to nod. "I know a guy who does good fake papers. I could probably get some ID and a passport and get out of here."

"Do it. That's what I want you to do." Maybe I wouldn't be able to see him, but at least he wouldn't be in jail. I could lie in my bed at night and know that somewhere my son was living free.

"Where is it?"

There was no need for me to pretend I didn't know what "it" he was asking about. I looked him directly in the eyes. "I burned it."

"Burned it?" He smiled, almost despite himself. "Gotta say, Mom, there's a wild side to you I never knew existed. Who would have guessed something that wholly illegal was in your repertoire."

"Yeah, well, when it comes to protecting my kids, I've found out there's not much I won't do."

"I guess you had to find that out the hard way." He continued to watch his foot plow across the dirt. "What made you burn it?"

"The Bible says, 'As far as the east is from the west, so far has he removed our transgressions from us.' Your transgressions have been forgiven in Christ's eyes. I didn't see the reason to bother with anyone else's opinion." I reached my hand up and cupped my son's cheek. "The person who swung that bat no longer exists. He died the day you went into rehab. The real you emerged from the drugged-out shell you used to inhabit, and once again became the person you were before all that. A person who deserves a chance at life."

"Are you going to tell the police that you burned it?"

"I think I'll have to. I can't exactly produce the thing, and I suppose they'll want to know the reason for that."

He nodded. "Won't that get you in trouble?"

"Probably. Lacey said destruction of evidence would likely be a misdemeanor, so maybe it won't be that bad." I didn't tell him what else she'd said about obstruction of justice and accomplice after the fact. I wanted him to leave here with as free a conscience as possible. "Kurt, I have to tell the truth, but you don't need to face this. Get out of here while you can."

He nodded slowly. "If you're sure that's what you want me to do."

"I'm sure." And I was. It was the only thing that kept me going.

Two days later I sat in church, wondering if it would be my last time to ever worship here. Who knew what next week would bring? I might be locked up somewhere, or at the very least ostracized from this group of people. I smiled and hugged everyone on my way in the door, feeling tears sting my eyes as I squeezed just a little tighter. These people had been such a support for me, so much a part of my life, but I knew it would all change when they found out what a sham I'd been putting on all these years. And what else could my life have been except a sham, if I was willing to do something as terrible as I had done?

We sang some songs, but I barely listened. My lips moved, and sounds came out—at least I think so—but my mind was somewhere far away. When Pastor Maddox began the sermon, I had no idea what he was saying. Somewhere in the middle of it, though, I began to hear snatches of phrases, occasional words that caught my attention. Things like "pretense" and "being less than transparent." Well, those things all applied to me. I'd been pretending to be so many things for so many people for such a long time. I supposed that one slip made the next easier.

At the very end of the service, he called for anyone who wanted to come kneel at the altar and pray to please come forward. I couldn't hold myself in my seat. I rushed forward, certain every eye was on me, wondering what dark secrets I had that brought me up here so quickly. I knelt there with tears running down my face, thinking how far I'd let myself slide. I'd been so busy trying to be brave and "Christian-like" in front of all these people that I'd managed to completely shut God out of the deal. I buried my face in my hands and prayed like I hadn't in weeks. I had been silent before God, thinking He wouldn't notice what I was doing. Well, now I was going to come clean.

After a period of time passed, I have no idea how long, I opened my eyes. I was shocked to see at least a hundred people also kneeling at the altar. Were all these people here because they, too, had felt the pretense in their lives? Was it possible that I was not as alone in all this as I supposed?

I stood and returned to my seat. Other than Ruth Ann Sparks, who reached out to pat my shoulder as I returned to my seat beside her, no one seemed to notice that I had gone forward. I could detect none of the knowing stares that they all now knew what a fake I was. Other people slowly returned to their seats, until only a dozen or so remained at the altar.

Ken Maddox walked to the podium and looked out toward the congregation. "And Alisa Stewart, director of our women's ministries, will be leading us in our closing prayer."

I looked up in shock. Closing prayer rotated among staff members, and I'd never before lost track of my turn. Until now. I certainly did not want to go to the microphone, to say a prayer in front of everyone—today of all days. Not at all. Somehow, though, my feet did not seem to understand this, because before I could stop them, I found myself standing at the podium. I looked out at the congregation, row after row of people, who just a moment or two before had confessed their sins before God. Every person out there probably thought they had a terrible secret. Well, they had nothing on me.

"Dear Father, you are a mighty and perfect God, perfectly holy. Unfortunately, people who do your work, well, we're not." I thought about my resignation letter, tucked safely in my purse. I would give it to Ken on my way out, but now was not the time for all that. "God, as you know, I have been living a lie for a long time now. I've pretended to be stronger and more in control than I am, because I felt like that's what I was supposed to do. Forgive me. Forgive us all. Amen."

I looked down at so many faces that were familiar to me. People I had counseled, people I had put on my bravest face for. I returned to my usual seat for perhaps the very last time. The life that I had always known, the one I had spent so much effort cultivating . . . it was over.

Thirty-Two

I waited until after dinner Sunday night before I called Rick. "I need to talk to you about something. Can you come over?" I could hear my pulse thrumming in my ears. I dreaded telling Rick almost more than I dreaded the police.

"What's up?"

"I'd rather talk in person."

He hesitated before he answered, and for a moment I thought he was going to refuse. Then he sighed and said, "Yeah, I'll be right over."

I made a big deal about setting Caroline up in her room with the portable TV and her latest favorite DVD. This was such a rare treat, she was too happy to be suspicious. After the movie began, I kissed her on her forehead and closed the door to her room on my way out. I hoped she wouldn't realize her father was downstairs until after the explosion. Then, of course, I would have to tell her. There was no way to keep something like this from her, and I wanted her to hear the truth from me. But I was going to tell Rick first.

I stood by the front window and watched for him. As soon as I saw the flash of his headlights as he pulled into the driveway, I went out to meet him. "Caroline doesn't know you're here, and I'd just as soon keep it that way while we talk."

After studying my face for what seemed like forever, he simply nodded. "All right."

I led him into the sunken living room—not because it had always been our favorite room in the house, nor because the leather sofa and matching recliners held such fond memories of family times from years past. No, I chose this room because it was the farthest possible from Caroline's room. Even if she did hear voices, which likely she would after Rick got started, we'd at least hear her coming down the stairs before she got to us.

"I've got some things to tell you." I rubbed my temples between my two hands. "You're not going to like this very much."

"So I've gathered. What is it?"

"When Kurt was in rehab, Coach Brooks brought over some boxes of his things. Kurt had been living in a small cabin near one of their avocado orchards. After Kurt went to live with Jodi, I remembered the boxes and decided to go through them and get all his things cleaned up for him. You know, wash clothes, things like that." I squeezed my eyes tight together, trying to shut out the images that were flooding my mind. It only made the picture more vivid, so I opened them and looked at Rick. "I found something at the bottom of one of the boxes."

"What kind of something?"

It was too late to turn back now, but oh how I wanted to. Still, I had no choice at this point, so I took a deep breath. "The bat."

"The bat?" He looked at me in total confusion.

I didn't bother to answer him. Instead, I watched his face as the pieces slowly fell into place. I knew the exact second he understood. A string of expletives flew from his mouth that could make an average mafia guy blush. "You've got to be joking! You've known all this time, you've had the bat all this time, and you didn't say anything to me about it? How could you have kept something like this from me?"

"Of course I didn't say anything about it. I knew exactly what you'd do."

"Oh really? And exactly what would I have done, Miss Mind Reader?"

"You would have gone straight to your new best friend Bruce Thompson. That would put an end to Kurt's new life." I took a deep breath and forced myself to lower my voice. Upstairs or not, Caroline would be here in a flash if we didn't calm it down. "The boy who killed Rudy Prince doesn't even exist anymore. He died when Kurt was reborn as his old self. I just didn't see any reason to punish him for something he no longer was."

"And he's just been playing along all this time?"

I shrugged. "I don't think he really knew. When I brought his stuff to him, he asked me if that's all there was. I told him yes. Then, a couple weeks ago, I asked him directly if he had any part in Rudy Prince's murder. He told me that he'd been having dreams about waking up beside the bat, but he didn't know if they were real or not."

"A dream. How rich."

"Maybe he really didn't know for sure. He'd spent so much time taking drugs, I would think the line between reality and fantasy blurred for him a lot. Wouldn't you?"

Rick picked up a book from the end table and threw it across the room. "And I just gave him three thousand dollars. I can't believe I was so stupid. He probably bought some drugs and sat around with a few of his old friends and laughed about how he'd gotten away with beating a man to death, and even conned his father into paying for his fix."

"No, he didn't." I barely whispered the words. I knew the truth, it was on my side, but Kurt's actions had been too noble to be shouted in anger, used to win an argument.

"Of course you don't think so. You probably think that bat just happened into his stuff and he had nothing to do with it, too. Right?" He kicked the arm of a sofa and it scooted several feet across the carpet. "This is unbelievable. *You* are unbelievable. To think you've known this all this time and didn't tell me."

"I'm telling you now, and your reaction is showing me just exactly how understanding you would have been if I'd told you earlier."

He spat out a few more curse words, then dropped onto the couch and put his face in his hands, his head shaking from side to side. "I can't believe this. I just can't believe this."

I perched on the far edge of the sofa. "I have an appointment with Detective Thompson tomorrow morning at nine. I'm going to tell him everything."

Rick looked up at me, surprised. "What made you decide to tell him?"

"When that other boy was arrested, I started having doubts. Then, after I read the story of his mother, I knew I had to come forward. I couldn't put her through that."

"Have you told Kurt?"

I nodded. "I went and talked to him Friday."

"What did he say?"

"He was upset, but I think maybc a bit relieved. It had been haunting him for a while."

"So he plans to confess to everything?"

I laced my fingers together and studied the raised veins on the back of my hand. How had so much time slipped through my fingers? Now there was nothing left to hold on to.

"Alisa?"

I wondered what he would do if I told him Kurt was running. Would he call Detective Thompson right here and now, cut Kurt's lead by a good twelve hours? I looked into his eyes and saw the face of a man who'd just lost everything. I knew exactly how he felt. I reached across and squeezed his hands. "I told him not to." I couldn't force myself to tell Rick what I had told him to do instead. "There is something else you should know. He didn't use the money you gave him to buy drugs."

"You know this because?"

"Because I've met Pamela—the soon-to-be

mother of our soon-to-be-born grandchild. Kurt's been helping her with some living expenses."

When he looked up at me this time, I wasn't sure if I saw anger or desperation. "Are you sure?"

I shrugged. "As sure as I can be, I suppose. She plans to put the baby up for adoption. I think Lori Radcliff's daughter and her husband are the intended parents."

"I see." Rick nodded briskly and stood. He started up the short steps that led to the main level of the house, but stopped and turned on the third step. "This is one time in my life when I wish I was wrong. He really did try to turn his life around. I think you were right about that. I wish there was something we could do to save him."

"Me too." I looked at his face, suddenly a dozen years older than his current forty-seven years. "I'm sure I'll get in a fair amount of trouble for my part in this, but I know you'll take good care of Caroline." Tears choked my words.

"You'll get in trouble? For hiding the bat you mean?"

"Destroying it."

"You what?" His voice rose loud enough to shake the roof. "How could you have done something so stupid?"

"Mom? Dad, is that you?" Caroline came running down the stairs. "Dad, what are you doing here—" Her voice disappeared into a cloud of fear when she looked at his face. She came to stand behind me. "Mom?"

I reached an arm back and around her. "It's okay, sweetie. Your father was just leaving."

Rick stormed out the door, slamming it behind him.

"Mom, what's going on?"

Now came the hardest part of all. Telling Caroline.

"Marshmallows too?" Caroline clearly knew that something was wrong, but she was far too crafty to question late-night hot chocolate until she'd drained it for all it was worth.

"Why not?" I pulled out the bag and sprinkled a liberal helping on the surface of the frothy liquid.

"Whipped cream?"

I considered for just a moment, then shook my head. "Let's not push it to the point of an upset stomach."

She shrugged and reached for the mug. "I won't get an upset stomach." She took a sip, then looked up at me. "How about some graham crackers?"

By now it was more than painfully obvious that I either needed to start talking or empty the cupboards of anything sweet. "Caroline, there's something we need to talk about."

Her face went solemn and she poked at a

marshmallow with her spoon. "It's about Daddy, huh? You two are really mad at each other now, aren't you?"

"No, sweetie, you just happened into the room at the end of an especially difficult conversation." Come to think of it, it was the same discussion I was about to have with Caroline.

She took a sip of her cocoa and considered this. She didn't look convinced. "Then, what do we need to talk about?"

I opened my mouth to speak, but not a single sound came out. Nothing. I took a sip of water, which caught somewhere in my throat, coughed, and tried again. "There's something you need to know."

Caroline set her mug on the table and crawled into my lap. She wrapped her arms around me and laid her cheek on my shoulder. "I love you, Mommy. You can tell me anything."

Any other time, the words would have made me laugh. How many times had I said the exact same phrase to her? Tonight, it wasn't funny at all.

"Caroline, before Kurt came back to us, he did something really bad."

She leaned back and looked at me, her face solemn. "I know." Her huge blue eyes blinked, the long eyelashes only adding to the innocent look.

"You know?"

"Yeah, he was using drugs. I know that it's bad

to use drugs, Mom. You don't have to tell me that."

How I envied the parents whose tensest moment with their children would be the " just say no" talk. "Yes, he did take drugs, and that was very wrong. But the drugs made him do some other bad things, too."

"Like what?"

"Well, there was a drug dealer who sometimes hit people with a baseball bat. One night, Kurt got really angry and took the bat away from him."

"What's bad about that? Sounds to me like it was something good."

"It would have been . . . if he'd stopped there. Caroline, Kurt got the bat and started hitting the drug dealer with it."

"Seems to me like he deserved it."

"Maybe so, but Kurt hit him hard enough that he killed him."

Caroline's huge eyes filled with tears. "But it wasn't his fault. That drug dealer was mean."

I stroked the silkiness of her long blond hair. "The police don't really look at it that way."

"What do they say?"

"Nothing yet. They think someone else did it. But . . . tomorrow morning . . ." Each syllable caught in my throat. "I'm going to the police station to tell them the truth."

"You're what? You're going to snitch on Kurt? Why would you do that?"

"Because someone else has been arrested. Caroline, if we don't tell the truth, an innocent man will probably go to jail."

"Jail?" Caroline screeched out the words. "Jail? Kurt is going to jail because you're going to tell on him?"

"It's the right thing to do."

She shoved herself out of my lap and returned to her chair, the cocoa apparently forgotten for now. "I don't think that's what a mother should do."

I gripped my hands together on the kitchen table and stared at them. "There's one more thing I need to tell you."

"What?"

"I found the bat a couple months ago. At the time, I sort of agreed with what you're saying, and I burned the bat so the police couldn't find the evidence."

She looked at me, eyes huge. "You did?" She couldn't quite contain her smile—mad at me or not, she approved of this part of the story.

"Yes, I did. But, Caroline, it was the wrong thing to do. It was a crime, and tomorrow when I go talk to the police, I've got to tell them that part, too."

"Will they be mad?"

I nodded. "Yes, I'm afraid they will."

"Mommy, you can't—I won't let you. I won't let you go." She launched herself at me and wrapped her arms tight around me. "I'm not letting you go to jail."

"I don't think I'll go to jail. But Daddy will be here to take care of you, even if I do."

"Nooooo! Noooo! I hate Daddy. If you go tell the police to put you and Kurt in jail, then I hate you, too." She ran out of the kitchen. I heard the thud of her feet as she ran up the stairs and the slam of her bedroom door as it closed behind her.

The weight of the words, of what was before me, pressed against me so hard, I didn't think I could lift myself from my chair. I braced my palms against the table, used my arms and legs to push myself upright, and somehow managed to move forward. I used the handrails to pull myself up the stairs, one at a time, toward Caroline's room. I turned the knob but wasn't surprised it was locked. "Caroline, open the door."

For the space of a full minute there was no sound at all. I was just about to issue a more forceful order when I heard the slip of the lock. She opened the door and looked at me, eyes already red and puffy. She threw her arms around me. "Please don't go, Mama, please don't go."

Thirty-Three

At five o'clock Monday morning, I reached over and turned off my alarm. I supposed the bright side about not being able to sleep was not having to wake up to a loud buzzing sound. I looked at the unmoving lump in the covers next to me, the wisps of sandy curls that stuck out from beneath the blanket, and how I wished I could go back and change things. What I wouldn't give to be able to erase the memory of Caroline's tears, the absolutely brokenhearted wailing that had finally silenced into sleep sometime after midnight.

The day I chose to get rid of the bat, I had never imagined that this awful morning would come. If I could turn back the time, maybe I would have done things differently.

But even now, as I remembered the smell of sulfur from the moment when I struck the match against the side of the box, I could still feel my desperation. My son needed a chance, and I had to make certain he got one. Would I be able to make a different choice now?

I padded down the stairs and went into the kitchen. If this was going to be the last morning I spent with my daughter, then I was going to make it a breakfast to remember. I mixed pancake batter, scrambled eggs, put in a couple of extra pieces of bacon. Soon the entire house smelled like . . . well, like a happy home. It was amazing how the scents of favorite foods could have that effect. I realized that after this moment I would never smell bacon with the same affection I had for the last forty-five years. It would always remind me of this day. Of the end of everything.

I heard the clomp of Caroline's footsteps coming down the stairs. She appeared in the kitchen a moment later, dressed in a red velvet jumper, white tights, and black patent shoes. This was not an outfit my tomboy would ever put on of her own free will. In fact, getting her to wear it to the Christmas Eve service had taken begging, pleading, and downright threats. "Don't you look pretty." I kept my tone noncommittal because I wasn't sure exactly what she was up to, and I wanted to leave all my options open.

"Yep." She sniffed the air. "Smells good. What did you make?"

"Come see." I set a plate at her seat, and within seconds she had popped a piece of bacon in her mouth. "Mmm."

I took a small bite of bacon, but it almost made me gag. Regret filled my stomach until there was no room for anything else.

"I figured I needed to look nice for the police station." She said the words matter-of-factly, but she stared at me with all-out defiance in her eyes. She had made up her mind and had no plans to back down.

"Oh, sweetie." I went to her and wrapped my arms around her, burying my face in the hair that still stood on end from a rough night's sleep. "That makes me so happy to know that you would go with me if you could."

"What do you mean, if I could? Of course I can. I'm coming with you, and that's final." Her use of the same words I often threw at her would have been comical had it not been so altogether heart-breaking.

"Sweetie, you can't. I don't know what's going to happen to me today. I don't think I could stand it if I didn't know that you were safe at school, and then safely home with Daddy."

She started crying, every bit as hard as she had last night. "Please don't make me go to school today. Please, I want to go with you. Please let me go to the police station with you." She wrapped both arms and legs around me. "You can't leave me. I won't let you."

"Oh, honey." I held her tight while my own tears poured over her. "I love you so much. I love you so much." Somewhere during this, I ended up sitting on the floor with her in my lap, our arms woven around each other like a safety net—one we both knew would not be able to hold.

What had I done?

After a long time I pulled back. "Come on, let's brush your hair and your teeth and then I'll walk you to school."

"I'm not going." Her arms went around my neck again.

"You've got to, baby. You've got to. Don't worry, though. Daddy will be there to pick you up when you get out."

"I don't want to stay with Daddy. I want to go with you."

I reached up and pried her arms away from my neck, then stood up and away from her. It took more strength than I knew I possessed. "Come on, you're already late."

She grabbed for me, but I backed away and pointed toward the stairs. "Brush your hair and your teeth. Now!"

She burst into a fresh bout of tears and ran up the stairs. I wanted to follow her, to spend every available second with her, but I knew she'd be more likely to finish what she was supposed to do if I wasn't in her line of sight. A couple of minutes later she came down the stairs, her hair slightly less tousled than before. She slung her backpack over her shoulder and looked up at me with a defiant look, but her lower jaw was trembling. "You said you'd walk me to school."

I reached down and scooped her up into my arms, and proceeded to carry her the block and a half to school. She wrapped her arms around my neck and buried her face in my shoulder. I could sense the stares coming from the cars that were making the drop-off circuit through the parking lot, but I didn't care. The two of us needed each other now, and there was nothing to be ashamed of in that.

The tardy bell rang with twenty yards still left to go, so I went straight to the office to sign her in. As soon as I signed on the appropriate line, I went to set her down. She started screaming. "I'm not staying, I'm not staying, I want to come with you."

I knelt down at eye level. "Sweetie, I need you to be strong for me. You're all in the world I've got left. I can't make it if you won't help me."

The school secretary watched this scene unfold over the lenses of half-glasses. She stood from her desk. "Good morning, Caroline. Why don't I walk you to your class?"

I nodded at my daughter and wiped the tears from her cheeks. "You need to go with her. I'll see you soon."

Caroline reached a trembling hand up and took the secretary's, but she shuffled through the door still turned, still staring at me.

Thirty-Four

My legs had become stones, but somehow I managed to force them to bend, lift, move, and step by heavy step, propel me back to my house. I collapsed at the kitchen table, put my head on my folded arms, and prayed out everything in my

261

heart. "I blew it, God. I know I blew it. This is my fault. I know I shouldn't have covered up and lied in the first place. But, God, how could I not do everything in my power to give my son a chance? Wouldn't you do everything in your power . . ." The rest of the thought died in my throat.

Somewhere deep inside me, I heard the ringing of the hammer against nail, the thud of nail against flesh, and the splitting of the wood as the nails were driven in. I saw a Son's face, contorted in agony, awaiting a slow and painful death. I thought of the Father who didn't save Him, although He could have done so with complete integrity. Instead, He left Him there to pay someone else's penalty. Mine.

I, on the other end of the spectrum, had been willing to sacrifice someone else to save my son, the one who deserved the punishment. It was so against everything God stood for that I wondered He hadn't knocked me dead by now.

"God, I'm so sorry. So very sorry. I've done everything wrong, everything the way that you wouldn't want me to do it. Please forgive me. I'm so grateful your Son shed his blood so I could be washed clean from sins just like this. Please take care of Caroline. And Kurt. And Rick, too."

I'd always heard people telling stories about things like this, and right about now they always said something to the effect of "The Spirit of God washed over me and filled me with complete peace," but that's not how it happened for me. There wasn't a single ounce of peace anywhere to be found inside me.

I stood up, picked up my keys and purse, and walked out the garage door to where my car waited to take me to my fate. I pressed the garage door opener, climbed into the driver's side of my car, and started the ignition. The song on the Christian radio station was something about being more than overcomers, but I reached over and flipped it off. I needed silence now.

Rap. Rap. Rap.

The sudden knocking at the passenger-side window startled me. I looked over to see Lacey, her hair perfectly styled so that it gently rounded into a single curl just at her shoulder, completely absent of headbands, bows, or sequins. She was wearing a navy blue suit, and I could see what looked like the handle of a briefcase in her hand. I used the power button to roll down the window. "What are you doing here?"

"You paid me a retainer, remember? I'm your lawyer, and as such, I say you can't go do this alone. Now, open the door and let me in. We've got an appointment downtown."

I hit the power locks, but even as she was relaxing into her seat, I said, "You don't have to do this, you know."

"Of course I don't. I want to. If ever there was

a woman naïve as to the way the law works, it's you. It would be like throwing Daniel into the lions' den if I let you go down there alone."

I looked at her and smiled. "I hate to break the news to you, Lacey, but it wasn't a lawyer who saved Daniel, it was God."

"Yeah, well, and if God wants to keep your mouth shut at the appropriate times like He supposedly did with those lions, then that will make my job all that much easier, now, won't it?"

I reached across and hugged her. "You're the best."

"So they tell me."

I backed the car out the driveway and started on the journey I did not want to take. I was glad that Lacey was in the car with me, in part just to answer the questions I thought I knew the answer to but wasn't sure.

"What's going to happen today? After I tell them, I mean? Will they arrest me and lock me up?"

"Well, that could go either way. They'll likely turn it over to the DA for now, but there is the possibility they will go ahead and lock you up today, to use you as bait."

"Bait?"

"You're a tiny player in this whole big opera. They want the big dogs, and in this particular case the dogs don't get any bigger than the boy who swung the bat. I'm guessing they will suppose that if they lock you up long enough, Kurt will be more willing to show his face at the station."

I wondered where Kurt was now, if he had made it across one border or the other yet. I hoped he was far enough away that he would never find out I was bait. I didn't want him to do anything because of me. He was gone, and I was here to face my part in this. That's all I could do.

We parked on Garden Street and walked around the corner to the imposing three-story white building that housed the police department. I stood at the bottom of the long procession of concrete stairs that led up from the street level and took a deep breath. I looked at Lacey. "I'm ready."

"Not quite, you're not. You seem to be forgetting something. Or someone, that is." Kurt's voice came from behind me.

I spun around and faced him. "Kurt! What are you doing here?"

"I knew you were coming here this morning, so I've been sitting on a bench across the street just waiting for you. I'm going in there to face this with you."

"But . . . I thought you were going to leave town."

He shook his head. "And leave my mother to face this battle alone? Besides, Dad was always telling me I needed to man up. Well, if ever there was a time to man up, I'd say this is it. How about you?"

I reached out and hugged him. "Are you sure you want to do this?"

"Yep. It's what Nick would want me to do, don't you think?"

I thought about my older son, his penchant for absolute honesty, even when it got him in trouble. I nodded at Kurt. "Let's go man up together."

We walked arm in arm up the steps, Lacey by my side. About halfway up, she grasped my arm. "Hold on. Need a quick rest." Her breathing was shallow and wheezy.

"Lacey, are you all right?" Kurt asked.

She smiled at him and nodded. "Police stations always have this effect on me."

He smiled, but I could see he was scared, too.

She leaned forward and put her hands on her knees, taking deep breaths. After a full minute she straightened up and nodded. "Let's do this."

We finished the climb and pushed through the glass doors that led to the lobby. I walked to the only open window. It said Records above it, but I didn't much care at this point whether we were at the right spot. "We're here to see Detective Thompson. He's expecting us." I looked over my shoulder at Kurt. "Some of us, at least."

"Have a seat. I'll tell him you're here."

We went and sat together in a row of blue plastic seats. An angry-looking Hispanic man sat directly across from us, and a woman who I assumed to be his wife sat crying in the seat beside him. They were speaking Spanish, but my immediate assumption was that they had a son in trouble. I'm sure it's the same way Rick and I had looked on several occasions.

"Mrs. Stewart?" Detective Thompson's voice came from somewhere to the left.

We all stood and walked to the open door. He looked from me to Kurt to Lacey. "You've brought some friends, I see."

"We've got some things to tell you."

"Please, come right this way." He held the door open and smiled, a cat that had all three blind mice lined up right there for the taking.

"There are several detectives at their desks right now. Shall I take us somewhere that we can have a little more privacy?" Detective Thompson stopped at the end of the hallway, waiting for our answer. Just past him I could see staircases heading both up and down. I wondered which direction led to the booking room—or whatever they call it.

"Privacy would probably be a good idea," I said.

"Well, there's the big conference room downstairs, but I think they're having some sort of meeting in it right now. Shall we just go sit in one of the interview rooms?" The gleam in his eyes told me more than I wanted to know about this suggestion. He knew something big was up, and he was ready to pounce with full force.

I understood that this was his job, to get to the truth. I just wished he hadn't been quite so happy about our impending demise. "Sounds good."

Lacey got between Kurt and me as we retraced our steps down the hallway. "Anything you say from here on out is likely to be recorded. Think before you speak. Got it?"

We both nodded as we turned down another hallway with several doors on the left side. Detective Thompson stopped outside a door that looked as though it might lead to your basic classroom at your basic high school. It was painted white, but where there might normally have been a Classroom 15 sign at a school, here there was a small red plastic sign with white letters, Interview Room 3.

The hallway began to tilt around me, and I reached for the wall with my right hand, taking deep gulps of air. I tried to put my focus some-where other than the door that was opening beside me. A little up ahead of us, I could see a room off to the right. I could only see part of it, but I could see enough to know that it was cov-ered in Plexiglas and bars. That's when dark spots started popping like paint balls before my eyes.

"Alisa, Alisa, are you all right?" The voices were coming from somewhere, I couldn't tell where. All I knew for sure was the deepening blackness and the strength draining from my legs until I could no longer feel them. Maybe I fell, I don't know.

The next thing I remember, I was lying on the floor in the middle of what could only have been Interview Room 3. Worried faces hovered all around me. I sat up and rubbed my head, which pounded with the movement. "I'm okay, I'm okay."

I made to stand up but felt a restraining hand on my shoulder. I looked up to see Detective Thompson. "Don't try to get up just yet. Give your body a little time to get the blood flowing in the right direction again."

I looked at the worried face of my son, and I knew the worry I saw was for me, not for himself, not for what he was about to go through. "Sorry about that." I looked up at Detective Thompson and tried to smile. "I guess you're thrilled you agreed to this appointment now, huh?"

He grinned. "Believe me, I've seen worse. A lot worse."

In an effort to restore my bearings, I began to look around the room and study my surroundings. It wasn't like you see on TV. Those rooms are always large, with a big table where the defendant is always leaning on his elbows, smoking cigarettes and looking nervous. This room was hardly the size of my closet. In fact, I wasn't quite sure how someone had fit through the door while carrying me. And as for the table, it was more like a small shelf, stainless steel and attached to the wall. Barely bigger than the tray on an airplane. Certainly no place to lean on and smoke, even if you wanted to.

I pushed myself up into one of the white plastic chairs, which put me shoulder-to-shoulder with Kurt and Lacey. Detective Thompson was in the chair on the other side of the room, but if we all stretched out our legs we could have touched his chair. No wiggle room here.

"Well, I guess it's time I tell you why I wanted to talk."

"Mom, you don't have to say anything. I'm here to do the talking for me. There's no reason for you to say anything." Kurt looked at Detective Thompson. "I'm the one who killed Rudy Prince. Not Gary Singer."

Detective Thompson set a pad of paper on the small table and pulled a pen out of his pocket, clicking the ballpoint out of its protective case. "Tell me about it."

"I owed him money, as you already know. He came to me one night down at De La Guerra Plaza. I was sitting against a wall, stoned out of my mind, and he started yelling about paybacks."

Detective Thompson nodded. "Did he threaten you in any way?"

"Rudy always threatened people. That was the way he operated. He swung that stupid bat around, telling me how he was going to let me have it if I didn't pay."

"But he never actually hit you?"

Kurt shook his head. "I don't think so. The memories have been coming back in flashes, but I'm pretty sure he never got too close to me." He stared at the wall for a minute before he continued. "There was this homeless guy named Mike—skinny, harmless as can be—who was always sitting on the bench right near where we were." Kurt rubbed the back of his neck and shook his head. "I keep seeing the smirk on Rudy's face when he stood right over the old man and swung as hard as he could. I think he must have killed him, because I can still hear the sound of the wood cracking against the guy's skull. Then he looks up at me and goes, 'That'll be you tomorrow night if you don't come back with my money.' And he started laughing. Laughing."

"And that's what set you off?"

"Well, yeah. He was still standing over Mike, and I thought he was maybe going to hit him again, and then somehow I thought it was Nick lying there." Kurt closed his eyes. "I charged him with every bit of the hate I felt inside. I was so angry nothing could stop me. I managed to get the bat out of his hands, and in my mind, I could see the guy who'd killed Nick. I was hitting him after watching him laugh over Nick's body. I hit and I hit and I hit, until I couldn't swing the bat another time. But I wasn't seeing Rudy, I was seeing Lonnie Vandever."

I looked at Detective Thompson, wondering then if he was going to ask who Lonnie Vandever was. Then I remembered all his little visits to my conferences and the church, and realized he probably knew more about that case than I did. "What happened then?"

Kurt shook his head. "I'm not really sure. The next thing I remember was waking up in my bed and seeing the bloody baseball bat lying there. I picked it up and carried it to the sink and tried to wash the blood off it. It had already been stained by then. I dropped back down on my bed, hungover and still a bit confused about exactly what had happened. I tossed the bat under the bed and called this rehab place I'd heard about, and they told me they had a spot for me. I got in my car and drove down there and checked myself in."

"What happened to the bat?"

"Somewhere during the middle of the detox process, I realized that I'd left it back at the cabin where I was living. I planned to come home and see if it was really there, because by that time I had begun to convince myself that maybe the whole thing was a drug-induced hallucination. By the time I got out of rehab, the Brooks family had sold the place and the cabin had been demolished."

"So the bat went down with the cabin, so to speak?"

"I guess so." Kurt made a point not to look at me. I knew what he was doing. He was turning himself in for the real crime, telling the truth about his part. He figured there was no reason to give more information that would only get me in trouble.

I looked at Lacey, who nodded almost imperceptibly. She knew what he was doing and agreed, as well. Kurt was giving me an out. All I had to do was take it.

What came first to mind was a story from the Old Testament, when Joshua was leading the Israelites into the Promised Land. They surrounded Jericho, walked around it every day for seven days, and the walls fell. They had the victory, just like God had promised.

Except, there was a problem.

God had told them not to take any spoils for themselves. None. Nada.

When the army went up against the small group from Ai, whom they should have defeated without even a thought, they were routed.

Turns out, one of the men from Israel, Achan was his name, had seen a few things in Jericho that he really wanted: some gold, some silver, and a beautiful robe, so he took them. None of the people of Israel knew that he had done this, but God knew. When they went into battle, God withdrew his hand of protection and let them suffer a humiliating defeat.

Here I sat, having the opportunity to walk away

from this room without any repercussions at all. I had burned the bat, but no one would need to know. My son had confessed to the crime; the guilty party was going to be punished. I wanted to walk out of here a free woman, to go home and see my daughter this afternoon and tell her it had all been a mistake after all. But what kind of example would that set for her about honesty? And what if, just like in the time of Achan, God poured out His displeasure on my son during his trial because I tried to hide the truth?

I looked at Detective Thompson. "There's something else that you need to know."

"No!" Lacey and Kurt yelled the word in unison.

I turned to Lacey first and then Kurt. "Yes." I looked back at Detective Thompson. "Now, where was I?"

"You were just about to tell me something I need to know."

"Yes, I was."

Thirty-Five

"Okay, Mrs. Stewart, I think that answers all of my questions." Detective Thompson made the last of a series of notes, then looked up.

My stomach twisted hard, because I knew what was coming next. Fingerprinting. A mug shot. The sound of clanking locks.

Detective Thompson stood and walked to the door, then turned and looked at Lacey. "I'm going to file a probable cause declaration with the district attorney's office."

Lacey nodded. "I expected as much. I'll get in touch with them."

"I expected as much," the detective replied, but somehow his attempt at humor didn't work for me, especially since I had no idea what they'd just been talking about.

Lacey looked at me. "I'll come with you. Kurt's doing just fine on his own." Her skin was turning a pale blue, and I knew the long hours without her oxygen were taking their toll. She squeezed his shoulder. "You're one fine young man. I'm proud to say I know you."

I managed to push myself up from my chair, and, remembering my episode from earlier in the day, I focused on trying to stay conscious and upright. I followed Detective Thompson down the hall, trying not to think about what was coming next. At least Lacey was still with me.

He stopped at a doorway and held it open for us. I could see the lobby just on the other side, the same blue plastic chairs we'd sat in this morning. What was going on here? I didn't understand, but thought maybe Lacey was supposed to escort me to the fingerprinting. It didn't make sense, but then, what did I know?

A flicker of movement drew my attention. Rick

had stood up and was walking toward us, his face as grim and pale as I'd ever seen it.

He nodded at Detective Thompson, who returned the gesture. "Tell you what, Rick, you've got a wife and son with more guts than most prizefighters even dare to dream about."

"Son? Kurt's back there, too?" He looked from Detective Thompson to me.

"Kurt decided to meet me here this morning," I said. "He turned himself in, told them everything."

Bruce Thompson said, "You should be proud of them."

"Believe me, I am."

I jerked my head around to see if Rick was joking. He was proud? That we were criminals? He waited only until I was through the door before he put his arms around me, and the sound of an involuntary sob spasmed somewhere in his chest.

The door closed behind Detective Thompson, and then it was just the three of us, alone in the lobby. I looked first at Lacey. "What just happened?" Then I looked at Rick. "And what are you doing here?"

He shrugged. "I came to see if I could help."

I wondered how exactly he thought he might help in this situation, but before going there I turned my attention on Lacey. "So I guess I'm a little confused. Am I under arrest or not?"

"Not yet." She walked toward the front door, and Rick and I followed her. "They're filing a probable cause declaration, which basically is Detective Thompson's sworn statement about what happened between you and the bat. They'll spend some time looking it over in the DA's office, and then they'll decide what they're going to do about it."

"So I'm free to go?"

"For now, you are."

"Well, I guess you won't need me to bail you out, then."

So that's why he was here. I reached over and hugged him with more emotion than I'd felt in years. "I can't believe you came down here to do that. I thought you were so angry you'd let us both rot in prison."

He held me tight. "That's what I thought, too, for about the first couple of hours after you told me. Then I realized what courage, what absolute gumption you had to come forward like you were." He leaned back just enough so that he could look in my eyes. "I'd forgotten." He shook his head. "No, that's a lie. It wasn't that I'd forgotten, it's that I'd taken it for granted so long that I no longer noticed."

We held each other for a moment on the sidewalk, until I became aware of the gentle wheeze of Lacey's breathing. I checked my watch. More time had passed than I'd realized. Lacey needed to get home and our daughter would be getting out of school soon.

"Caroline was supposed to be with you this afternoon."

"I called the school and Katrina's going to be at the house waiting for her."

"Our house?"

"Our house. I wasn't planning to leave here today without you, whether through bail or jail-break, but I was coming home to Caroline with her mother, no matter what it took." He grinned and said, "To tell you the truth, I don't think she would let me back in the house any other way."

"Well, we better go see that girl then."

We drove home in our separate cars, Lacey riding with me. I reached over and clasped her wrist. "Thank you so much for all you've done today. I can't even begin to tell you how much it means to me."

She shrugged. "Didn't do much." She rolled her head toward me. "I know how the system works, that's all."

"Thanks, Lacey." I pulled into her driveway, climbed out of my car, and started to help her up the stairs.

She pulled her arm away. "I don't want help up my own steps. I may be frail, but I'm not ready to go there yet."

I stopped at the bottom of the steps and watched

278

her unlock her front door. "I'll bring some dinner over in a little while."

"Don't have to."

"I know, but I want to."

She nodded and disappeared inside. I turned to find Rick's truck parked on the curb, him leaning against the passenger's door. I walked over to where he stood. "Why didn't you go in to the house?"

He put his hands in his pockets and stared at the sidewalk. "After we had that little blowup the other night, I got back to my apartment and I was just miserable. Because it wasn't until that exact moment that I realized whose fault this all is."

"What do you mean?"

"I've never seen you lose your temper and throw things. Or kick a couch halfway across the room." He looked up at me. "Or knock someone to kingdom come with a baseball bat. That temper, that part of Kurt that exploded, well, it didn't come from anywhere but me. I realized then that I've got some of my own facing up to do. As much as I hate to admit it, I've signed up for an anger management program here in town, and . . . I've been thinking . . . maybe we ought to try one of those marriage counselors."

"Really?"

"You know how I feel about those things, but I figure, what's it going to hurt at this point?" He opened the door to his truck and climbed in. "I just wanted to say that before we got home and Caroline was standing right there, and I lost my nerve."

"Thanks." I knew just how hard that had been for him, and I thought maybe his good heart might not be completely buried after all.

I returned to my car, but before I'd even pulled into the driveway, Caroline was already standing there. "You're home, you're home! They knew it wasn't Kurt's fault, right? They're going to let you go, and Kurt, too? Right?"

"Not quite, sweetie. Come sit in my lap and we'll talk about everything that's happened."

Thirty-Six

The story broke in a major way. The local morning news spoke of little else, and of course it made the front page of the *Santa Barbara News-Press*. Far beyond what I expected, it also graced the cover of the *Los Angeles Times*, and every single major news channel picked it up. It seemed that no one could quite believe the story of the mother and son who turned themselves in to save another boy.

My phone started ringing about seven in the morning and didn't stop. Reporters, reporters, and more reporters. I finally turned off the ringer. What would the women at church say when they saw today's headlines? I could just hear the phone conversations that were probably happening now.

The doorbell rang not long after Caroline left for school, and I considered just ignoring it. Instead, I tiptoed to look through the spy hole and saw Lacey standing there, staring directly back into my eyes. "It's me," she called.

I opened the door and saw that she was carrying a plate of scones. "I figured you'd be barricaded in today, thought you might need some reinforcements."

"Oh, Lacey, you're the best."

"Sure am." She nodded and followed me into the kitchen without another word. She was wearing a pair of gray slacks and a red sweater, which made me do a double take.

"What, no sweats again today?'

She shrugged. "I wore boring suits long enough I figure I deserve the change. But I wasn't sure if there would be photographers lurking around here today, and I didn't want to do anything that would look bad for you." She pulled at the sequined band holding her hair back. "I did add a little touch of individuality today."

I set out some plates, poured us both a cup of coffee, and we sat. Sometimes we looked at each other, sometimes we looked away from each other, and sometimes we just stared out into space. I took a bite or two of my scone, but it barely registered.

"I took the liberty of making some calls. Ryan

Scott is the absolute best criminal defense attorney in Santa Barbara, and he's agreed to take both you and Kurt as clients."

"But what about you?"

"Oh, honey, I don't have the strength to see this thing through. I've been retired a few years now, and I wasn't on the best of terms with a good bit of the legal establishment well before that. Besides, I was a civil attorney back in the day. You need someone who knows what he's doing." The doorbell rang. She looked at me. "You expecting anyone?"

I shook my head. "I've had several phone calls from reporters. I'm guessing they finally just decided to show up themselves."

"I'll take care of that." Lacey pushed to her feet, and I noticed she wheezed as she walked away. I heard the door open, and Lacey's scratchy voice. "What's your business here?"

I strained to hear the voice because I wanted to know. Then again, I really didn't.

"I . . . well, my business is Alisa. I came by to offer my support. And to bring this, too."

Beth? Was that Beth's voice I heard? I stood from the table, walked to the doorway, and peered at the front door. "Beth, you're here?"

"Yes I am. And I'm not the only one coming, either. The women have been burning up the phone lines this morning." She held out a casse-role dish, covered with aluminum foil. "I don't think you're going to have to worry about cooking again until at least the end of the decade."

"But . . . don't you realize what a hypocrite I've been?" I looked at this woman who personified the statement "God is the God of order," and could not begin to understand this visit. "Why would you want to even speak to me?"

"Alisa, the fact that you're willing to throw away everything to do the right thing, well, I've never been more proud to say I know you. I know a lot of others feel the same way."

I threw my arms around her and hugged her tight. "Thank you so much for being here for me."

"Honey, think nothing of it. This is what we're supposed to do, remember? Love each other, support one another, and pull each other back to our feet when life has knocked us flat."

Beth left after a few minutes, but half an hour later Carleigh arrived. Then Kristyn. Then Tasha. Some brought food, some flowers, but they all brought words of support.

Lacey looked at me. "Well, I have to say it. I underestimated them." She looked at me. "I daresay that you did, too."

I nodded. "Most of all, I think I underestimated God. I didn't trust Him to help me through whatever it was He asked of me. This is hard. So hard. But I can't believe the relief I feel at not trying to live a lie anymore. After this, I don't think I'll ever again feel the pressure to pretend to be perfect, because by now, everyone in America knows better."

Ryan Scott came by my house late that afternoon. He was in his midthirties, nice looking in a balding yuppie sort of way. He took the soda I offered him, then settled his briefcase on the coffee table. "Kurt's arraignment will be at ten o'clock tomorrow morning. They'll officially file charges then."

"How bad is it going to be?" Lacey had brought over her portable oxygen and now sat on the couch beside me.

"Murder, of course. They're talking about adding special circumstances, similar to the charges against Gary Singer, but with some differences. Mr. Singer's special allegations involved murder committed for robbery, and since we all know that Kurt is not the one who robbed Rudy Prince, that will be dropped. However, the use of a deadly weapon circumstance is still possible."

"It's that kind of thinking that's made me hate our legal system," Lacey said. "What kind of system adds a bigger penalty to Kurt for using a deadly weapon, when the weapon was taken off the thug he's accused of killing? Never has made sense to me, which of course has kept me in plenty of trouble with the legal system for years."

Ryan smiled at her with such affection that I began to suspect the two of them had crossed paths somewhere in the past. "I'm going to fight it, of course."

Lacey nodded. "Of course you are. It's downright ridiculous, that's what it is."

"Will Kurt be able to come home until the trial?" That's what I wanted more than anything. To have Kurt out of that awful place, back among family, back where he could get the support he still needed so desperately.

"I'm going to fight for bail, and a reduced bail at that."

"Reduced bail?" I hadn't even thought in financial terms. "How much do you think it will be?"

"We have a set bail schedule here, so everyone starts out on the same page. The bail schedule for murder is one million dollars." Ryan did not acknowledge my gasp, and I was grateful for that. He paused just a moment, then continued. "Actually, that's the good news. The bad news is, there is no bail schedule for murder with special circumstances, so we're going to have to do some fast talking to keep them from attaching use of a deadly weapon to his charges."

"Do you think it'll happen?" I felt the closest thing to hope I'd felt in a long time.

"That's my plan. We'll see how it goes." He

pulled off his glasses and looked at me with the gleam of self-assurance in his eyes. "They can't really claim he's a flight risk since he came and turned himself in, now, can they?"

I hoped he was right.

Thirty-Seven

Wednesday morning, the small courtroom was filled to capacity. A group of about a dozen— men, women, and a couple of teenagers—sat directly behind the prosecution's table. They were dressed in mostly baggy jeans and T-shirts, several of the men wore gold chains, and they all had a rough edge about them. I assumed this to be Rudy Prince's family, and I found myself wondering what his childhood might have been like.

The last two rows in both sides were filled by reporters and the likes. I made a point of not looking back.

Rick and I sat in the front row behind the defense table, Jodi beside me, Monte beside Rick. Lacey sat on the other side of Jodi, dressed demurely. She offered a single brief nod, her eyes broadcasting determined strength. About a dozen of my friends from church sat in the rows behind us. They all smiled at me and nodded their encouragement.

At the far end of our row, there sat a thin, dark-haired woman. She looked vaguely familiar, but I couldn't remember where I might have seen her before. I would have assumed she was Rudy Prince's mother, except why would she be sitting on our side of the courtroom?

Ryan Scott and Kurt entered the courtroom, and a buzz of whispers began to drone from the back rows. Kurt walked military straight and didn't look to the right or left until he passed our aisle. Then, he looked back at me and nodded, no expression on his face at all. It frightened me.

The district attorney took his place, looking confident and almost bored. This was just another day's work for him, I supposed, another day of wrestling with the power to change people's lives forever.

The judge came in through a back door and took her seat, and a battle soon emerged between Ryan Scott and the district attorney. Ryan seemed ever so confident, and he threw out words like "no flight risk" and "acting with courage and honor." The district attorney looked equally confident as he spouted phrases like, "the barbaric nature of the crime." A lot of legalese peppered their statements, and I lost all track of who I thought might be winning the argument.

"Excuse me. May I say something to the court?" The dark-haired woman at the end of our row was standing, leaning against the rail that separated the spectators from the front.

Ryan Scott turned toward her, his face showing

the first sign of surprise I'd seen all day. He glanced at the woman, then turned toward the district attorney, who appeared equally astounded.

"You are out of order." The judge's words were stern.

"Please, I'm Gary Singer's mother. This boy turned himself in to save my son. I know he's not going anywhere. Please grant him bail, for my son's sake. For the sake of rewarding justice."

The bailiff soon escorted the woman out of the room. However, as they made their way down the aisle, she was calling back over her shoulder. "You should show him the same respect he showed to my son." The rows behind me erupted in applause, just one or two people at first, then the entire back section—including most of the reporters, from what I could tell.

"You will be silent, or you will leave this courtroom." The judge's words silenced the claps. What it didn't stop was the buzz of whispers that ran through the reporters. I saw the district attorney turn and look at them. From the look on his face, I was sure I could practically read his thoughts. Tomorrow's news would report that Gary Singer's mother had pled for Kurt to be released and the district attorney watched, ice cold, as she was thrown from the courtroom. Or perhaps he could be the hero who honored her bravery and call for mercy. At least that's what I hoped he was feeling.

He turned back to the bench. "Given the unusual circumstances, and the fact that he did turn himself in, we could consider lowering bail. But I want a guarantee from the defendant and both his parents that he will show up in court. I want to hear from his drug counselors on a regular basis that he is making his daily meetings, and I want a guarantee from his uncle and aunt that he will remain employed for the duration."

All parties came to an agreement, leaving Rick and me to spend the next two days working out the financial details of Kurt's bail. By the time we finally arranged everything, we were well aware that if Kurt skipped town, we would lose our house and everything in it. It seemed a safe enough deal to me.

I couldn't believe how quickly things had changed. Hope sprouted from the tiniest of seeds. My son was going to come home.

Friday morning was the first time I ventured out of my house for something that didn't directly relate to legal proceedings. I needed to clean some things out of my office at the church, and I needed a few odds and ends at the grocery store. Since I most dreaded the office cleanout, I decided to get it over with first. The sooner I pushed myself past these unpleasant hurdles, the sooner they would be forever behind me. Right?

Somehow it seemed a little too optimistic, but I was willing to try.

When I walked down the hallway toward the church office, I could hear light-hearted chatter. Just the usual "Look at this typo" kind of office conversation. As soon as I walked through the doorway, however, conversations disappeared behind a saddening, deafening silence. It was amazing how fast sound waves could disappear. No echo. Nothing.

I nodded toward the empty cardboard box in my hand. "I . . . came to clean out my office."

Beth looked at me with tears in her eyes. She jumped to her feet, ran around her desk, and had me locked in an all-out hug before I even realized what was happening. "Oh, sweetie, how are you?"

Over her shoulder, I could see Jana sitting at her desk, studiously making a point of not looking my direction. I hugged Beth for just a moment and then pulled away. "I'm hanging in there. It's easier now that Kurt is out on bail."

"I can imagine."

I think we both knew that she really couldn't imagine, but she wanted to help and I appreciated that. I turned my attention to the suddenly industrious Jana and took a deep breath. "Good morning, Jana."

"Morning." She didn't look up from her computer.

The slight stung. We may not have been confidants, but we'd been what I would consider friends for the last few years. I had known when I came forward there would be some at the church who would have this reaction. Funny how the people who I most thought would judge me—like Beth—had been so supportive, and the people who I thought were my friends—like Jana—were the first to turn away. I didn't want to stand here and prolong the agony any longer than necessary. I started toward my little office.

"I'll just be a few minutes."

I closed the door behind me and sat at my desk. Where to start? I removed my own books from the small bookshelf, pulled a few personal items from the desk drawers, and then put a framed family photo on top of it all.

Someone knocked at the door. "Come in."

Ken Maddox entered, careful to leave the door open behind him—as he always did when in an office alone with a female. "I hate to see you go."

I knew that he meant it from his heart. I also knew that if I stayed, the backlash would fall on him, probably even harder than it would on me. I'd caused enough damage to the people I cared about. I couldn't do it to one more. I gave him a wry grin.

"Care to give me a rough estimate of how many irate calls you've gotten from people who didn't know I'd resigned, demanding that you fire me?"

He smiled sadly. "I've had a few."

I opened my desk drawers for one last look, to make certain I wasn't leaving anything behind. "Can't say as I blame them. If the situation were the other way around, I'm hardly the person I'd want directing the women of our church. I mean, when I decided to tell a lie, I made sure I did it in a big way." I closed the drawer with a final snap and felt my throat closing in. "I've loved every minute here. I'd really like to apologize to you for all the trouble."

He shook his head. "As far as I'm concerned, you're welcome here anytime."

But we both knew I wouldn't be coming back.

Thirty-Eight

"Mr. Scott would like to see you this afternoon to discuss your case. Would you be available at three o'clock?" Ryan Scott's ever-efficient secretary had the perky voice of a cheerleader turned receptionist.

"Sure, I'll be there." Like I had anything else to do besides hide inside my house as I'd been doing for the last six days. The story surrounding the case was still news fodder, and with my fate about to be decided, I didn't see it vanishing off the front page anytime soon.

I called Lacey. "Ryan Scott wants to see me this afternoon. You want to come with me?"

She paused for such a long time that I began to wonder if she were still on the line. "I think . . . you should call Rick and see if he wants to go with you."

Over the course of the last few days, Rick had given a support I would never have thought him capable of. He'd even been staying in the guest room since Monday. "I don't know."

"He wants to help you, Alisa. It's time that you quit pretending like you can handle everything, and let him be the man he wants to be."

Let him be the man he wants to be. The words slammed into me. Is that what I'd been doing in all the years since Nick's death? Had I been so preoccupied with putting on appearances, with showing everyone what strong faith I had, that I'd completely shut out the people God had put in my life to help me? "I . . . uh . . . maybe you're right. I'll give him a call."

My fingers shook a little as I pushed the buttons. Whether or not Rick wanted to help me, he didn't like personal calls at work. Unless it was an emergency. Wouldn't this qualify?

"Alisa? Everything okay?"

I could hear the roar of heavy equipment in the background. "Well, Ryan Scott wants to see me in his office this afternoon at three, something about my case. I wondered if you would want to come with me?"

I could hear shouting in the background—

something was obviously going wrong at the jobsite. "Hey listen, I've got to go." I heard a shuffling sound like a hand over the phone and could just make out him saying, "I'll be right there," then the shuffling again and, "I'll be by to pick you up at two thirty." He hung up without another word.

I spent the afternoon wondering if he was mad that I called. Would he resent this because of a busy afternoon at work he'd be missing?

I watched out the window for his truck to appear. I didn't want to inconvenience him by making him wait. If he was upset already, there was no reason to add to it. At 2:27 I saw his truck coming down the street. By the time he pulled into the driveway, I was standing ready at the passenger's side. I climbed in. "Sorry to disrupt your day like this. I know you were busy."

"Yeah, well, you happened to call at the exact minute that Kevin hit an underground waterline. You should have seen the geyser." He laughed. "Lucky for us, Carroll Plumbing was working on the business across the street. Between us and those guys, we had it fixed in record time."

"Good." I looked out the window, relieved that he wasn't angry, but found myself worrying about what I was about to hear. Was I about to be locked up? Were official charges about to be filed?

Ryan Scott's office was upstairs in a chic little

shopping alcove just off State Street. I climbed the stairs, looking at all the shoppers, the sidewalk diners laughing and enjoying the carefree spring day. What I wouldn't have given to be able to do that again. Live my life carefree.

Rick and I sat in the upholstered leather chairs across from Ryan's large desk and waited for the news. I wasn't sure I wanted to hear it.

"I spent some time talking with the DA's office today. There are several areas where they can charge you. Destruction of evidence, which is a misdemeanor, but there's also obstruction of justice and accessory after the fact, both felonies."

"What are they going to do?"

"They tell me they're going to file charges for all three."

Rick reached over and took my hand. "What does that mean?"

"For now, it means that there will be an arraignment hearing where Alisa will be formally charged."

"Will we need to post bail?" I was thankful that Rick was here to carry on this conversation, because I'd lost my ability to think or speak.

"I expect them to release her on promise to appear. She turned herself in, your son is under arrest, they don't expect her to be a flight problem. What they will do is use her to keep the pressure on Kurt. That's why the full slate of charges—they want to make sure he knows something bad could happen to his mother if he chooses to run."

I finally found the gumption to at least nod. "Okay. When will all this take place?"

"They're taking their time so they can keep their options open. Next week at the earliest. I'll call you as soon as I know something for sure."

Rick squeezed my hand and looked at me. "It's going to be all right. We'll be fine. We'll all be fine."

I wasn't sure how he felt he could make that statement, considering there was no way things were going to be "fine," but I didn't have the strength or the desire to argue. I just needed him to somehow be right.

Thirty-Nine

Sunday morning, I arrived at church just seconds before the start of the service. I didn't want to put myself in the position of having to stand around and make small talk. Instead of my usual spot, I found a place on the back row, hoping to remain mostly undetected. It was a hope that proved utterly unworkable.

"Oh, Alisa!" Kristyn almost yelled when she spotted me. "I'm so glad you're here." She made her way over and hugged me, followed closely by Carleigh and Beth. It felt good to be welcomed. "Do you want to come sit with us?"

I shook my head. "Go ahead and sit with your families. I'm fine." As they walked away, I took my seat, feeling less self-conscious than I would have expected. That's when I noticed the young couple a few rows up. He turned to look at me and then whispered something to his wife. She slowly turned her head, but jerked around straight when she saw me looking at her. She said something to him, and soon I could see their shoulders shaking with silent giggles. As I looked away and scanned the room, I could almost feel the whiplash of heads turning. I'd expected no less, but that didn't make it any easier.

I felt someone take the seat beside me and turned to look. Rick said, "Okay if I sit here?" His face looked as uncertain and insecure as he'd looked when he'd asked me for our first date—some twenty-five years ago.

"Of course." I looked at him and smiled. I leaned a little closer and whispered, taking care to keep my tone light so that he didn't understand it for anything but the light-hearted teasing it was. "What are you doing here?"

"All this time I've thought God was only a crutch for weaklings, but after watching what you and Kurt just did, I'm thinking He's much more than that. And that's what I want to be. More."

He sat beside me during the service, and I prayed the whole time that he would hear what he needed to hear, that he would be moved to action, and that he would be open to the Spirit. As the service ended, he stood up and looked at me. "Well, how about I take my two favorite ladies to lunch?"

"Sounds great, and I'm sure Caroline will be thrilled."

"Good. Maybe next weekend we can drive up to Templeton for a visit. Do you think Jodi and Monte would be okay with that?"

"I think they'd love it."

It was Rick's first visit since not long after Monte and Jodi bought the place. He drove slowly up the driveway, looking all around. "Wow, they've really fixed this place up since I was here last."

"Yeah, your son has played a big part in that. He and Monte have been working themselves ragged, I think."

Just then, a puff of dust began moving up the driveway toward us. I squinted into the sun and saw Kurt approaching fast on the quad. He skidded to a stop right beside the truck. "Hey. I saw you guys pull in. Thought I'd come grab Short Stuff and see if she wants to go for a quick thrill ride through the hills with me."

Caroline was out the door and had her hand on the back of the quad, before she turned and looked at me. "Is it okay?"

"I guess it better be, since you're already half-way on the thing." I tried to give her a scolding look, but she'd stopped paying attention.

She climbed on behind her brother. "Go fast, Kurt."

"You got it." He peeled out down the driveway, and the sound of her squeals covered the hillside.

Rick watched them go, then turned to me. "I look at Kurt and how well he's doing now, and I realize that once again Monte has been a better father than I ever was."

"What are you talking about?"

He shook his head, and I was certain I saw tears in his eyes—something I'd seen only at his mother's funeral and no other time. "During Christmas before Nick died, I heard him on the phone with a girl from school. He was telling her about our Christmas feast and about Monte and Jodi. I heard him say, 'Monte has always been my role model.'" Rick's voice cracked here, and he shoved his fingers through his hair. "My own son preferred Monte over me."

"Is that why you've been so upset with Monte for the last few years?"

"I wasn't going to blame myself for that, so I placed all my anger directly on Monte's shoulders. Yep, that's why."

"Oh, Rick." I reached over and put my hand on his shoulder. "It didn't mean that you weren't a good role model. Monte just shared the same faith, and that was very important to Nick."

He put his hand atop mine. "Well, maybe I should have been more open to it then, instead of always . . . well, you know."

"Nick loved you. You were a wonderful father and he knew it. I heard him say it a thousand times when he was telling me about one of his friends from a broken home. He always said how blessed he was to have you."

"I'll just bet."

"Really, he did."

"I wonder what he would say now, about his own family. It's as broken as they get."

I put my right hand on his cheek. "Yeah, well, I share plenty of the blame for that."

We leaned toward each other then, and before any of our baggage could get in the way, Rick was holding me in his arms, kissing me like he used to before all this. I tasted the salt of tears, and wasn't sure if it was Rick's or my own.

The moment was too good to last long, and it didn't. Too much distance had grown between us and too many barriers had risen in that space to be forgotten in an instant. When we pulled apart I felt everything—hope and doubt and fear and love and anger. We parked the car in front of the house, and I knew there was still much work to be done before all was well between us again. At least now, though, we were committed to getting there.

Forty

Five more days passed before the morning of my arraignment finally arrived. During those days I thought of Paul and Daniel and Joseph in the Bible, those who'd faced prison. But in every case they were innocents suffering for God. I was guilty, and day by day my prayers boiled to a simple plea for mercy. Not that I deserved it, but for Rick and Caroline. I'd also hoped that the event would escape everyone's notice. I wanted to go in quietly and get this all over with. But of course that's not what happened.

Ryan Scott and I walked toward the courthouse together. He pointed toward a clump of people gathered around a sidewalk. "Those are reporters. I'm not sure who they're talking to, but when they see us, they're going to be right in our faces. Keep your head down, your expression neutral, and don't say a word."

"I've got no problem with that."

As if they'd heard him, the pack looked up and immediately began to run in our direction. I looked at the sidewalk just a few feet in front of me. "Mrs. Stewart, is it true that your son confessed to the crime, and that justice in this case could have been served without your ever coming forward? What made you decide to turn yourself in? How are you feeling?"

How am I feeling? Okay, that was the dumbest question I'd heard in a long time. As we got closer to the front door, I turned to the side and tried to catch a glimpse of the person they'd been talking to. I recognized her at once. Gary Singer's mother.

We walked into the small room, filled mostly with the same crowd that had been present at Kurt's arraignment a few weeks ago, except there were no members of Rudy Prince's family that I could see.

Beth, Ken Maddox, and several other friends from church smiled and waved up at me. Noticeably absent were Jana, Julie, and Marsha. Just as well. I'd gotten enough of the grapevine chatter to know what the three of them were saying about me. I was glad I didn't have to face them, now that I'd sworn off putting on a happy face and pretending.

Rick, Kurt, Monte, Jodi, and Lacey all sat in the front row, with an empty seat beside Lacey. A jacket lay across it, obviously holding someone's spot. I had no idea whose it might be.

Just then, Theresa Singer entered the court-room, picked up the jacket, and sat down. She and Jodi exchanged some sort of small talk. Then she looked me directly in the face and nodded. I returned the gesture and turned back in my seat.

"All rise." The bailiff's announcement caused my heart to skip a beat.

The proceeding was quite short. The judge was middle-aged, and had a rather pleasant demeanor, or at least I would have thought so until he looked up at me. "Mrs. Stewart, you are charged with obstruction of justice, destruction of evidence, and accomplice after the fact. How do you plead?"

"Not guilty, your honor." Of course everyone in this courtroom knew that I was guilty. They all knew exactly what I'd done. But Ryan Scott had assured me that now was not the time to state any of that in front of the court. There was lots of legal wrangling to be done before we reached that point. I didn't argue.

A few minutes later everything was over. I was free to go home on the promise I would return when summoned back to court.

I turned just in time to see Theresa Singer step quickly out of the courtroom. I walked around the rail and hugged my family. "That wasn't too terrible."

Jodi hugged me. "Did you see all the press out there, talking to Gary Singer's mother?"

"Yeah."

"I heard her tell them you were a brave and good mother."

Kurt came to stand beside me. "And she's exactly right."

Forty-One

Two Months Later

"She's a beautiful baby." I looked down at the pink-cheeked darling wrapped in a striped hospital blanket and it made me gasp. The oval shape of her eyes, the dimple in her chin—it was like holding Kurt as a baby all over again.

"She is, isn't she?" Pamela blinked back tears and looked from me to Kurt. "The Tuttles will take good care of her."

"They're good people." Kurt's voice was thick. He reached down and kissed the baby on the forehead. "Good-bye, little one. Enjoy your life. Always remember that your daddy loves you."

"And your grandmother, too." I stroked the baby's cheek, then turned away.

Kurt put his arm around my shoulder as we walked from the hospital room together. "It would be so easy to say I want to be tested, to prove beyond the shadow of a doubt I'm her father, to demand custody." His words mirrored my own thoughts, and after seeing the baby, I had a pretty good idea what the tests would show.

"I know what you mean."

"But it wouldn't be the right thing to do, and we both know it. I'm going to end up in jail, and even though I know you would take care of her for me, she deserves a stable life, with a loving mother and father who will be there for her."

My head knew he was right, but the rest of me desperately wanted to hold on to her forever.

Kurt squeezed me a little tighter. "It's the hardest thing I've ever done in my life."

"Harder than turning yourself in?"

"Yeah. I mean, that was scarier because I knew I was looking at jail, but there was no question about what was the right and wrong thing to do. Here, if I think about it long enough, I can convince myself that it would be best for her to be with her biological father. It's much harder shutting out that voice."

We walked into the parking garage, where Rick waited for us, leaning against the side of his truck. I reached up and kissed Kurt on the cheek. "I'm so proud of you. Again."

"Me too." Rick pushed off the car and hugged his son. "So proud."

"Thanks, Dad."

I thought of how few times Kurt had heard those words over the course of the last few years. It was strange how a tragedy like this sometimes turns things for the better. The problem was there were still more turns to come, and not all of them, I was sure, would end so well.

Forty-Two

Three days later, just after lunch, the phone rang.

"I need to see the three of you in my office as soon as Kurt can get here. We've been offered a deal that I think we might want to consider." Ryan Scott's voice kept its usual lawyer monotone, but somehow I knew he was excited. Or at least, I hoped that was what I knew.

"Okay, I'll give Kurt a call."

"I just did. He's on his way."

Wow, Ryan Scott must really be excited. As soon as we hung up, I called Rick at work and told him what I knew. "I'll be home within the hour." "I don't think Kurt will be here that soon." "That's the idea. I want to be ready to roll when he gets here."

I hung up the phone and looked at Caroline, who had come to stand behind me sometime during the phone conversation. "I'm coming, too."

"No, sweetie, this is not for you. I'll call Lacey and see if you can go stay with her."

Caroline crossed her arms across her chest and stomped her right foot. "I'm a member of this family, and this affects me, too. You guys all think you are so smart trying to hide stuff from me. The kids at school know more about this than I do."

The reality of that slammed me hard. She was right. The only way she would be able to fight the rumor mill was if she knew the truth and knew when something was and was not true. I reached down and gave her a hug. "You know what? You're right. You can come with us."

She pumped an air fist. "Yes."

"But, you have to sit very still and very quiet in the lawyer's office."

"*Pffft*. I'm not a baby. Of course I will."

After Rick arrived home, we all paced the floor until Kurt pulled into the driveway. He climbed out of his beater car, looking somewhere between terrified and hopeful. "Did he give you any idea what the deal is?"

I shook my head. "I was hoping you knew something."

"Well, let's quit wasting time, get in the car, and go find out what we can find out." Rick jingled the keys in his hands. Caroline had already climbed in the backseat and was calling out the door, "Come on, everybody, let's get moving."

When we got out of the car, Rick waited for the three of us, but I could tell by the stiffness of his step and the impatient lift of his shoulders that he didn't want to. He hurried down the hall, and the moment we were inside Ryan's office he demanded, "A deal for whom?" He didn't bother to take a seat.

I, on the other hand, couldn't stand. I dropped into my usual chair and pulled Caroline up into my lap. "What is the offer?"

"They've offered something of a package deal." He looked at me. "Everyone involved understands the situation and realizes the decision Alisa made in coming forward. And if they didn't realize it before, after all the editorials in the paper and Theresa Singer interviews on TV lately, they realize it now." He actually laughed a little as he said those last few words. "For you they're willing to settle for three years probation and a couple hundred hours of community service."

I slowly exhaled. I could definitely live with that. But now came the hard part. "What about Kurt?"

Ryan pulled at his tie. "He's a bit more complicated. He killed a man. But given the amount of public support for the two of you, and given the fact that there is arguably a self-defense argument that could be made, they've offered voluntary manslaughter."

That didn't sound all that good to me. I looked up at Rick, who looked as confused as I was. He cast a furtive glance toward Kurt, then turned back to Ryan. "Will he go to jail for that?"

"Yes." Ryan paused a moment, giving us time to take in this fact.

"For how long?" Rick asked.

"California is a determinate sentence state. What that means is, for each felony conviction, there are set amounts of time a person can go to prison. There is a low level, a mid level, and a high level. For voluntary manslaughter, the high level is eleven years."

I gasped. "Eleven years? That's too much."

"The low level is three years, which the DA says is not enough. They've agreed to recommend the mid level to the judge, and that's six years. Of course, the judge makes that final decision. He could choose to go high."

Kurt leaned forward, hands on knees. "What do I need to do?"

"He'll want a write-up of your background, et cetera. I want you to tell him about every good deed you've done in your entire life."

"But if Kurt's got to go to jail, why can't we ask for the low end?" I knew it sounded whiny, but I didn't care. My son was going to prison; I felt whiny.

"Mom, it's the right thing." Kurt's voice was firm with resolve. He sat so erect in his chair, like a person trying to face the firing squad bravely.

I looked toward the lawyer. "But Rudy Prince threatened him first. It wasn't Kurt's fault."

"Yes, he threatened me, and then he turned around and walked away. I'm the one who went after him and killed him."

There was truth in every word, I knew there was, but I wasn't ready to give up my trench. "After you watched him viciously attack a homeless man. Why should standing up for another human being be a crime?"

Ryan Scott cleared his throat. "If you'd rather, we could take it to trial, hope that a jury sees it the same way you do. *If* we do that, the DA's obligated to go after first-degree murder charges. If you win, great. If you lose—you'd lose everything."

Kurt shook his head. "No, manslaughter is good." He came over to kneel beside my chair. "Mom, you've been saying we need to leave the past behind us, and I agree with you. But if I'm going to leave yesterday behind, I want to do it with as clear a conscience as I can get in this case. The fact is, Rudy Prince died because of me, and I need to pay for that."

We called Monte and Jodi, and they drove down to Santa Barbara, where the entire family sat huddled around the living room, saying little. There was a mixture of grief and relief and regret, which seemed to choke back all conversation.

Finally, Monte spoke. "I hope I'm not overstepping my bounds here"—he cast a glance toward Rick—"but I went on the Internet this afternoon and looked up some information on Prison Fellowship."

Rick looked at him with hollow eyes. "Prison Fellowship, what's that?"

"It's a Christian group that works through local churches in the prisons. They teach classes, have discipleship groups set up among the inmates, help with transitioning back out, all those things." He reached inside the duffel bag at his feet and produced a pile of papers, clipped together. "I downloaded their *Guide to Prison Survival*. I thought it might be helpful. And I took down the numbers for the offices that work with the Southern California prisons. I didn't call anyone. I thought I'd leave that up to you."

Kurt took the packet of papers from his hands. "Thank you. I'll look into this."

I looked toward Rick, wondering how he was taking all this, especially since it was coming from Monte. I didn't have to wonder long, because he spoke up. "Thank you. For being here for my family time and again."

"We're family. That's what we're supposed to do."

"Yes, it is." Rick reached over and took my hand.

Forty-Three

I stood before the judge and pled guilty to obstruction of justice and destruction of evidence while a dozen women from my church sat in the courtroom and watched. I could hear them sniffling in the rows behind me.

Then it was Kurt's turn. He stood before the judge, his shoulders square, his back straight. Personally, I found it difficult to remain upright. What if the judge decided to go for the high end of the sentencing spectrum? I didn't think I would be able to stand it.

The judge read a lengthy statement, none of which I heard. My mind could wrap itself around nothing but the length of the sentence, not all the legal hithertos and thithertos. "Due to the violent nature of this crime, my inclination would be to go for the high end of the sentencing spectrum." I heard a gasp from the row behind me. I knew it was Jodi. The judge looked over his glasses in disapproval before continuing. "However, due to an overwhelming amount of the paper work recommending otherwise, including a rather lengthy affidavit from the lead detective on the case . . ."

I turned my head to see if Bruce Thompson was in the courtroom. He nodded at me and offered something akin to a smile. I turned back to the judge.

". . . a low-end sentence of three years." Once I heard those words, the tears started. They weren't happy tears—how could they be when my son was about to go to prison? But they were at least grateful tears. It could have been so much worse, there could be no doubt about that. I would thank Bruce Thompson later.

The bailiff approached our table. Kurt locked me in an embrace. "I love you."

"I love you, too." The words were choked by sobs. My sobs.

The bailiff motioned for Kurt to step toward him and produced a pair of handcuffs. Kurt nodded and extended his hands, but he never took his eyes off me. "We did the right thing—never doubt that. We did the right thing." The metal made a clinking sound as the cuffs were set in place, then my son was led away from me. He turned just before they pushed through the back door and called out, "I love you, Dad."

"I love you, too." Rick's strangled words carried through the room.

I slowly turned and walked toward Rick. I fell into his arms and we simply held each other and cried for a moment. Then he pulled back, put his left arm across my shoulder, and started to lead me from the courtroom. "Let's go home."

Jodi came and linked her arm around me, Lacey on her other side. Monte did the same on the other side of Rick, and we walked out of the courtroom, one big human chain. One step at a time we would get through this. With the dawn of each new day we would shake off the dust from yesterday, learn from it, then leave it behind as we walked toward tomorrow.

Acknowledgments

Thank you, Father in heaven, for allowing me to, yet again, see my dream come true.

Lee Cushman—For the continuing love and encouragement.

Caroline Cushman—Your smile can brighten the darkest day.

Ora Parrish—The most amazing mother, friend, and all-around cheerleader in the world.

Carl Parrish—The coolest father ever!

Leah Cushman—Thanks for researching the olive farms for me. You're a terrific mother-in-law.

Carl, Alisa, Lisa, Katy—Your unwavering support makes me so happy to be your sister.

Lori Baur—A great friend, neighbor, and marketing champion.

Sally Turvey, Carolyn Horwald, and Kara Horwald—For great feedback on the early drafts.

Dave Long—Thanks for never letting me take the easy way out.

Natasha Sperling—For cleaning up the grammar mess I leave in my wake.

The Bethany marketing team—Steve, Debra, Noelle, Jim, and Carra, you continue to amaze me.

Mike Berrier and Shawn Grady—It's been great

to walk this writing journey with the two of you.

The Winklings: John Olson, Jenn Doucette, James Rubart, Katie Vorreiter—For your support and friendship.

Carrie Padgett and Julie Carobini—Great friends and great writers.

Scott Campbell—Thank you for all the "I'm not a defense attorney, but . . ." answers.

Adam Pearlman—For taking the time to answer my copious questions and walk me through the criminal defense process.

Sergeant Lorenzo Duarte—For heading up the amazing "Citizens Police Academy."

Boots Cushman—for being the second Cushman pet to make a cameo appearance in one of my books.

Questions for Conversation

1. One of Alisa's coping mechanisms was: "If I pretend it doesn't exist, it will go away." What are your own ways to cope when things get too awful to face head on?

2. Lacey and Alisa's belief systems differed quite a bit, but the two women still had a strong friendship. Why do you think Alisa felt she could show her true face with Lacey more than with her other friends?

3. Alisa and Rick practiced tough love on Kurt when he was at his lowest point. When thinking about it, Alisa makes the statement that her head tells her one thing, her heart another. What's your opinion?

4. Jodi and Monte sold everything and moved to an olive farm in Templeton because they "felt led." Have you ever felt deeply called to something? To what have you attributed that inner confidence?

5. Alisa spent a lot of time wondering whether Kurt was guilty, and trying to convince herself that he was not. Would you have asked him the question as soon as you found the

bat? Would you have told the detective? Or would you have done what you could to help your son succeed in his new life?

6. In all likelihood, Lacey was correct: Gary Singer would almost surely end up in prison again, even if Alisa saved him by coming forward. Would you be able to trade your son for this man?

7. After Alisa saw the baby, she had a pretty good idea it really was Kurt's. Did she do the right thing by letting another family adopt the baby without ever knowing for sure?

8. Both Alisa and Theresa Singer blamed themselves for the path their sons' lives went down. Do you agree that they were at least partly responsible?

9. When Kurt confessed to Detective Thompson, both he and Lacey wanted Alisa to keep quiet about destroying the bat. She chose to come forward. What would you have done?

10. If you were on the jury, would you say that Kurt was guilty of murder?

About the Author

Kathryn Cushman is a graduate of Samford University with a degree in pharmacy. Her two previous novels were *A Promise to Remember* and *Waiting for Daybreak*, which was a finalist in Women's Fiction for the Inspirational Reader's Choice Award. Kathryn and her family currently live in Santa Barbara, California.

She enjoys hearing from readers at
www.kathryncushman.com

Center Point Publishing
600 Brooks Road ● PO Box 1
Thorndike ME 04986-0001 USA

(207) 568-3717

US & Canada:
1 800 929-9108
www.centerpointlargeprint.com